VICTORIA BROWNLEE

Brioche in the Oven

AMBERJACK PUBLISHING

CHICAGO

AMBERJACK
PUBLISHING

Amberjack Publishing
An imprint of Chicago Review Press Incorporated
814 North Franklin Street
Chicago, Illinois 60610

Library of Congress Cataloging-in-Publication Data

Names: Brownlee, Victoria, 1985- author.
Title: Brioche in the oven / Victoria Brownlee.
Description: Chicago : Amberjack Publishing, [2019] | Summary: "A mature cross-cultural romance about an Australian transplant to France whose relationship is tested by cultural misunderstandings, a surprise move to the French countryside, and the tiny matter of a baby on the way"-- Provided by publisher.
Identifiers: LCCN 2020005757 | ISBN 9781948705660 (trade paperback)
Subjects: GSAFD: Love stories.
Classification: LCC PR9619.4.B78 B75 2019 | DDC 823/.92--dc23
LC record available at https://lccn.loc.gov/2020005757

10 9 8 7 6 5 4 3 2 1

ISBN 978-1-948705-660
eBook ISBN 978-1-948705-677

To my parents,
for sending me to France
when I was young and impressionable.

*Each sort of cheese reveals a pasture of a
different green, under a different sky.*

—ITALO CALVINO

• PART •

One

AUTUMN

Chapter

1

I **STARED AT THE TEST** in disbelief. It was hard to come to terms with the fact that such a life-changing moment could be happening while my pants were around my ankles. A baby, *un bébé*—no matter what language I said the word in, it sounded terrifying.

Merde! I thought, pulling up my pants and flushing. *How did I manage this?* When I'd picked up the test the night before, it had been more as an aid to settle what I thought was just an overactive imagination. I'd never dreamed that it would come back positive. I stuffed the tiny, life-changing blue dye stick into my bra and took a deep breath.

"*Bonjour, ma belle,*" Serge's voice called out from the kitchen.

"*Bonjour,*" I said, joining him.

"Did you sleep well?" he asked me in French, handing me a large mug of coffee.

We're going to have a baby, we're never going to sleep again! I wanted to scream. Instead, I replied with: "*Très bien. Et toi?*" I felt like I was on autopilot, not really thinking about what I was saying, and distracted by trying to figure out when I was going to tell Serge that he was going to become a *papa*.

He nodded and walked over to hug me. I ducked away from his embrace, figuring that a test stick falling out of my bra might give the game away rather quickly.

"I've got to run," I said, switching to English and blowing him a kiss. "I need to stop at the chemist before work . . ."

And pick up a few more pregnancy tests, I added in my head.

"Is everything OK?" he asked.

"Of course, just stress headaches," I said. At least the "stress" part was true.

I took a quick sip of coffee—and immediately spat it out, remembering that too much caffeine wasn't good for pregnant women.

Serge looked at me sideways, and I waved my hand in front of my mouth. "Too hot," I told him with an apologetic look as I regretfully tipped the remainder of the delicious liquid down the sink.

"No problem, Bella," he said with a smile. Serge had taken to calling me Bella recently. A combination of *belle* and Ella. It was charming and adorable, just like him. I had a vision of me telling him the news then, of his muscular arms engulfing me, and of his face beaming with joy, but for some reason I couldn't quite make the words come out of my mouth. I had to get my head around the implications of being pregnant in France first.

I'd only started dating Serge earlier in the year, although our friendship had been brewing since my first day in Paris when I'd stumbled into his *fromagerie* and had christened him Mr. Cheeseman. We'd been through a lot together, from my innocent bet that I could eat 365 types of French cheese in one year, to him then helping me win the bet; from him stealing a kiss after a decadent cheese dinner, to me stealing a kiss back after realizing I was in love with him.

When I first arrived in Paris, I hadn't been looking to get into a relationship. Regardless, I had quickly fallen head over heels for a villain named Gaston. It was a ridiculous rebound tryst that, in hindsight, was as foolish a relationship as I could have gotten myself into. But Gaston was suave. And at the time, nursing a broken heart from a failed long-term relationship in Australia, I fell under the spell of his French charms—the very same "French charms" that led me to walk in on him in bed with two other people—neither of them me—a few months later. That was, I hoped, the last lesson I'd ever need on how to stop falling for idiots.

After my own rather dramatic down-and-out-in-Paris moment, I realized what a fool I'd been to remain oblivious to the real hero in my story, Serge. He wasn't the type of guy I'd normally go for—which mostly meant that he was kind and cared about what was important to me—but I'd been blind to true love for long enough. So, I'd fled Paris to accost him on a cheese-buying trip in the Loire Valley and tell him how I felt. It was a grand gesture and, thankfully, for both my happiness and my pride, it had worked.

And Serge had ended up being everything I'd never imagined I could have in a boyfriend. He was sturdy and sweet, adventurous and determined, a hopeless romantic, and a fierce advocate for French culture and tradition, which manifested in his absolute devotion to, and adoration of, French cheese.

Since my declaration of love, our relationship had blossomed beautifully, and I adored the man. Sure, we had our differences, including his abhorrence for all things technological—including my own cheese-devoted Instagram account, which had gained his *fromagerie* a bit of a cult following among Anglophone tourists—but in other matters, we mostly saw eye to eye.

Still, I couldn't help wondering if thrusting a baby into our relationship was just asking for trouble. We'd been seeing each other for less than a year. We hadn't even had a major argument yet. We certainly hadn't discussed having children together. Could a mutual love of cheese, Paris, and each other be enough to get us through this?

I was relieved to have the day ahead of me at work to continue to mull things over. All this introspection felt a little too serious for this early in the morning.

It was cold when I stepped outside. The summer warmth had seemed to evaporate as soon as I'd flipped the calendar over to October. There's a specific smell in Paris that I'd come to associate with autumn and winter. It is a combination of warm air escaping from the Métro grilles and of cooking aromas wafting from school canteens. Occasionally sneaking into the mix is a slight waft of urine, but thankfully the frequent autumn rain helped wash that away.

I wasn't surprised to find Tim already in the Food To Go Go office when I arrived. Since getting additional funding earlier in the year, he had been putting in long hours at the office. The company was understaffed but somehow managed to keep growing despite everyone, including Tim, wondering how it was even staying afloat. But Tim was determined, and his passion for good-quality delivery food seemed to fuel our success.

"Oh, hey, Ella," he said. He sounded exhausted.

"Everything OK?" I asked.

"Rough night with the baby."

I sympathized. "She's still not sleeping?"

"No, she's like the devil. I feel like I'll never function normally again."

"How old is she now?" I asked.

"She's nearly ten months," he lamented.

"And it's still bad?" Normally I would have dismissed Tim's baby complaints. *Why have kids if you enjoy sleep?* I'd figured. But I had more at stake now.

"Oh, God, yes and more. My advice is don't have a baby—at least not if you want to maintain some semblance of a normal life. Compared to being a parent, this shite is easy," he said, waving around at the empty desks in our office.

I laughed, hoping Tim was exaggerating, but his face remained somber, the dark circles under his eyes almost making him look like a zombie. *Shit,* I thought, sitting down and turning on my computer.

I raced through some work but kept getting distracted by thoughts of the pregnancy. I needed some time to obsess over the morning's events and figure out what the hell I was going to do. I asked Tim if he wanted me to grab him a coffee. He got up and hugged me.

"Get me a three-shot latte, Ella. It's going to be a long day."

Thankfully our new office was a short walk from Flat White, which I consider to be one of Paris's best coffee shops (completely unbiased by the fact that I'd worked there for close to a year, or by the fact that I still received a friends-and-family discount). I was relieved to see Chris's smiling face behind the machine when I walked in.

I fell onto a stool by the counter. It felt comforting to be in the café, on familiar turf, the warmth of the oven and the aroma of chocolate chip cookies almost making me forget about the pregnancy test that, by now, I'd stashed away in my hand-bag. I often found myself pining for the ease and familiarity of working at Flat White. As much as I liked working in an office, I certainly missed the social interaction that came with the café.

"So, what can I get for you, El?" Chris asked, his Australian accent making me feel even more at home. "The usual?"

"Sure," I said without thinking. "No, wait . . . Do you have decaf?"

"Huh? Of course, we don't have decaf. Blasphemy! What's going on?"

"Nothing's going on," I said, while hoping that the sudden rush of blood to my cheeks wasn't as visible as it felt. "I'm just cutting down on coffee. I'll grab a hot chocolate."

Chris raised his eyebrows but didn't say anything more. He was always the gentleman with me, which was surprising because he was quite the ladies' man about town otherwise. Despite both of us being from Melbourne, we'd only met when I'd started working at Flat White shortly after arriving in Paris, and we'd been friendly ever since. I'd found him handsome in those early days, but nothing had ever happened between us because I wasn't French, and Chris had a penchant for dating (mostly emotionally unstable) French women. But now, I was grateful for his friendship. Outside of his relationship dramas, he was serious about coffee, and he was a sturdy friend. He almost felt like the brother I never had.

"And I'll get a triple-shot latte for Tim," I said.

"Still with the baby troubles?" Chris asked, all too aware of Tim's change of pace since becoming a father, not so secretly mourning the loss of his drinking pal.

"Yep," I said. "Better give us some of those cookies as well."

"You bet ya."

I walked slowly back to work, cradling our takeaway cups to keep them warm. Taking a sip of my drink, I was rudely reminded that it wasn't coffee, and that I was destined to be ordering hot chocolates for some time to come. And then I started thinking about how having a baby would affect my life in France, and how it would affect my relationship with Serge.

Is it even a good time for us to be considering a baby? I was in a good place at work, and I felt at home in Paris. I had colleagues and friends and felt like I had a good support network. And Serge had just decided to open another branch of his *fromagerie* and was scouting locations. He was motivated and was looking forward to expanding his business. Surely a baby would slow that down. Perhaps he would even come to resent this interruption to his plan.

And does he even want children? I'd been shocked when he told me that he'd been married before, but I knew that things with his ex-wife had been tense long before they decided to divorce, which was why I'd assumed they'd never had a child themselves.

And what about me? Do I *want a baby? And do I want a* French *baby?* Back when I was in Australia, I'd thought I wanted to have kids. Then, after my sudden breakup with my long-term boyfriend Paul, I told myself I'd need to be 100 percent certain with a man before even contemplating adding children. And while I was certain about my love for Serge, I couldn't be certain about how he'd react to my news. *Oh, God! Will I have to raise this baby alone? Just when life was finally trotting along smoothly . . .*

I was then struck by another harsh realization. Being pregnant meant no more French wine, no gooey cheese—*Oh, mon Dieu! No gooey cheese!*—and I could only imagine what else.

Plus, I knew nothing about growing a child, let alone what to do with one once it was born.

I tried to calculate when I became pregnant. I figured that it couldn't have been more than six weeks earlier. Serge and I'd had a pretty raunchy weekend in Provence toward the end of summer, and I was sure that we hadn't been as careful with protection as we could have been. *I guess that much is obvious now!*

I'd like to say the sex had been worth it, but that would have to be assessed over the next eighteen years or so. Regardless of how it happened—and not to get distracted by the memory of the delicious act itself—it was a relief to realize that the pregnancy was still sufficiently early to leave us with options. Even so, these were decisions I'd have to make with Serge. He was my life in Paris, and our relationship was the whole reason I'd stayed in France. *But how can I tell him that I'm worried about how much pressure a baby will put on our relationship? That if things don't work out, we'll have even more difficult decisions to make?*

It was in moments of agonizing like this that I desperately missed working with Clotilde. She'd recommended me for the job at Food To Go Go, where she was working, after we'd become flatmates, but she'd moved on months ago to pursue a career in modeling. Now, she spent most of her time travelling and working overseas. She would have known what to say to make me feel better. Pretty much since the day I'd met her, she'd been great at helping me sort out my life in France. Even when I'd busted Gaston—who, in a complicated turn of events, turned out to be her cousin—she'd taken my side, navigating me through with plenty of wine and moral support. After Serge, she was the person I was closest to in France, and her recent string of trips abroad had made Paris a little lonelier. Thankfully, she would be back this weekend from her month-long work stint in New York. If I didn't have the guts to tell Serge about the baby by then, I was sure she'd help me figure out a plan.

I forced myself to ignore any more thoughts of having a child so I could focus on work. Somehow, I even managed to shelve the question of how to tell Serge as a future-Ella-problem. But when six o'clock rolled around and the office emptied out, the pressing feeling was back in my tummy. Hoping it was in part due to hunger, I used my phone to check the food safety recommendations for pregnant women just in case we were destined for a cheese dinner (not an unusual occurrence, as *fromage* was pretty much a prerequisite at any meal with Serge).

The search results were as bad as I was expecting. No soft cheeses unless they were pasteurized (which in France they hardly ever were, so *au revoir,* Chabichou, Sainte-Maure, and Valençay); no mold-ripened soft cheese (bye-bye, Brie and Camembert); and no blue-veined cheese (farewell, Roquefort). I tried to look on the bright side; there was still Comté. And Cantal and Gruyère. All was not lost.

"What shall we eat tonight?" Serge asked with a raise of his eyebrow when I got home. He held up a Neufchâtel, the heart-shaped cow's milk cheese from Normandy. I could see more cheese varieties lining our kitchen bench.

"I'm not sure I feel like cheese," I said, trying to sound cheery despite wanting to cry.

Serge looked at me like I was a stranger. "Ella, *ça va?*" he asked.

"Of course, I'm OK, I just thought maybe we'd eaten enough rich food recently. Perhaps we should have a cheese break. A cheese detox?"

"This seems like a very bad idea, Ella."

"You're right. Can we just keep it simple then? Some thirty-month-old Comté?"

I knew full well that aged Comté was hardly "simple," but if I was to live through the next nine months on a cheese-restrictive diet, then why not go all out on those varieties I *could* still consume? I was sure *bébé* would agree with my logic.

"Good idea," Serge said, seeming relieved. As he began placing packages back in the fridge, I thought about all the wheels of Brie and ash-coated goat cheeses that were screaming to be eaten, regretting not having had the chance to organize one last sweet goodbye party with them.

Serge made us pork chops and Puy lentils while I pretended to have some work to finish on my laptop. He brought me a glass of red wine, which taunted me as I googled the chance of getting a false-positive result with a pregnancy test (very slim) and then looked up ways to tell your boyfriend that you're pregnant. I felt uneasy as I read through articles suggesting things like: "Why not present the father-to-be with the positive pregnancy test and a little baby outfit?" or "Give him a t-shirt that says 'World's Best Dad.'" But all this seemed a little contrived, especially for a down-to-earth guy like Serge.

It was too hard keeping the pregnancy a secret with offers of coffee, wine, and gooey cheese flying about. That, and I knew I'd need Serge's help figuring out how to navigate the French medical system.

Part of me was also desperate to know whether he'd be supportive of the news. It almost felt like a relationship test—one that I wasn't yet ready to administer, but that I was still keen to know the results of.

When Serge sang out that dinner was ready, I grabbed my untouched glass of wine, shut my laptop, and took a few deep breaths. *It's now or never, Ella! You've got this!*

I began to eat immediately. I was ravenous. *Is it because of the pregnancy?* Perhaps it was just nerves. While I was inhaling dinner, Serge started telling me how an American lady had visited his store earlier that day looking to buy a tower of different cheeses for her wedding.

"And she kept insisting that she wanted all the cheeses to be piled on top of each other, from big at the bottom to little at the top. And I kept telling her that each type of cheese should be kept separate so she didn't ruin the flavors, but she wouldn't listen."

"You can't buy taste," I joked, but Serge was already all worked up.

"She told me that she didn't need advice; she just wanted to order the cheese. But I didn't want her to be disappointed at her wedding—after all, it's such an important day—so I also informed her that the formation of the cheese, all piled into a 'cake' format, would make it impossible to cut. But then she showed me a picture of one—I knew logistically it wouldn't work but, yes, maybe it looked quite appealing . . . It was incredibly frustrating."

I laughed. Serge was very particular about how cheese should be served, and the American bride sounded like she couldn't care less. I wished I'd been there to witness the exchange.

"So, did she end up ordering something or did you scare her off?" I asked.

"Of course, she placed a large order, but I will write strict instructions for cheese serving and include them in the delivery. Then it is her loss if she chooses aesthetics over flavor. At least that way I don't have to lose sleep."

"Speaking of sleep," I said, figuring this was as good an entry point as I was going to get, "I have some news."

"As do I," he countered.

"Oh," I mumbled in surprise. *What on earth could Serge have to tell me?* "You first, then."

"I think I've found the location for our new *fromagerie* in the sixth *arrondissement*. It looks perfect. Apparently, the old store-holder—a shoemaker, of all things—had been there for thirty years. But he died," he said matter-of-factly.

"Oh," I said, about to express my condolences.

"So, it's now available," Serge continued. "I need to let the agent know as soon as possible. Even tonight. What do you think?"

He pulled out the real-estate listing with photos of the location. I still wasn't sure how, if at all, the pregnancy would affect Serge's ability to take on another store. I wondered if maybe I should wait to tell him.

"Are you sure you want the responsibility of a second store?" I asked.

"*Mais oui*," he said. "It is already decided, *non*?"

"Yes," I said, stalling. "But do you have time? You've been so busy recently."

"Fanny has already agreed to take on more at the original location while it gets off the ground," he said.

"Oh, good," I said flatly.

"You don't think it is a good idea?" he asked.

"It's not exactly that . . .," I said.

"What's the problem, then?" he asked.

"No problem, it sounds great," I said, forcing a smile.

"*Bon*," he said, as though that was that.

"*Bon*," I said.

"And what did you want to tell me?" he asked, slicing off a huge chunk of pork and putting it into his mouth. I waited a few seconds and let him chew, worried he might choke.

No point beating around the bush any further, I figured.

"I'm pregnant."

He coughed awkwardly. "You're what?" he asked.

"*Je suis enceinte*," I repeated. I'd learned the French word for "pregnant" while taking the test that morning—a pretty handy addition to my vocab list, all things considered.

"*Bébé*," I said pointing at my stomach for extra effect.

Serge looked at me, mouth agape, and took a large gulp of wine.

"*Oh là là*," was all he could say, shaking his head.

Chapter

2

RIGHT WHEN I WAS GETTING worried that Serge had suffered a silent heart attack, I asked him if he understood what I was saying.

"It's hard not to understand, Ella, but are you sure?" he asked. My heart sank, as his expression remained blank.

"I'm pretty sure, yes. But it's still early so anything could happen. I think it must have been from our weekend in Provence," I said.

He let out a chuckle and gave me a knowing nod with raised eyebrows. I waited for the gravity of what I'd told him to sink in. I kept wishing that he'd get up and hug me, tell me that everything would be perfect.

Instead he said, "Right," and stood up, clearing our plates and whisking away my still-full wine glass.

"Is that all you have to say?" I called after him, getting progressively worried. He started doing the dishes loudly, and I left him to process while I waited nervously at the table. I'd had all day to try to come to terms with what that tiny cross on the pregnancy test meant (and still, I wasn't sure how my life, or our lives, would change because of it). Maybe he just needed a few minutes.

Serge came back to the table with the Comté, another (very) full glass of wine for himself, and a glass of water for me.

"*Ma Bella*," he started, drawing out these two simple words, making me feel like minutes elapsed before he continued, "Are you OK?"

"Sure. I mean, it's a bit of a shock, but I don't have any symptoms or anything. Not yet anyway," I bumbled, not really understanding what he was asking.

"No, not physically. With the news. Is this what you want?" I could tell he was judging my reactions, feeling me out in the same way that I was trying to feel him out.

So, I rambled. "Well, I hadn't really thought about it before, to be honest. I'm so happy with you, and we're in such a good place relationship-wise, and I'm not sure I've actually considered the repercussions of having a child here."

Serge looked a little lost, so I slowed down. I often forgot that English wasn't his first language, despite his dreamy accent when he spoke it. I took a breath. "I think it could be good," I said, feeling immediately like I was out on the edge of a bridge begging for a reason not to step forward.

"Me, too," he said after a short pause. I leaped back to safety. Relief surged through me, and I got up and hugged him. He pulled me onto his lap and kissed me.

"It's what you want?" he asked, wrapping his arms around me again.

"As long as you want it, too," I said, enjoying feeling cocooned and safe for the first time since peeing on the stick that morning.

"*Ah, oui.* A very happy accident," he said.

The moment of bliss was, however, short-lived. Serge sat me back down on my own chair, grabbed both my shoulders, and said to me seriously, "Things will have to change, Ella."

"Huh? Why?" I asked.

"Well, I think it would be silly to take on a new lease and open a second branch of the *fromagerie* now."

"Oh, no," I said. I'd worried that this might be the case.

"*Mais oui*, I think we'll have enough to worry about with the pregnancy and the baby's arrival."

"But what about the perfect location you found? You've been planning the second store for ages," I said.

"These things can wait, Ella," he said, pragmatically.

"But are you sure they have to?" I asked, feeling guilty that he could so easily put a dream on hold.

"Of course, and we'll have to move," he said, which seemed even more out of the blue.

"To where? Not back to Australia?" I asked, shocked.

Despite it seeming like a logical conclusion in retrospect, it hadn't yet occurred to me that I might move home. My life was here in Paris.

"*Non, non, non,*" he said. "Unless you want to?"

"*Non*," I said, offended. "*J'adore la France!*"

Serge looked relieved. "But still, we can't have a baby here," he said.

"Huh?" I asked, looking around at Serge's gorgeous apartment and wondering why we'd need to relocate. "Babies don't take up much room."

"A baby cannot grow up in such a cramped home. It's not good for their creativity and development. Nor for our relationship."

I sat mute, surprised at Serge's sudden sure-headedness on the topic. I wondered if he'd already thought this through.

"Yes, we'll need to move somewhere with more space," he added. "We could get a house with a garden. Maybe even get some animals."

"That sounds idyllic, but can we afford that in Paris?" I asked.

He laughed. "Ella, you do know there is a France outside of central Paris, don't you?"

My jaw dropped.

"Not for me, there's not," I said. Admittedly, a garden sounded nice, but the thought of leaving our neighborhood and setting up somewhere new terrified me. Besides, I was an inner-city person. And it had taken me long enough to learn how to live here like a local. I didn't want to go through that again.

"Do you remember when you came to meet me in the Loire Valley?" he asked.

"Of course I do," I said.

"Well, that is the real France. The France where people still say 'Bonjour' when they pass each other in the street, where they return home from work to eat lunch as a family, where you can walk down the road without smelling somebody else's piss."

"And?" I asked.

"And maybe it's time you experienced what life can be like outside of the capital."

"Let's not get ahead of ourselves, Serge. Maybe we should just wait and see how things play out with the pregnancy."

"Let me take care of things, Bella. You go rest."

"I'm hardly even pregnant. I don't need to rest," I protested.

He shushed me, handed me the plate of Comté, and told me to go to the couch. Wide-eyed, I obeyed—I mean, eating

Comté on the couch was one of my favorite things, and I figured that Serge probably just needed more time to acclimatize to the news.

Lying down and feeding myself slivers of cheese like a Roman goddess might feed herself grapes, I tried to imagine leaving Paris. I didn't get far. I loved our *quartier*, Le Marais, and I loved living near my work and Serge's *fromagerie*.

I couldn't imagine leaving our cosy apartment simply because a tiny little human was about to enter our lives. I was sure all Serge's talk of changing his work plans and moving was just an immediate reaction to the shock. I'd let him freak out for a while and then I would talk some sense into him.

It'd been an anxiety-inducing day, and the mix of the hard, salty cheese and the blanket Serge had insisted on putting over my legs was too comfortable. After a few unintentional head-nods, I gave up trying to fight my eyelids and promptly fell asleep.

I woke up at midnight and saw Serge sitting behind his computer. It was a strange sight. Normally he avoided technology. He leaped up when he saw I was awake and ushered me to bed.

"What were you doing?" I asked, so sleepy I could hardly form words.

"Never mind, Bella, just getting a few things organized."

I was too tired to protest and allowed him to tuck me in under the blankets.

"Are you coming?" I asked.

"Two more minutes," he promised, although I was hardly in any state to adjudicate because, within seconds of my head hitting the pillow, I was out cold.

When I awoke the next morning, Serge was missing from our bed. I couldn't be sure if he'd joined me at all the previous night, and the sheets didn't give away any clues. I stumbled out into the kitchen, where I found him, still on his computer and looking slightly deranged in an old gray sweatshirt and faded blue boxer shorts.

"Have you been up all night?" I asked, hugging him from behind and trying to get a look over his shoulder at what he was doing.

"I had a few hours of sleep," he said, folding his screen shut.

"Serge, are you sure everything is OK?" I asked.

"Of course, this baby really is the most wonderful surprise!"

I breathed a sigh of relief.

"So, what's with the research then? You do realize that we have nearly nine months to figure all this out, don't you?" I asked him.

"I am just getting my head around things. But I think I have found a solution."

"Oh?" I asked. I hoped I wasn't about to regret sleeping last night.

"But let me get a few things in order before I explain my idea," he said, evasively. "Coffee?" he offered.

"I'll have tea," I said.

"Right, no coffee because of the baby," he said, sympathetically.

"Apparently so."

He leaned down and kissed my belly, saying hello to the tiny ball of cells currently residing somewhere deep within. At the idea of our little family, I felt love coursing through my body.

I sipped my tea and replayed our conversation, looking for clues. Finally, I said gently, "Serge, I'm worried that you think having a baby has to completely change your life."

"Oh, Ella, now is not the time to worry," he replied.

I wondered what there was to *not* worry about.

"Why don't we get out of the city sometime soon? Go see more of the France that I was telling you about," he suggested. "The fresh air will do us good."

The idea of long walks in the countryside did sound nice. Serge and I could ponder and discuss the future, and I could convince him that our current living arrangement would be totally fine with a new addition.

"Yes! A weekend away, just the two of us," I said.

"Or we could go visit Jacques and Marie."

Jacques was Serge's friend. He ran a bed and breakfast with his wife, Marie, near Sainte-Maure-de-Touraine. Jacques was very French and very friendly. He'd actually been witness to my declaration of love to Serge when I'd hunted him down in the Loire Valley in a manic state at the end of the previous winter. His property was beautiful, and it was as far from Paris as you could get in terms of nightlife or any life other than goats and the occasional spotting of a ruggedly handsome farmer.

"Sure, I guess that could work, too," I said, not wanting to shut him down. Besides, it actually made sense that Serge would want to visit the Loire. He probably needed to go back to where he'd grown up with his own parents to come to terms with the news.

He nodded, and I felt like we were slowly getting on the same page.

"So, I guess I should make an appointment to see a doctor," I said.

"Good point. I've taken care of that. I made you an appointment for this morning at 9:30 a.m. The doctor apparently speaks English but I'll come with you for support." Serge had clearly sprung into productivity mode.

I checked my watch. It was already half past eight. I'd desperately wanted to call my mum or Billie, my best friend back in Australia, to share the news, but it looked like that would have to wait.

Serge shuffled me into the bathroom and told me he was popping out to get me a croissant. I had a vision flash through my mind of him never coming back and of me telling our future child that Papa had gone out on a pastry run and didn't return. Thankfully, I knew this wasn't his style.

Serge's reaction had mostly been reassuring. He didn't fight me, he didn't seem disappointed, and he didn't run for the door. If anything, he just seemed to become even more protective. And I did love him. Although we'd only been together for a short time (especially compared to Paul, whom I'd been with for close to a decade), I thought he'd make a great *papa* to our little one.

I inspected my stomach in the bathroom mirror, but it looked the same as ever. Not particularly taut, but also not giving any indication that it was harboring a human. I gave it a rub before getting ready for the doctor's appointment.

Chapter

3

"SO, YOU THINK YOU ARE pregnant?" Doctor Caron, a petite and quite pretty woman who must have only been in her late twenties, asked in French.

I nodded, wondering when she would switch to English.

"Well, before we get to any of that, I have a few general questions about . . ." She spoke quickly, and I lost track of what she was saying about halfway through her sentence. My heart was beating loudly in my ears, which didn't help matters. I looked desperately at Serge. He nodded and told the doctor that he'd help interpret for me. So, the questioning about my medical history began, all passed through a surprisingly un-squeamish-looking Serge.

"So, when was the first time you had sex?" Serge relayed.

"Oh, um . . ." I blushed hard. "I think I was sixteen," I said, attempting an apology at Serge with my eyes.

"And your monthly periods, were they regular?"

I nodded, mortified. Serge and I hadn't even peed in front of each other, let alone spoken in detail about our most personal bodily functions.

"Were they painful?"

I shook my head no.

"And when did you last get checked for . . ." Serge faltered, looking for the right word. "Sexy diseases?" he continued.

"Ah, yes, sexually transmitted diseases," the doctor chimed in, by now obviously enjoying the free English lesson.

Oh, God! I thought, wanting to disappear. I shot Serge another apologetic look and told him that it had been a couple of years since I had been tested. She tapped away on her computer, and I wondered what she was noting down.

"And now the doctor would like to know if this was a planned pregnancy," Serge asked, waiting to follow my lead.

I almost burst out laughing, but held it together.

"*Non*, but we're happy," I told the doctor. Serge grabbed my hand under the desk and squeezed it.

After more questions about our families' respective medical histories, the doctor ordered me onto the scales (normally a pastime I tried to avoid) and mentioned something about me not eating too much bread. I looked at her in shock. *Is she telling me to watch my weight? How does she even* know *how much bread I eat anyway?* Thankfully, she didn't mention anything about cheese. I might have short-circuited if I'd had to cut back my already-pared-back consumption.

While I was still reeling from the idea of eating fewer baguettes, Serge asked the doctor something about whether it would be too stressful moving house during the first trimester. *He's still hung up on that?* I thought. She gave a hurried response that included something about not lifting anything heavy, and then asked Serge to step outside so she could perform the dating scan. I was ripped back into the present moment.

"What the hell is a dating scan?" I asked, grabbing Serge's hand desperately.

"To tell how old the baby is," he replied, sounding surprised about my lack of knowledge. "It will be fine," he said as he left the room.

But it didn't feel fine, it felt terrifying. Even if I made it through the nine months of pregnancy in a foreign country, how the hell was I going to deliver this child in French? It was one thing ordering a wheel of Brie, but delivering a baby in a different language? *Oh, God!*

Doctor Caron was clearly oblivious to my distress and directed me to take off my pants and hop on the examination table. Normally at this point in Australia, you would have been offered a gown in a fairly feeble attempt to preserve your modesty, but in France, it was more of an open book, or open legs, policy. I still wasn't sure why I even needed to take my pants off, because as far as I knew, she just needed to access my abdomen. *It must be to avoid ruining my clothes*, I told myself. I'd seen pregnancy ultrasounds a million times on movies and in TV shows and figured I'd just lie back, have goo squirted on my belly, and then get to see my tiny baby. But it turns out Hollywood glamorizes most aspects of pregnancy and giving birth, and I was about to learn that the hard way.

She wheeled over a machine and grabbed a long, thin instrument that couldn't have looked more like a dildo if it tried. *Right*, I thought. *And what the hell is that?* A wave of panic rushed over me as I wondered if this was just the "French way."

A little lube later and the "ultrasound wand" was doing its job. I'd barely had time to register the shock when a blurry image appeared on the screen. Doctor Caron started pointing out the "baby," which resembled a jelly bean more than any humanlike figure. She fiddled around with the machine, moving the camera about as she went, and said with certainty, "*Six semaines*." Six weeks pregnant.

So, it was *the weekend in Provence that did it*, I thought.

"*Et voilà, le battement de cœur.* The heartbeat," she said.

I'd had no idea that something so small could even *have* a heart, but as I listened to the quick thudding sound coming out of the machine, I realized just how attached I'd already become to the prospect of this child. Tears welled in my eyes.

The doctor handed me a rough paper towel. *That's sweet,* I thought, wiping my eyes. She looked at me like I was deranged, handed me a fresh paper towel, and then instructed me to wipe before getting dressed.

I was more than grateful when the appointment was over. I wasn't prudish, or had never considered myself to be so in the past, but the color of my face told me I still had a way to go before I was completely comfortable stripping in a doctor's office.

"Six weeks pregnant!" I said to Serge as I showed him the printout of our tiny babe, not knowing whether what I was feeling was joy, panic, or an odd combination of both.

He hugged me and said, "You've made me so 'appy." The way Serge said "happy" made me happy, too. And then I started to cry. It was unintentional but the tears flew out of me like drops being flung from a particularly violent waterfall. I carefully folded our first baby picture and put it in my jacket pocket.

Things had definitely moved quickly since I'd peed on the stick the previous morning. Now I just had to come to terms with the fact that my glamorous Parisian existence, where I frequently indulged in eating cheese and drinking wine, would have to be put on hold.

One step at a time, Ella, I repeated over and over under my breath.

The next morning, I called Mum. I waited until Serge had gone out for a baguette (at my request—pregnancy cravings were already in full force, I'd told him, happily ignoring the doctor's advice) so I could have some privacy.

I wasn't sure I should even tell Mum about the pregnancy before the twelve-week mark, but I still felt like I needed to talk to her. I needed a dose of support.

"Ella, darling. How are you? How is Serge?" Mum asked. Since their last visit to Paris in August, she and my stepfather-to-be, Ray, had fallen even harder for Serge. He'd wooed them with cheese and charm, just like he'd wooed me. Every time I called Mum, she now asked about him in a concerned tone, as if she was worried I'd do something that would jeopardize the relationship.

"He's well. He just popped out for fresh bread," I told her truthfully.

"How wonderfully French," she replied, always one to blindly love a cliché.

"So, what's been going on, Mum? How are things with you and Ray?" I asked. Despite my original perspective that no one would ever be good enough for Mum, I now quite liked the man who'd whipper-snippered his way into her garden, and then her life. So much so that I, too, feared she might do something that would jeopardize their relationship. Like mother, like daughter, I guess.

"Well, actually, Ray and I finally chose a date for our wedding, this time next year. We're thinking just a small ceremony, family and close friends, that kind of thing. You know the garden looks so lovely at the start of spring, and the timing should give you and Serge plenty of notice to book tickets. It's not a peak time for travel either, so it shouldn't be too expensive," she rattled on.

"Sure," I said before realizing that, at this time next year, I'd have a tiny baby. It was an idea I was still trying to wrap my head around. "Actually, next year might be difficult," I said.

"Why? What could you possibly have planned for this time next year?"

"Nothing in particular," I lied. "Anyway, I'll have to check with Serge. I think he was considering a holiday around then."

"Perfect. You can holiday in Australia. Serge said he'd love to see where you came from."

"Mum, it's not always that easy to come all the way to Australia."

"Are you trying to tell me you can't be bothered flying home for your own mother's wedding? Ray will be devastated. You know how much he likes Serge. Do you not want to come either?" I could feel her starting to get angry.

"Of course I want to come," I tried to convince her.

"Then tell me, Ella. What's stopping you?" she asked.

There was clearly no way I was going to get away with not telling her about this baby.

"Well, I'll most likely have a baby by then," I said.

The phone went silent.

"Mum?" I asked.

"You'll most likely have a *what*? Is that your cute way of telling me you're getting a kitten or something?"

"No. A baby, baby. You know, when two people love each other very much, sometimes they have a special cuddle and—"

"Ella," she scolded.

Now obviously wasn't the time for jokes.

"I'm pregnant," I said in a more serious tone.

"By Serge, I hope," she said.

"Of course by Serge."

"Is this something you were planning? How far along are you?"

"I wouldn't say we'd planned it, but we're happy about it. I'm only six weeks, so it's still too early to really be telling people, but you were very persuasive."

"Right. Well, I won't mention it to anyone," she said coldly.

"You can tell Ray if you want," I said, trying to get her to warm up, or at least not just dismiss the conversation.

"As you wish," she said. "Anyway, I should go."

"Don't you have anything else to say?" I asked, hoping for congratulations, or perhaps some words of encouragement.

"What would you like me to say? That it's great that you'll miss my wedding? That it's great that I'll miss the birth of my grandchild?"

I rolled my eyes. *Of course my unborn baby is all about my mother.*

"It's not like that, Mum," I said.

"And have you even considered moving?"

"Serge did mention it," I said.

"Back to Australia?" she asked, her tone lightening.

"Oh, no," I said and she sighed. "Serge mentioned moving to a bigger place so we'd have more room for the baby. I'm trying to convince him we don't need to go anywhere. I think he's just in shock."

"You probably *will* need more room once the baby arrives," she said. "You can't stay in a one-bedroom apartment forever.

And it's certainly smarter to do it while it's just the two of you."

In a way, I knew Mum was probably right, but what she was forgetting was how hard I'd fought to make this little part of Paris my home. Besides, I was the one who was pregnant, and I felt like everybody was suddenly telling me what to do.

"But what about where I want to live?" I said.

"Ella, it's no longer only about you. You have a baby to consider. And you have Serge to consider. You're all linked now. Did you not think about that before getting pregnant?"

Her words hung in the air.

The silence was broken by Serge's key turning in the front door.

"Mum, I've got to go," I said. "And sorry about the wedding," I added, but she'd already hung up.

⌒

"I booked tickets for Friday," Serge announced when he walked inside.

"What tickets?" I asked, thinking perhaps he'd heard me talking to Mum about going back to Australia.

"To see Jacques and Marie. I've arranged for Fanny to look after the store all weekend," he said.

"Oh," I said, still confused. "I didn't realize you meant this weekend. I can't go anyway. Clotilde is in town."

"She's already agreed to join us. She'll come with Jean," he said. Clotilde and her father, Jean, had a very close relationship; however, it was a traditional one and there was a lot that Jean didn't know about his little girl. Back when Clotilde and I were still flatmates and he'd found out that she'd been working as a foot fetish model, he'd threatened to cut her off completely. He was rather old-fashioned in his values, but he had eventually come to accept Clotilde's modeling career.

"You spoke to Clotilde?" I asked, surprised at how onto everything Serge suddenly was. Normally our social calendar was my domain.

"I hope you don't mind," he said.

"No, that's great. Seems like it's all sorted." I tried to sound positive but felt completely out of the loop.

"You just relax and let me take care of you," he said.

I ripped into the baguette and slathered a hunk of it with butter and raspberry jam. It was hard relinquishing control, but I knew I needed to trust Serge in order for any of this to work out.

Chapter

4

JACQUES MET US AT TOURS train station, and as we drove to his bed and breakfast, I had the most glorious flashback to when I'd fled Paris to come here and meet Serge, and of our perfect first date that had followed.

Marie welcomed us warmly and ushered us into her garden, where she'd set an outdoor table under a large chestnut tree. Little posies of wildflowers set off the cream tablecloth, and colorful cushions lined the chairs. I felt my shoulders soften as the sun speckled and warmed my skin. Clotilde and Jean arrived shortly after in Jean's convertible.

The wine flowed over lunch, although not in my direction, as Marie dished up leeks in vinaigrette, followed by a plump roast chicken and a decadent tray of local cheese, which mostly taunted me.

"It must be such a relief to get out of Paris," Jacques said to our group. "I don't know how you cope living like sardines."

"I was saying the same thing to Ella recently," Serge agreed.

"But Paris has everything we need," I said, defending my city.

"Except easy access to local wineries," Jacques said.

"Isn't there a winery in Montmartre?" I asked.

"Only one?" he said with a chuckle, and I had to restrain myself from listing off the other million things I loved about living in Paris.

I'd just bitten into Marie's fruit tart with pears fresh from her garden—and was thinking to myself that I now had the perfect excuse for accepting seconds, thanks to *bébé*—when Marie asked Serge, casually and out of the blue, "And how is Françoise?"

I nearly choked on my rather large mouthful. *Why is she bringing up Serge's ex-wife in front of me? Perhaps she thinks I'm not listening, or that I might not understand her French.* I tried not to take it personally, reasoning with myself that it was only natural that she'd come up in conversation every now and then, especially here, considering her family was also from the Loire.

Still, even the prospect of Françoise made me nervous because I knew so little about her. Other than a few general discussions about their marriage, Serge preferred to, as he would say, "leave the past in the past." And I didn't push the topic because I understood the desire to not rehash old relationships. Just thinking about Paul or Gaston was enough to send me into a rage.

I surreptitiously watched Serge's face for a reaction as he finished chewing. He avoided looking at me and then said, somewhat sharply, to Marie, "I have not spoken to her recently." I appreciated the sense of finality in his response, but it also managed to kill the vibe around the table.

Clotilde gave me a look and, clearly trying to dissipate the tension, announced, "Ella, want to help me with these?" She got up and started to gather the plates.

As soon as we were out of earshot of the rest of the group, she asked, "So, Ella, what's going on?"

Is it that obvious how uncomfortable the mere thought of Françoise makes me? I wondered.

"Nothing's wrong," I said and attempted a smile.

"Bullshit," she said.

"Seriously, it's nothing. I'm just being stupid. I don't even know why I'm getting so worked up."

"Well, it's kind of a big deal," she said.

I panicked. *Is Serge's ex-wife that big of a deal? Should I be* more *worried?*

"You think?" I asked.

"Well, yeah. When I saw you skip the unpasteurized cheese, I pieced together what was going on," she said.

"Huh?" I asked, suddenly confused. *What does Françoise have to do with me not eating cheese?*

And then I twigged.

"Oh, you're talking about the pregnancy," I said, almost relieved that my anxieties about Françoise weren't totally transparent.

"So, you *are* pregnant? Ella, this is huge!" Her voice was a mix of excitement and concern.

"In a few more months, I'll be huge . . .," I said, attempting a joke.

She gave me an obliging chuckle.

"I haven't quite gotten my head around it all yet," I continued. "I shouldn't even really be telling people."

"Gosh," she said.

"Is it a terrible thing?" I asked anxiously.

"Do *you* think it's terrible?" she countered.

"Perhaps a little premature," I admitted.

"But are you unhappy about it?" she asked.

"I don't think so," I said honestly.

"Well, then, it sounds like congratulations are in order," she said, kissing both my cheeks.

It was nice to have somebody close to me, other than Serge, celebrate the news. Especially after my own mother's reaction had been so reserved.

"Thank you," I said, wholeheartedly. "Now I just need to initiate my plan to get you to move back to Paris so you can help me get through all this pregnancy stuff."

"You might not need to try too hard. I've been considering coming home. I'm sick of travelling back and forth," she said seriously.

"What? Why didn't you say so sooner?" I asked. "I thought everything was going well."

"I miss life here. I miss you, I miss Papa. For now, I'm just mulling it over," she said, looking out the window. "Anyway, we should probably get back to lunch."

I squeezed Clotilde's hand as we returned to the table. Her levelheadedness and positivity were comforting. *I could do with a dose of her French poise right about now*, I thought, sitting back and trying to relax.

I caught the tail end of an intense-looking conversation between Jacques and Serge: ". . . and with the low interest rates, it probably makes more sense to buy rather than rent," Jacques said.

"Are you planning on moving, Jacques?" I asked, trying to join the conversation.

"Me?" he asked, looking at me blankly and making me wonder if I'd misunderstood what they'd been talking about.

"Jacques was telling me about a goat farm that's just gone on sale in the region," Serge jumped in. "Apparently it's on a beautiful piece of land, and it's not too expensive, either."

"And?" I asked, confused.

"Well, Jacques is planning to go visit tomorrow morning. Perhaps we could join him," he said.

I was about to suggest to Serge that we should probably spend some time talking about our future when Clotilde piped up cheerfully, "I'll come. I love looking at properties," which led to our whole group agreeing to the pre-lunch outing.

As everyone discussed logistics, I worried about Serge. *Could he seriously be considering a move to the country at some point in the future?* I wondered. I knew he wanted us to live somewhere with more space, but here? Really?

When the discussion turned to politics, I quietly asked Clotilde what she thought of the whole situation.

"It's a common phenomenon," she said.

The confused look on my face prompted her to clarify: "Many people in Paris, at least those who weren't born there, dream of returning to where they grew up when they have a family. Maybe Serge has had this plan for years. I guess he just didn't need to enact it until you came along."

"Seriously? You think that's what's going on? I couldn't live in the country. What on earth would I do all day?" The thought of all that fresh air was terrifying.

"Don't worry. I'm sure it's just a flight of fancy. Is that the right expression?" she asked.

I nodded. "So, it's something he might get over?" I asked nervously.

She gave me the type of French shrug that made a confusing discussion even more ambiguous.

After lunch, Marie showed us to our rooms and told us to enjoy the property for the afternoon while she and Jacques ran some errands.

As soon as I'd shut the door, it was impossible not to notice the lack of sirens, car horns, and general noise that I'd come to expect in Paris. All I could hear were birds and the wind. The silence was almost ominous.

"Is there anything you want to tell me about why we're going to look at a farm for sale tomorrow?" I asked Serge.

"Do not worry, Bella. Jacques had already lined it up before I told him we were coming to visit. Maybe we can just go so we do not offend him," he said, rubbing my shoulders.

"So, it's just for Jacques, then? Or is this what you had in mind when you said we needed to move out of central Paris?"

"There is no harm in looking, right?" he said, avoiding my question.

"Serge, are you sure everything is OK? I'm starting to worry that the news of the baby has made you feel like we need a complete life overhaul," I said as gently as I could. Meanwhile, I was furiously trying to figure out why he was even entertaining the idea of looking at property out here. I certainly didn't believe that it was only for Jacques's benefit.

"But you agree we need to make changes, yes?" he asked.

"We've got plenty of time before the baby comes," I said. "I don't think we should rush into anything."

"But you will at least come?" Serge asked. "Everybody else seems interested."

"I guess. I'm just not sure if there's much point. I thought we were out here to clear our heads and come to terms with the news of the baby. This farm visit seems like an unnecessary distraction."

"We can probably taste some goat cheese," he added, obviously having kept this selling point up his sleeve.

"Why didn't you lead with that?" I joked, resigning myself to the fact that Serge would be going, with or without me. At least if I was there I could do damage control if need be.

Seeing Serge's face relax now that I'd agreed to join them, I felt even more skeptical of his motives. He seemed oddly attached to us both going. Perhaps he was nostalgic for his father's old goat farm. Or maybe he just needed to see firsthand what running a farm would entail in order to reinforce that we had things pretty damn good in Paris.

"What should we do now? Fancy a walk?" I asked.

"I actually have some work I need to do," Serge said.

"I thought Fanny was looking after things in the store," I said, frustrated that we couldn't at least enjoy the afternoon off together.

"I just need to figure this one thing out. Why don't you lie down," he suggested.

"I *am* exhausted, come to think of it," I said.

Just before falling asleep, I saw Serge pull out a pencil and a calculator.

⸻

The next thing I knew, I was waking up to the breeze that gently slipped through the window. Serge was still hard at work, tapping away and jotting something down. I called him over for a hug, and he was wrapping his arms around me within seconds.

"Everything is going to be perfect," he said, excitedly.

"What's going to be perfect?" I asked.

"*Everything*," he reiterated unhelpfully.

Chapter

5

THE NEXT MORNING, I WOKE to the crowing of roosters through our still-open window, and I couldn't help but smile at how clichéd that felt.

After a few minutes of this, however, the novelty wore off. I was left wondering how long the roosters would keep at it, and if it was more of a daily or a weekly wake-up call.

Serge must have heard it, too—it was impossible not to— because he soon began smothering me in sleepy kisses, telling me how much he adored the sounds of the country. *Each to his own*, I figured, as he pulled me under the covers.

We set off to meet farmer Michel in the town of Chinon. For some reason, everyone seemed to be dressed in "country chic," autumnal-colored knits and stylish gum boots, making them look like they'd taken wardrobe inspiration from a Ralph Lauren catalogue. I felt out of place in my blue jeans and striped jumper, which Clotilde jokingly informed me was only appropriate when holidaying by the seaside. *Of course, the French have rules about holiday attire*, I thought.

As we drove, Marie was busy pointing out particular vineyards and cheese producers, as well as some of the most popular castles to visit. Where normally I would have loved nothing more than a discussion about French wine, cheese, and culture, I was distracted by the conversation that was quietly taking place between Jacques and Serge in the front seats.

"And don't be deterred by the house itself," Jacques said.

"But the farm justifies the price, right?" Serge asked as a follow-up.

"You won't be disappointed."

"And the structural work?" Serge asked.

"Leave it with me," Jacques replied confidently.

Serge nodded, and my worries about his intentions returned.

Approaching Chinon, I was immediately charmed. The wide Vienne River merged with vibrant grassy banks leading up to uniform lines of houses, with the imposing Chinon Château looming in the background. It was hard to deny that it was one of the most picturesque places I'd ever visited.

Papa Jean and Clotilde tooted their horn as we caught up to them, and we all headed across the bridge toward the center of town. From the impatient look on Jean's face, I guessed they'd been waiting for us for a while.

Coffee was apparently the first stop on our farm visit, because, well, this was France. We met Michel at a café in the Place du General de Gaulle.

Michel was tall, weather-beaten, and muscular. It was hard to pinpoint his age, but given he wanted to sell the property because he apparently felt too old to run it, I was guessing he had to be at least seventy. He wore jeans and a beige knit jumper, and when he shook my hand, I could feel his years of hard work rubbing against my smooth, office-worker skin.

His French was husky but slow, and I delighted in the fact that I could mostly understand everything he said. *We're not in Paris anymore, Toto*, I thought.

We sat near an old fountain, surrounded by trees that were losing their leaves to the season. It was the perfect backdrop. I almost wondered if Serge had orchestrated this whole weekend to be a seamless exhibition of the wonders of country life. I reminded myself to stay alert and decided that if I saw a wild deer crossing our path or something similar, I'd know I was being set up.

My musings about getting caught up in a *Funny Farm*-esque plot line were quickly shot down, however, when the coffee arrived and tasted terrible. I was reminded of my early days in Paris before I discovered Flat White, when I was drinking the bitter sludge that the old coffee machines spat out all day long. I thought that perhaps it was just the decaffeinated version, so I snuck a sip from Serge's espresso, and it confirmed my fears. If I needed another reason not to leave Paris, it would be the distinct lack of drinkable coffee.

Everyone was chatting away in French, so I let myself tune out and began to enjoy some people-watching. I hadn't spent a lot of time outside of Paris since I'd arrived in France, so I was keen to check out the scene.

I was intrigued to see a relatively young—and, by young, I mean young compared to the rest of the people I'd seen out here—man tapping away on a laptop at a café across the square. I put him in his late thirties, but he had the kind of face that made it hard to guess his age. He was quite tall for a Frenchman and wore thick glasses with a dark rim. I couldn't help but notice that he was handsome, despite Serge's hand resting warmly on my thigh.

I wondered what he was working on. Notebooks and books surrounded his laptop and overtook the small round table where he sat. The spines and covers were too far away for me to read, but I guessed they were all terribly intellectual. He appeared to be slipping in and out of deep thought, resting his fist on his chin for a few moments and then furiously tapping something out on his laptop, or scribbling in his notebook. Whatever he was doing, he seemed to be taking it seriously.

Suddenly, he looked up and busted me staring at him. I blushed and hoped I was sitting too far away for him to notice the color of my cheeks. He gave me a little grin and a nod before going back to his work.

I tried to figure out why I was so interested in what he was doing. Perhaps he just caught my attention because he looked so out of place. There weren't many other younger people around, so he'd been elevated to become the most interesting out of an average bunch. Whatever it was about this stranger, he shattered my impression that country life had to revolve around gardening and cooking.

"How is Françoise?" farmer Michel asked Serge in French, forcing me abruptly back into the conversation. *How was it that everyone in town seemed so interested in Serge's ex-wife?*

My eyes shot to Serge to see how he'd respond this time, but his face didn't give much away. He muttered something about her being well last he heard, and I thought that would be that.

But then Michel followed on with, "*Et son papa?*"

I wasn't sure why the recent mentions of Françoise—or her father for that matter—continued to bother me so much, but I could feel my cheeks burning. *Doesn't anyone consider how I might feel about being so casually reminded of Serge's ex?* Regardless of everybody's intentions, these brief discussions reinforced how completely in the dark I was about Serge's former marriage. Before, it hadn't seemed particularly important, but now, with the baby on the way, it felt like there was more at stake. Perhaps if I understood what had led to the degradation of the relationship and, ultimately, the divorce, I could get to the point where I could hear Françoise's name without flinching.

After coffee, we followed Michel's beat-up old Citroën van out of town and toward the farm. When I saw his turn indicator start to flicker ten minutes later, I thought, *At least we don't have to go too far out of our way for this whole debacle.*

The long and dusty driveway led to a modest, but not entirely ugly, farmhouse made of large stones with a slate-tiled roof. The house was surrounded by other buildings, which I guessed made up the "farm" aspect of the property. These were less appealing than the house itself, and I imagined that the property would be much more aesthetically pleasing without them, but given the farm was set up to make goat cheese, I figured they were a necessity. Less of an eyesore was a gorgeous little pond that had come into view.

I wondered why Jacques had been so keen for us to check this place out. It was hardly the grand country château that might persuade someone to pack up and move here immediately. In fact, it looked like many of the other rather nondescript properties we'd driven past on the way over. Sure, the garden was quite pretty, but then we'd been blessed with the type of perfect autumn weather—big blue skies contrasting with juicy green grass and trees of varying shades of yellows and reds—that might convince people that moving to the country would solve all their problems. *Fools*, I thought with a silent chuckle.

Michel pulled up to the open garage next to two other cars. (I'd always wondered why people living in the country needed so many cars; perhaps I'd finally get to figure this out.) After we got out, he started explaining about the property. Apparently, the barn, milking shed, and cheese-making rooms were another hundred meters down the road. The random hangars and other buildings nestled beside the house were simply for all the cars and excess crap you ended up with when you weren't confined by tight spaces in Paris. *Lesson one in country life*, I told myself.

Clotilde and Jean came over to me, neither of them looking particularly impressed.

"Not quite what I was expecting," Clotilde said.

"No, rather underwhelming, really," I replied.

"*Papa*, what do you think?" she asked.

"It's certainly not Paris," he answered with raised eyebrows.

"I'm with you, Jean," I said.

The three of us stood looking out over the farm, and I got the impression we were all asking ourselves what we were doing there.

"Shall we start with the house?" Michel suggested.

"Yes, let's go," I said. *The sooner we start, the sooner we'll be done and on our way to lunch.*

Serge looked at me enthusiastically and took my hand.

The front door led into a gloomy hallway that led into a gloomy living room. As we walked from room to room, my heart sank for Michel. I was certain that the house would be difficult to sell in its current state. The décor was dated, with floral wallpaper in the bedrooms and ugly brown tiling in the kitchen and bathroom that burned into my retinas.

"Just imagine the bones, Ella," Serge said to me as he saw my expression change to one of horror as we walked into the miserable kitchen. "There's so much potential."

"For someone, maybe," I said, being generous.

"I can see it now."

"See what now?" I asked.

"A family home," he said.

"Serge, you can't seriously be considering this!" I said. "Just look around."

"For the price, it's hard not to."

I finally acknowledged that I could be in a little trouble.

After rushing through the rest of the house to avoid Serge getting any further ideas, we walked across to the farm. It was impossible not to notice the sound of the bells that hung around each goat's neck. At one point, Serge raised his voice to talk over the clanging, but just as quickly seemed to decide to wait until we were inside to finish what he was saying. Some goats came toward us bleating loudly. I was taken aback by their dark, elongated pupils and was relieved when we finally got away from their collective gaze.

To my surprise, the interiors of the farm were modern and well maintained. The milking machinery and cheese-making facilities (lessons two and three in country living) looked shiny and professional, and the buildings were well maintained. It was evident that Michel's passion resided firmly with the animals.

He talked us through the different aspects of the business—the milking, making the goat cheese, and his aging process—and Serge nodded along enthusiastically, stopping him often to ask questions.

We were then led into what Michel called "*le grand plus*," or "the big plus," of the property. It was an airy room with a large bar at one end and floor-to-ceiling windows overlooking the fields of goats. A long trestle table was plonked in the center of the room, and through a side door, I could see a small kitchen with a barbeque and an old oven.

"This would be the perfect space to sell direct to the public," Michel said.

"So, you're already set up for that?" I asked, wondering if the rustic look was perhaps intentional.

"*Non, non, non*," he said sternly. "I'm too old for all that. Besides, this is where I host my hunting dinners."

"Right," I said, surprised that he'd gone to the effort of setting up a rudimentary restaurant just for hunting dinners with his mates. *What a waste!*

Stepping behind the bar, Michel pulled out a few wax-paper-wrapped packages from a small fridge. *Cheese!* I thought with glee. But my plans to finally make the most of this farm visit were quickly thwarted as Michel proudly explained that none of his cheese was pasteurized. Serge gave me an apologetic look, and I spent the next few minutes trying to convince myself that it wasn't the end of the world.

Our party unanimously liked Michel's produce, and their appreciation only increased as they sampled their way from the day-old goat cheese to the aged ash-coated log. I smelled each variety and eyed the texture and had never felt such an intense desire to pick up cheese remains and run away with them. *To hell with this unpasteurized malarkey. One bite can't hurt.* I took a small slice of the fresh cheese and ate it. It melted onto my tongue like a scoop of ice cream dropped on a hot pavement. Serge looked over at me as I dragged out eating my tiny sample.

"*C'est bon, oui?*" he said.

"*Oh, oui,*" I said, unable to articulate anything more.

And it was *bon.* It was overwhelmingly light and fresh. The perfect balance between fluffy and creamy, a little sweet, with a hint of citrus. If clouds were edible, I decided, they would taste like this cheese. Michel had done himself proud.

When we arrived back at the car, Serge pulled me aside.

"Ella, I need to talk to you," he said.

"Can't it wait until after lunch?" I asked. "I'm starving!" It felt like days since Marie had served up big bowls of coffee and hot chocolate with warm baguettes, butter, and homemade raspberry jam. Since arriving in France, I'd really come around to French-style breakfast, or *petit-déj*, even though it wasn't as filling as my old go-to of eggs and bacon. There was something about the way a buttered baguette softened yet retained its crunch when dipped into a hot, milky drink, that drove me wild with joy.

"I will be quick," Serge reassured me, leading me to a little tree by the pond.

I was chatting away idly about how delicious Michel's cheese was when Serge suddenly got down on one knee and took my hands in his.

Oh, shit, what's he doing down on one knee? I thought. *This can't be what I think it is, can it?* I shook any possible feeling of excitement out of my head and decided that the last thing I needed on top of what had already been an eventful week was a pity proposal from my boyfriend just because I was up the duff, knocked up, had a brioche in the oven. Au revoir, *romance!* I lamented.

"Ella," he said, looking deep into my eyes.

My mind sped through how I should respond. There was no way I was going to accept. I didn't want him to ask me to marry him out of some archaic sense of obligation just because we were going to have a baby together. But what was the best way to let him down gently?

"Will you move in with me?" he asked, quickly shaking me from my marital flight of fancy.

Huh, I thought, momentarily offended that he didn't actually want to marry me, despite my intention to turn him down.

"Serge, we already live together," I said.

"But not here," he replied, motioning to the farmhouse with his hand.

"Oh, do you mean as a holiday house?" I asked, suddenly feeling relieved. I could definitely get on board with us having a country farm if it meant we still lived the majority of the year in Paris.

"*Non, non, non!* We'll move here permanently," he confirmed.

I looked at him, trying to figure out if he'd gone mad.

"It is *fantastique, non?*" he prompted. His cheeks were flushed from the excitement of the "proposal."

"Perhaps we should discuss this back in Paris," I said, looking over to see Jean, Jacques, and Marie still waiting by the cars, and Clotilde, mouth agape, giving me a "What the hell is going on?" look.

"Too late," Serge said, joyfully. "I bought it for you!"

"You what?" I yelped. My head started pounding in panic.

"It's ours," he said. "I've already paid the deposit. We will move here in a couple of months!"

Considering what Serge would be giving up in Paris—his apartment, his *fromagerie*, his whole life—I couldn't figure out why he looked so happy.

"But, Serge, I don't want to move here. I love Paris."

"You don't love the farm?" he said, his smile fading quickly.

"God, no!" I said. "I mean, the farm is fine. But it's not for us . . ."

"*Merde*. I thought you'd love it," he said.

I was speechless. If it weren't such a clichéd move, I would have pinched myself to make sure I wasn't dreaming. My mind was spinning, trying to figure out how my perfect Parisian life had just been sliced through like a slab of Comté.

"Why would you have thought I'd love it here?" I asked.

"I saw how your eyes lit up when I mentioned us moving somewhere with a garden. I thought this would be a step up."

Oh, God! This wasn't how I'd imagined our country weekend panning out.

A wave of nausea rushed through me, either from fear or from the pregnancy. It was impossible to say which major life change caused my need to run behind the tree and be sick, but as I lost my breakfast, I decided it wasn't a good sign.

In the absence of a tissue, I used the printout of the baby scan that was still in my jacket pocket to clean off my shoes. *This is definitely not a good sign*, I thought, apologizing to our unborn child for using his or her first baby picture so appallingly.

· PART ·

Two

WINTER

Chapter
6

"OK, SERGE," I SAID, GEARING myself up once we were back in the privacy of our room at Jacques and Marie's B&B. "Please tell me you can get your deposit back."

"Well . . .," he stalled.

After the initial shock of the morning had worn off, I was finally feeling recovered enough to unleash some of the thoughts and emotions that had been buzzing through my head since he "popped the question."

"Serge, this is crazy! What about our life in Paris? Did you even think any of this through?" I asked.

"Of course, I have thought this through. I've done nothing but think about what is going to be best for the baby," he said.

"Thousands of people have kids in Paris, and they seem to get along just fine," I reasoned, a little more gently now I knew the intention behind his hare-brained scheme was to give our baby a proper home. "Yes, we might have to make some slight adjustments when he or she arrives, but I feel like this is perhaps an overreaction."

It's next-level panic! I wanted to add, but held my tongue.

"Ella, I don't want to raise a child in Paris. The noise, the pollution, the cold and dark winters; these are not good for little lungs, hearts, and brains. We need to leave the city if we're going to do this right. Don't you want our baby to be happy?" he asked.

To me, the baby's happiness was still a faraway concept. A future travel plan you made with a friend that neither of you planned to commit to, but you enjoyed discussing anyway. And now I suddenly felt like Serge was trying to guilt me into agreeing to move to the farmhouse. Yes, this might have been his vision for his family, but surely my vision had to count for something, too.

"And what about *our* happiness? Could you really be happy living out here?" I asked.

"I could never be happy knowing our child is not getting to experience nature and fresh air," he replied.

"But the house is a mess."

"We'll renovate!"

"Do you even know how to renovate?" I asked.

I'd never renovated anything before and had zero concept of what Serge and I would even be capable of. *And isn't renovating supposed to be as stressful as the death of a family member or a divorce?* I thought nervously. *We haven't even made it to marriage!*

"I've done a few odd jobs in my life," he said, rather unconvincingly. "And did you see the lake outside? I can already see the family picnics we could have. Perhaps there are even some fish."

I couldn't believe how cavalier he was being. *Does he really expect me to move to the country? And if I don't agree to go, will he move without me?* I closed my eyes and focused on my breath for a few seconds.

"And what about the *fromagerie*?" I asked, trying to bring some focus back to our discussion. Clearly Serge was emotionally invested—or perhaps emotionally unstable—when it came to discussing anything baby-related.

"That is the best news," he said.

Merde, I thought.

"I do not even need to sell," he continued. "Fanny had already agreed to manage things for me full-time when I was planning to open the new store. So, there is really no risk. And financially, the farm is a great investment."

"You've completely given up your dream to open a second store, then?" I asked.

"I have already messaged the real-estate agent to let him know my plans have changed," he said. "Some things are bigger than dreams."

Since I'd met Serge, he'd always been tenacious in going after what he wanted, me included, and now he seemed determined to make the farmhouse his next project. He appeared to have already committed fully to the idea.

"So, you know how to farm, then?" I asked.

"It's only a hundred goats. And why walk when you can run?" he said.

"I'm not sure that's how the expression goes."

"Besides," he added confidently. "My father was a farmer, so I guess I'll just be going back to my roots. It's in my blood."

Serge didn't talk about his parents often, but I knew he'd chosen to leave his family's farm as soon as he'd finished school. I got the impression that his parents had wanted him to take over, Serge being their only child and all, but that he hadn't been interested.

After Mama Serge had passed, Serge had asked his father for help establishing his *fromagerie*, sort of rekindling their relationship. They'd worked together for a couple of years, but visiting suppliers was really as close as Serge had gotten to "working the land" himself. A few years later, Serge's father had died from a heart attack, and although Serge treasured those memories from the early days in his cheese shop, spending time with a farmer did not necessarily a farmer make.

"Can't you see this is absurd?" I asked Serge.

"No, I think it will be perfect," he said with a frustratingly adorable grin, which only served to make me angrier.

"What part?" I asked. "The run-down house? The goat farm you don't know how to run? Cheese you don't know how to make?"

I was on a roll now.

"And what about my job?" I continued. "I doubt I'll be able to find work in Chinon. And my visa is tied to my job."

"There are ways around this," he said with a wink, and I quickly ran through all the alternative visa options I'd researched, and wondered if he was implying that I could get a spousal one.

"Serge, enough!" I said, raising my voice. As if adding a tiny human into the mix wasn't an adequate shake-up, now he wanted to add renovations, a possible wedding, and a bunch of goats—was it a herd? A flock? A tribe? The fact that I didn't even know the appropriate collective noun reinforced how little I understood about life in the country.

"Enough what?" he asked.

"This is ridiculous. We're not packing up our life to move here and start a farm. Honestly, I think you're just freaking out a little about the baby. And don't worry, so am I, but we just need to get through these early days together. In Paris. And then see how we're feeling."

"We don't need to move immediately," he said.

"Oh, great," I said, sarcastically, although my tone may have been lost on Serge.

"Yes," he added. "There will be a few months before we move."

"No, no, no," I said.

"What do you mean, 'no'?" he asked, earnestly.

"I mean exactly what I said. I'm not moving. I think you'll come to the same conclusion after you've had time to properly process our news, and in the meantime, I think it's for the best if we don't discuss it any further."

Looking at Serge's disappointed face, I almost started to feel guilty. But then I reminded myself that my boyfriend just unexpectedly bought a farm in the French countryside without even consulting me. And yes, he may have done it all for our unborn baby, but in the process, he seemed to have forgotten about me completely.

Besides, this whole absurd idea revolved around a pregnancy that was still in its most fragile trimester. I'd be a fool if I let something like this drive Serge and me apart now. End of discussion.

Chapter

7

A COUPLE OF WEEKS LATER, back in Paris after our life-altering weekend in the Loire Valley, the ice had finally started to thaw.

The relief I'd felt at returning to the buzz of the city had been immediate, because although autumn in the countryside had been pretty, in Paris it felt magical. With the leaves changing color across the city, there seemed to be a sense of excitement in the air as people squeezed the last moments of warm weather out of the year. Christmas was still far enough away not to need worrying about, and every sunny day was treated as though it would be the last—terraces brimmed with people, and the parks filled with picnickers and families enjoying time out of their apartments.

That first week, Serge and I had hardly spoken. Any time he'd mentioned anything to do with moving to the country, I'd cut him off. We'd fallen into a semi-awkward existence of him wanting to talk and me resisting. He'd surely quickly come to realize, I thought, that he should have at least consulted me before ambushing me at the farmhouse.

With time, though, my feelings toward the whole experience had actually started to soften somewhat. As the days passed, and as I reflected more on what had happened, my emotions edged away from anger to doubt and then, eventually, a little toward guilt. I tried to imagine if our roles were reversed, and if Serge had left me in a similar state of limbo after I'd gone out on a limb for him.

After ten long days of us essentially not speaking beyond the minutiae of daily life—a rather dramatic first fight—he'd almost begged me to talk it through with him properly. And he really pulled out all the stops, compiling a cheese plate including all my pasteurized favorites, even though I'd already had a few "accidental" soft cheese slipups that week. He also baked a Mont d'Or (possibly the world's most comforting cheese, and also the variety that had prefaced our first kiss) and promised that he'd researched the necessary cooking temperature to make it safe for me to eat.

Not that I was going to allow any amount of cheese to convince me to leave Paris, an idea that I was still—mostly—firmly against.

I came to the table armed with a list of arguments against Serge's plan, but also prepared to listen to his take on things. After all, he'd shown nothing but good reasoning and judgment since we'd started dating, so not hearing him out now would have been unfair.

The mountain of cheese sat between us, waiting for one of us to yield. I hesitated before ripping into a baguette and cutting a slice of Comté, because despite feeling like I was accepting Serge's peace offering, I was hungry.

Serge talked while I chewed.

"Ella, let me start by saying I'm sorry," he said.

"Mmm," I said, thinking things were at least getting off on the right foot.

"I should not have surprised you."

"No, you shouldn't have."

"But now that you've had time to consider the move, you must think it's for the best," he said.

Oh, God, I thought. *Nothing's changed!*

"Serge! It's not just the way you went about telling me that's the problem, it's the whole concept."

"What whole concept?" he asked, and my frustration returned.

"You're forgetting that my whole life is here in Paris. I moved to France *for* Paris. This is where we met, where we fell in love. I have friends, a job, a life here."

"But you could have an even more wonderful life in the Loire," he said, like it was the most obvious thing in the world.

I struggled to see how. Unlike when I'd moved to the City of Lights, fuelled by thoughts of becoming a glamorous, cheese-eating Parisian, I couldn't even imagine what a move to the country would look like. Raincoats? Tractors? Herding animals? It didn't have quite the same appeal. And it wasn't me, at all.

In fact, the idea of starting again out in the country, of meeting new people and having to make new friends, made me anxious. I knew we'd have Jacques and Marie, but they were more Serge's friends, not mine. And establishing relationships with the French was a slower process than with Australians. I thought back to when I'd arrived in Paris and it'd taken weeks of living with Clotilde to establish trust and get to that "comfortable in silence" point; with Billie, all it had taken was a couple of pints.

For each concern I raised, Serge remained blinded by the romanticism of moving to the country and of giving our baby the best start to life that we could.

"Ella," he said. "So many people want to do this, but they don't have the means. We can actually make it happen."

His words reminded me of something Billie had said when I'd spoken to her earlier that day. "It actually sounds really dreamy, and kind of reasonable," she'd said once I'd explained the situation. "Some people spend their whole life wishing they could move to the French countryside. Why not just give it a go?" Billie had always been a guiding light for me in moments of panic and indecision, but could she be right on this occasion? *Could I actually get used to a gum-boot lifestyle?*

I sighed and cut a slice of Cantal, wishing I could explain my apprehensions to Serge as easily as I could to Billie. But that's the thing with old friends: you can let down your guard, and there's not quite as much at stake. How could I sit here and ask Serge outright if he thought our relationship was strong enough to withstand the pressure of moving, renovating, and having a baby all in the same year?

"I just think we should wait until after the baby arrives and see how things go," I said, reiterating my perspective that we didn't need to give up absolutely everything in order to raise a child.

"But why wait?" he said.

I felt like Serge was already too emotionally and financially invested in this country move. The mere fact that I thought we could, and should, stay in Paris seemed to bother him. I couldn't figure out whether I was being selfish for putting my desire to stay in the city before the supposed well-being of my child, or whether Serge was being unreasonable asking me to even consider it.

We were both showing signs of frustration as we went back and forth discussing the pros (mostly from Serge) and the cons (mostly from me) of leaving Paris, and as we spoke late into the night, part of me began to wonder if Serge knew something that I didn't about having a baby here. He was French, after all, and perhaps he'd had firsthand accounts from friends or customers about life in the city with kids.

Eventually, exhausted, Serge reached across to hold my hand and made a final plea.

"I'm not asking you to move there for the rest of your life, Ella," he said. "I'm just asking you to consider it. To try it."

"And what if I hate it?" I asked.

"If you really hate it, I will not force you to stay," he said.

"Seriously? You'd leave just like that?" I asked.

He nodded, his face softening; perhaps he realized I was finally breaking down.

"Do you trust me?" he asked, grabbing my other hand.

"I do," I said, after a moment's hesitation, wondering where this question was leading.

"So, trust me that this will be a wonderful experience. And if it's not, we will move."

"Back to Paris?" I asked.

"We will consider all options," he said.

I thought this over for a few minutes. Venturing into the unknown was scary, but I only had to look back at my experience since arriving in Paris to realize that so much good could come from taking a big leap. *What is the worst that could happen? I'll hate farming, and we'll move back to Paris?* I thought.

"OK," I said, just like that, finally giving in to the man who'd already made me happier than I ever realized I could be.

"OK?" he confirmed. "You're serious?" His face lit up with joy.

"But I have some terms," I said.

"Whatever you want," he assured me. The relief in his voice was palpable.

"Good," I said, and I got a paper and pen.

He intercepted me and gave me a hug that almost left me breathless.

"*Je t'aime, je t'aime, je t'aime,*" he whispered into my ear, while I prayed that I'd done the right thing by agreeing to go along with this mad plan.

So, I'd agreed to move to the country on the condition that Serge agreed to three simple terms.

My first was that we'd treat the move as a trial, a sort of sabbatical, to see how things went, and if at any stage I were desperate to leave, Serge would stand by me.

The second was that Serge would arrange to have the house renovated as soon as possible, to make it both baby-friendly and less of an eyesore.

And my final term was that Serge couldn't sell his Paris apartment to finance the farm, just in case we needed to come back. This last condition started another fight—officially our second ever—because it meant that Serge would have to take out a loan, and that he'd then be relying on cheese sales from day one to repay it. We eventually agreed to a compromise:

Yes, he'd get the loan, but we'd also rent out his apartment to relieve some of the financial pressure.

Lying in bed that night, with Serge's arms wrapped around me, I felt relief for what seemed like the first time since he'd gotten down on one knee at the farm. I'd agreed to a trial period in the country, which actually made the whole move feel like a fun experiment. *An extended holiday of sorts*, I told myself, *except with a lot more at stake*.

The following morning, Serge confirmed with farmer Michel that the move would happen in early December, and then the prospect of actually moving began to feel very real.

Suddenly, I only had six weeks left in Paris. My home away from home. My Paris! Anything that had ever bothered me about the city was quickly forgotten, and I was fully in love.

I was determined to make the most of my remaining time; after all, most people went on much shorter holidays. I was going to do everything I could in this magical city before we had to move. It was almost like I'd been given a few weeks to live, although somewhat less extreme.

I'd fill my heart with food and culture to keep me going over the winter in the country. I'd picnic, I'd walk through the Luxembourg Gardens, and I'd wander the museums. I'd gaze at people clinking wine glasses in bars and ogle the rows of unpasteurized cheese in all the magnificent *fromageries*. To warm up, I'd drink tea and eat the rainbow of macarons at Ladurée, sip rich hot chocolates at Café Pouchkine, and devour a very sweet Mont-Blanc at Angelina (I felt like the French expression *belle laide* was created specifically for this dessert, which was both beautiful and ugly).

Six weeks is better than no weeks, became my mantra. It was time to live large, French style—well, at least pregnancy-friendly French style.

Chapter

8

BUT SIX WEEKS IN PARIS—packing, trying to figure out what I was going to do about work, and arranging to leave—flew by quicker than either Serge or I had been prepared for. And as each passing day brought us ominously closer to our move date, I'd been living all my "last" moments with immense nostalgia.

We'd said our goodbyes to friends and colleagues, and also to the city. I'd walked the streets, lost in thought about how Paris had swept me into her arms when I'd arrived heartbroken from Australia, and about the life I'd managed to carve out for myself since then. When I'd gone to meet Serge in his *fromagerie* for the very last time, I'd even shed a few tears. Fanny, as usual, had looked at me like I was mad, and that she was mad at me.

Before I knew it, the moving van was arriving and a duo of already dusty men had started stomping their heavy steel-capped boots through our little Parisian oasis. I watched with regret as our apartment was slowly emptied of furnishings and looked less and less like our home.

Feeling useless, I tried to help lift boxes, but Serge was swiftly on top of me, telling me that I shouldn't be doing anything in my "state." I protested, to no avail, and was instead instructed to go get espressos and croissants for the movers.

As I walked to the bakery, I thought back over the past few days, and mulled over a discussion I'd had with Serge that had made me realize that his desire to farm might have a deeper meaning than I'd initially understood, or at the least that perhaps it wasn't born solely from the news of my pregnancy. While packing, I'd been looking through a box of Serge's old photos when I'd found a particularly cute picture of him mostly naked on a bike. I'd put in on the fridge, hoping it would make him chuckle.

"Did you see what I found?" I'd asked later, pointing out my discovery. "You were quite the cute kid. And who's the looker next to you?"

"My father," Serge had said quietly.

I'd only seen photos of Serge's dad as an old man, and I'd been surprised by how healthy and fit he looked in the picture.

"He was very handsome," I'd said, sensing Serge's sadness.

"He was so physical, always fixing things, making things better."

"Sounds like you."

"If only I could be half the man he was," he'd said.

I'd wondered what Serge was referring to. Yes, his father sounded like a very capable farmer, but from what I understood he hadn't always been the most supportive dad in the world, especially when Serge had wanted to follow his own path. And Serge was so great at so many things—being my favorite cheese-seller, in particular—I hated seeing him doubt himself. I'd hugged him and had reassured him that he was the best man I knew.

"I just wish I could have spent more time with him, especially now," he'd said.

"He'd definitely be proud of you buying a farm," I'd said, trying to cheer him up.

"It's far too late for that," he'd replied.

The conversation had hung over my head since then, and I'd decided that Serge must have regretted not taking over his father's farm when he'd had the chance. Perhaps now he was in part buying a farm out of a sense of obligation. I'd tried to bring it up again, but he'd been completely unwilling to open up any further. Father–son relationships were complicated, and I felt completely out of my depth when it came to dissecting them, so eventually, I left it alone.

The truck was fully loaded in no time, and the only thing left to do was sweep up the debris before closing the door on what had been one of the happiest periods of my life. My heart broke a little.

We got into Serge's little blue Citroën and Clotilde waved us off, promising to come visit us at the farmhouse soon. In a happy turn of events, she'd decided to move back to Paris full-time and had jumped at the opportunity to rent Serge's apartment.

Knowing she'd be there, keeping the place warm for us, it was even easier for me to pretend that we were just going on an extended country jaunt. I clung to this idea dearly; it was pretty much the only thing stopping me from bursting into tears as we drove through the streets that I'd known and loved so well. But as we got farther out, past neighborhoods I hadn't even had a chance to properly discover, the full reality of the situation settled in.

I was still feeling a little shell-shocked from the hustle of the morning and couldn't think of anything to say that wouldn't come off as being extremely pessimistic. I wasn't sure what I'd expected from our last few hours in Paris, but the words *romantic, dreamy*, and *slow* came to mind now. Instead, it'd been dusty, manic, and loud—*perhaps a sign of things to come on the farm*, I told myself. At least I'd managed a croissant.

Serge finally broke the silence. "I won't miss the traffic in Paris," he said, rubbing my leg.

"Oh, yeah?" I asked, feeling glum that all we had to talk about was the traffic. Perhaps I should mention the gloomy weather just to round things out.

"Is everything OK, Ella? You seem quiet."

"I'm just exhausted," I said. "I didn't sleep well last night." This was mostly true. I hadn't gotten a good night's sleep, in part due to my anxiety about leaving behind life in Paris, and in part because I'd been trying to decipher another discussion I'd had with Serge while we'd been packing.

When I'd been looking through his old photos, I'd also found a (very nineties looking) wedding photo of him and Françoise, buried even deeper in the box. Seeing as he'd always been unwilling to open up about her, I'd taken this as the perfect opportunity to ask a few questions.

"Cute tie," I'd told him, showing him the picture.

"Oh, Ella, put that away," he'd said.

"No, it's sweet," I'd encouraged. "Besides, why do you never talk about her?"

"There's not much to talk about," he'd said.

"So why did everyone in the Loire keep asking about her?"

"Well, we were married for years. I guess old habits die hard," he'd replied.

"And what was Michel asking about her father? Or did I misunderstand him?"

"Oh," he'd said. He'd seemed to mull things over for a few seconds, as if trying to decide what to elaborate on. "Her father lives in Chinon. Many people there know her and her family."

"Oh, great," I'd replied, trying to maintain my composure while wondering how often I'd soon be running into Serge's ex.

"But Françoise lives down south near the beach, now," he'd rushed to add. "I don't think she spends much time in the region."

"How much time?" I'd asked.

"Ella," he'd said softly. "You have nothing to worry about. She used to spend her time *avoiding* her father in Chinon, if that is any consolation."

"And were you close with him?"

"He is a very nice man but I have not seen him since the divorce. I think he was not happy about the outcome of my relationship with his daughter."

"Oh," I'd said, wondering if there was anything else about the divorce that Serge hadn't told me.

I'd lain awake for hours trying to figure out how Serge could have decided to move us back to where he'd met his ex-wife, a place, no doubt, full of memories of them falling in love. But asking him the question felt futile now. The paperwork had already been signed and our bags were already packed. All I could do was hope that Françoise would stick to her part of France and leave the Loire Valley to me.

After almost half an hour of driving in silence, Serge suggested I shut my eyes.

I sat back and did just that, and by the time we got on the motorway to the Loire, I had fallen into a deep sleep.

I woke up, and we were still driving. I looked over at Serge, so handsome behind the wheel of such an adorable car.

"Where are we?" I asked, groggily.

"We're nearly there," he told me joyfully. "You have been sleeping for most of the drive."

"Sorry I wasn't better company," I said.

"You didn't miss anything," he said, trying to reassure me.

A fog had descended over the Loire Valley, giving it an ethereal and spooky feel. While this isolation—the picturesque void—might be desirable on weekends away from the city, the prospect of it becoming my day-to-day still terrified me. I cranked the heater in the car and rubbed my hands against the fan to try to keep warm. Winter in the Loire wasn't shaping up to be a cosy experience. *How am I meant to stay warm without nipping into wine bars, shops, or the Métro when I get cold?*

We arrived through the mist and haze at our new home. I hadn't been back to the farmhouse since our first visit and, as we approached it, everything looked starkly different. The trees had all lost their leaves, and there was an unnerving silence that seemed to accompany us as we got out of the car. And then I heard them: the goat bells, the noise that would become the soundtrack to my new life in the country.

I hurried toward the house, keen to get out of the cold, but also keen to see what state it was in. I crossed my fingers, hoping that it was better than the grim image I'd painted in my head.

It was worse than I remembered. Emptied of its former furniture, the cold shell of the walls, ceiling, and floors gave off no life. The wallpaper was faded in sections where it'd been blocked by furniture, leaving what looked like the chalk outlines at a murder scene on the walls. I wouldn't have been surprised if someone told me that the house had been empty for a century. It was dusty and smelled of mold. The cold had crept past the wooden shutters and into the bones of the house, and as I moved between the rooms, it began to creep into mine, too. I couldn't even have a glass of wine—or a decadent cheese plate—to remind me of how much I loved France.

Thankfully, Serge decided in that moment to hug me. As I nestled into his chest I fought back tears. *Why did I agree to move here? What on earth have I done?*

Chapter

9

SERGE LOCATED AND FLICKED THE main power switch and the lights came on, which also meant that we had heating. If getting the mains turned on in time for our arrival had been left to me, we would have been without power for days, possibly weeks, but thankfully Serge knew how to deal with EDF, France's behemoth gas and electricity provider.

But, as I was about to learn, having the lights switched on turned out to be both a blessing and a curse. It meant that we could actually see what we were doing once the weak winter sun had set, early in the afternoon, but it also meant that I was better able to see the state of shabbiness of our new digs. Cracks and stains that had been hidden in the gloom now became apparent. We certainly had our work cut out for us. I opened the shutters and windows to let some of the freezing country air circulate.

The moving guys arrived shortly after us and started unloading things haphazardly in the living room. Although Serge's furniture had seemed perfectly normal-sized in his cosy one-bedroom Parisian apartment, piled up now it almost looked like doll's-house furniture. Whole rooms were left empty, and I worried about how we were going to afford to furnish all this extra space.

We unpacked the essentials, with Serge stopping every now and then to spin me around the living room. I wondered if my anxiety was as intense as his excitement. I had my doubts.

At five o'clock that evening, the two moving men shook our hands, wished us good luck, and left us alone. After they'd gone, driving their truck into the fog, the silence and the darkness surrounding us was overwhelming.

I hunted desperately through our boxes, looking for our portable speaker to add a little life to the house. I pumped some Édith Piaf to remind me I was still in France. *I love this country*, I kept telling myself, but it did little to cheer me.

I dug out the kettle, made a cup of tea, and then wandered the halls and rooms trying to get a feel for how we'd set things up.

The hours slipped by as we cleaned and arranged as best we could. Gradually, as our belongings started to fill the cupboards and bench-tops, I started to relax a little and as soon as I did, the hunger of a hundred men descended over me. I asked Serge if we had anything to eat.

"I have a *saucisson* in the car," he said. Of course, he had dried sausage in the car.

"Serge, I'm not meant to eat that during pregnancy," I said.

"*Ah, oui*. I forgot. I'll go get something," he said, kissing my head. "Have you found the towels? Why don't you go have a relaxing shower?"

"You're leaving me here alone?" I asked, suddenly realizing that, for the first time in a long time, I'd have no neighbors nearby, just fields, goats, and empty space. The prospect of being so isolated made me uneasy.

"Just for thirty minutes while I go get some food," he said.

"Can't we just get some delivery?" I asked, and he laughed, grabbing his car keys.

"I wasn't joking," I called after him, but he'd already slammed the door.

With Serge gone, the house felt even emptier. And despite me turning up the heating, it was still cold. I hunted around for the bathroom boxes and was met with a nasty surprise: Body wash had leaked all over the towels. I sat on the floor and burst into tears. Between the state of the house and my general state of distress and anxiety, heightened by pregnancy hormones, I felt like I'd made the biggest mistake of my life by agreeing to move to the country. The idea of calling my mum and moving home to Australia flew to my mind. But it was around three o'clock in the morning her time, and I didn't think she'd appreciate such an early-morning call from her pregnant daughter.

I bit my lip, rubbed my eyes, and went to the bathroom. I'd found a hand towel and a foot towel that had survived the great soap spill and made do with them. Inside the brown-tiled shower, I let more tears flow as I attempted to wash the dust and odor from the house off my skin.

After a good twenty minutes, with only a slight concern of running out of hot water, I finally felt warm. I got out and was immediately freezing again. I put on clean clothes, layering on nearly everything I owned. Perhaps the beanie, gloves, and thermal underwear were overkill, but I couldn't seem to get my body to accept the change in temperature.

Serge met me at the bathroom door as I was emerging. He laughed, looking me up and down.

"You going skiing tonight?" he asked.

"It's not funny, Serge. The country is freezing."

"*Ma Bella*, it's really no colder than Paris during the day."

"Seriously?" I asked, shivering.

"*Mais oui*. In the city, the buildings absorb heat and that makes it feel warmer," he said. "Also, the pollution contributes to rising temperatures."

I raised my eyebrows. "Paris isn't even that polluted."

"But it's more polluted than Chinon, *n'est-ce pas . . .?*"

I looked at him dubiously.

"But enough about the air, come with me," he said, leading me into the living room.

He'd spread a picnic rug out in the living room and had covered it with baguettes, pre-made salads, cheese, and fruit. He'd also found candles and a little red rose, which he'd dumped in a plastic water bottle. The *saucisson* did make an appearance, but I could get over that.

I hugged him hard through my many layers of clothing.

"Serge, where did you find all this?"

"Carrefour," he said.

"The supermarket?" I asked, surprised. He nodded. In Paris, we were spoiled by food stores and delis that stocked ready-made meals, which made throwing together dinner ridiculously easy. I wasn't used to shopping for this kind of fare at the supermarket, though, and I wondered if the quality would be as good. I was hoping to be pleasantly surprised.

We sat and feasted, and I avoided telling Serge about the knot of dread I was harboring in my stomach. I hoped my eyes weren't still red from my tears in the shower, because I didn't want him to know how I was feeling. I'd been hit with a weird mix of emotions and I knew that, if prompted, I wouldn't be able to articulate them well. I'd promised Serge to give country living a fair trial, and I didn't want to break down on our very first night at the farmhouse. Besides, he'd gone to such an effort to make everything as nice as possible. It wasn't his fault that I was madly in love with our former life. Nor was it his fault that the farmhouse would probably never live up to its Parisian predecessor.

Serge pulled out a bottle of sparkling apple juice and two plastic champagne flutes and toasted our "successful" move.

Chapter

10

THE NEXT MORNING, I FELT motivated to make a start on the renovations, but seeing Serge lying next to me made getting out of bed a mission. I blamed his strength, with his toned arms wrapping sneakily around me. And I blamed his face. Really, I was just destined to fail.

I was surprised to find that I'd slept really well, despite our bed sitting awkwardly in the middle of the bedroom. I'd relished the quiet when it came to falling asleep, and I'd savored the feeling of waking up without the background hum of motorbikes and ambulance sirens that seemed synonymous with Paris.

"Ten more minutes," Serge whispered into my ear, having felt me wriggling about restlessly.

"OK," I said, as if the idea of unpacking more boxes could ever trump staying in bed with my Frenchman.

When we eventually managed to get up and shower—and I sadly confirmed that the brown tiles in the bathroom looked no better in the light of day—I made a cup of tea and squeezed every possible ounce of caffeine out of the bag. I was going to need a lot of energy to get this farmhouse looking somewhat decent.

I grabbed a piece of paper and a pen and called out to Serge.

"Let's do this," I yelled. "I think we should definitely start with the bathroom. And maybe the kitchen," I added, looking around at what else needed to be renovated.

Serge appeared, fully dressed and holding a pair of work boots.

"Oh," I said. "Where are you going?"

"Michel is coming to show me how the milking machinery works and to explain the production room. Did you forget? Why don't you join us?" he asked.

"Maybe," I said, not too excited about the idea of going out into the cold.

"Don't you want to see how the cheese gets made?"

"I'd rather eat the cheese."

"It'd be good if you knew how things work," he said.

"I think it's best if you look after the goats," I replied, wondering if Serge had completely forgotten about his promise to renovate.

Before I had the chance to bring this up and potentially start our third official fight, he had the good sense to butt in: "But don't worry, Bella, I will be back in no time and we can call some local tradesmen and ask them to come and look at what work we might need."

Good save, I thought, looking at him. I didn't like having to rely on him to coordinate the renovations, but at the same time I was relieved that he'd be doing it. If I had my way, I'd probably just knock everything down and move into a hotel.

"Have fun, Farmer Brown," I said, as Serge opened the door to leave.

"Who is Farmer Brown?" he asked earnestly.

"I'm actually not sure. Just a cute nickname, I guess," I said.

I got to work cleaning out more cupboards and managed to unpack a few more boxes, figuring I could at least liven things up in the house while we were waiting for the renovations to start. I found some rugs and cushions and scattered them around and by the time I was done, and if I squinted slightly, the overall effect wasn't nearly as grim as it had been when we'd arrived.

As I was looking for vases, I stumbled on a box that I hadn't helped pack. *That's weird*, I thought. It appeared to be a bunch of old yearly planners and notebooks. I figured that they might be private, and hesitated. Perhaps I'd just unpack them onto the bookshelf and Serge could decide what to do with them later. As I transferred the books out of the box, an envelope slipped out. It was addressed to Serge.

I flipped it over to see the sender and felt the blood drain from my face. It was from Françoise. *How have I gone from hearing virtually nothing about this woman to her popping up left, right, and center?*

I checked the envelope for a date stamp, but couldn't find one. I wondered when she'd sent it.

Logically, I knew I shouldn't worry—Serge had told me before that his divorce was the result of mutual unhappiness. But emotionally, there was no way I could be that reasonable.

The letter began to feel like it was starting to take up more and more space in the room until there was only one way around its cumbersome presence. I pulled it out of the envelope.

Mon Serge Cheri . . .

My heart skipped a beat as I started reading. The handwriting was very pretty, big and voluptuous. I paused, feeling guilty for invading Serge's privacy, but couldn't draw my eyes away. I translated on the fly, as if by only skimming the letter I wouldn't feel as guilty.

It's been a long time since we have spoken. I miss you. I know our last call ended badly, which is why I wanted to write. I think we should talk about what happened. Let's not ruin so many happy years together. I'll be in Paris next week. Can we meet?

With love, Françoise

I finished reading and felt as though I might pass out. I suddenly wished I could go back in time to when Françoise was still an unknown entity.

I took a deep breath and tried to reason with myself. I'd found the letter in a box of old planners, so I figured it couldn't have been too recent. Still, I wondered if Serge had met up with her in Paris. And if so, what they'd discussed. And why did their phone call end badly? I had so many questions.

I spent the next hour or so simultaneously debating whether to even mention the letter to Serge and trying to figure out how I could nonchalantly bring it up. I didn't want him to think I'd been snooping through his things or that I didn't trust him.

Finally, I decided that the letter had to pre-date me. If it were recent, Serge would have mentioned it. And anyway, it really wasn't any of my business who Serge had met up with before we'd gotten together. I thought back on the feisty email exchange I'd had with Paul when he'd tried to suggest us getting back together. And although I'd knocked him back with a hearty dose of sass, it wasn't a conversation I'd chosen to share with Serge.

I buried the letter back in the planner and figured I'd just wait for a more appropriate opportunity to question him. If the past couple of months were anything to go by, Françoise would pop up in conversation again soon enough.

As I waited—and waited—for Serge to come back from the farm, I continued unpacking. Although I didn't find anything else incriminating, I couldn't help wondering what else he hadn't told me about his former life. And the more I thought about it, the more I found it strange that Françoise had referred to their years together as being "happy." From what I'd understood, things between them had started deteriorating pretty much from the get-go and, according to him, they'd been civil in the end, but certainly not joyful. Maybe I was just going slightly mad with all this country silence.

I considered going to look for Serge, but it was cold outside. I was sure he'd be back soon. We'd had an agreement, after all, to plan out our renovations. When he did finally return, I leaped into his arms. It was a relief to just see another human after a long few hours at home by myself, and I couldn't be mad at the one and only person I knew out here.

Chapter 11

IT WAS STILL ONLY EARLY days on the farm, but I already felt relieved to have arranged to continue working remotely for Food To Go Go. I'd pitched the idea to Tim after agreeing to the move and spending a few days subsequently wondering what the hell I was going to do for work in the country.

And as I'd been hoping, Tim had been so desperate to avoid any further upheaval in his life that he'd agreed to a remote-working trial within seconds of me raising the idea. And I'd get to keep my working visa. *Marriage proposal not required*, I'd thought, feeling mostly relieved at this outcome.

When I'd told Serge that I'd be keeping my job, he'd said, "Don't you think we will be too busy with the kids?"

Kids? Plural? Did the doctor forget to mention we were having twins or something?

"What do you mean?" I'd demanded.

"Kids are baby goats in English, *non*?" he'd said, and I'd breathed a rather dramatic sigh of relief.

"Yes, they are," I'd reassured him and myself.

"If it will make you happy keeping your job in Paris, then it is a *bonne idée*," he'd said.

And it *was* a good idea. I still had my security, independence, and, perhaps most important, a job if we ended up back in Paris. Even if it wasn't a long-term solution, it would buy me some time while I figured out what to do next.

I set up my laptop and phone on our dining table, ready to bury myself in work. Serge had told me he'd come across some issues down on the farm and would need the rest of the day to sort them out. To me, it seemed like he'd spent most of his time so far just wandering around with the goats, moving them from paddock to paddock. That, or he'd spent hours in the production room turning his cheese. Who knew cheese needed so much turning? I'd even seen him staring at the cheese for long stretches. I wondered if he wasn't feeling a little lost in his new job. I figured I'd give him a few weeks' grace period while he found his farming feet.

A frustrating few hours later, Serge and I were both in the car driving toward Chinon. He was annoyed because he didn't have the right tools to fix a broken fence, and I was pissed off because I couldn't even get a photo to upload for work because of the weak wireless mobile connection. There were a few things in France that moved quickly—like the line at the *boulangerie*—and others—like the line at the butcher's or getting a web connection at home—that would take an eternity, or at least, in our case, another couple of weeks.

I just hoped that one of the cafés in town would be connected.

"So, Serge, how do I go about getting my driver's license here?" I asked, thinking that I couldn't keep relying on Serge every time I needed a ride somewhere.

"Oh, it's a *very* big project. And very expensive," he said.

I should have guessed.

"What? Why?" I asked. "You know I have my Australian license already, right?"

"Yes, but you know in France we do things differently," he said.

I bit my tongue, thinking, *That's a lesson I've already learned a dozen times over since arriving.*

"What's the process then?" I asked.

"Well, you'll need to do a certain number of lessons. I don't know how many exactly. And then you'll pass a test. But you're not guaranteed to pass. Actually, you'll probably have to try the test a few times," he said seriously.

"But I already know how to drive," I reinforced. "I've been doing it for years. I started when I was sixteen!"

"Ah, yes, but do you know how to drive like the French?" he asked.

I thought about the French drivers I'd come across: going the wrong way up one-way streets, reversing long distances to avoid going around the block, and attempting to squeeze into too-small car parks by "nudging" the bumpers of the cars on either side until they pushed their way in.

"Hmm," I said. "I'll look into it." The thought of wading through more French bureaucracy made me want to hurl, but being stuck on the farm with no way out seemed like an even more dire option.

Serge dropped me in Chinon, and I started my hunt for a café that had Wi-Fi. Walking the streets, the first thing I noticed was the lack of people. I thought back to the many hours I'd spent by the Canal Saint-Martin in Paris where, no matter how warm or cool the evening was, crowds of people would gather, drinking wine or an aperitif. The diversity of the groups was representative of that which I'd come to appreciate in the city, the pursuit of a convivial and relaxed time being the greatest priority. I'd spent hours people-watching along the canal in the many cafés that lined the waterfront—Chez Prune, La Marine, Hôtel du Nord—using any hint of sunshine as my compass.

It had been easy to mix into the crowd in Paris, to read a book or to just wander the streets feeling like a *flâneur* rather than an outsider. In Chinon, I felt like the few people whom I did pass looked at me warily, like a foreigner. Perhaps it had something to do with how I was dressed, or maybe I just had a "Parisian air." I convinced myself it must be the latter, feeling rather chuffed at the prospect.

Considering I was in quite a touristy part of France, surprisingly few cafés had that little Wi-Fi sticker in their window. I headed toward where I'd seen the man working on his laptop on our visit to Chinon back when we were still Parisians and life felt a lot easier.

The waiter confirmed that they had Wi-Fi. *Finally somewhere that's connected to the outside world!* I thought, slipping into a booth seat by the window.

"*Oui?*" another waiter, middle-aged, grunted at me. I could only assume by the way he was hanging by my table that he was after my order. *Not at Flat White anymore,* I thought.

"*Un thé, s'il vous plaît,*" I said with a smile, thinking it was wise to try to befriend all the café staff in town just in case one of these places were to become my local. "*Et le code Wi-Fi?*" I asked, to his already-turned back.

A Lipton tea bag arrived, next to a chipped cup, a silver pot of lukewarm water, and two bags of sugar. I figured not even a dash of milk would have been able to resurrect the sad state of affairs as I poured the water into my cup. *What's so hard about making a good cup of tea?*

I kept telling myself that I was there for the free internet; that it was only temporary; that in seven or so more months, I'd be able to get back on the afternoon wines . . .

I was relieved to find the connection was at least much stronger than at home. It was still far from quick—and I'd likely waste a lot of time—but I could get my work done here. While I watched the spinning dial, I began to feel very isolated. Normally, if I were waiting for something to load, I'd just chat with a colleague.

I thought back to my last day at work in the office. Even though I'd still technically be working with them, Tim had forced our team out for a boozy lunch (although sadly *sans* booze for me) at one of the English pubs near work to say a farewell to me. I think he'd just needed an excuse to let loose during office hours.

Chris, who'd clocked I was pregnant after my second hot chocolate order, had come along for a drink, too, and had slipped me a takeaway cup. I'd taken a sip. It was a rich and creamy coffee, and as I'd swallowed, I'd been hit with happy memories of working at Flat White and overdosing on lattes.

"Thanks, Chris, but you know I'm off coffee for the moment," I'd said, handing him back the cup to finish.

"You can't ever tell anyone about this," he'd said.

"Tell anyone about what?" I'd asked, concerned.

"I snuck in some decaf beans just to make you a coffee, El. It's totally against our policy but I thought you should have one last decent brew before you go out bush," he'd said.

I'd hugged him, and he'd slipped the rest of the beans into my bag. "Just to get you started," he'd told me. "Let me know if the bean situation in Chinon gets too dire, and I can send you some more. I found a decaf guy and he seems OK."

Chris's dedication to my coffee cause was admirable.

"I honestly don't know how to thank you," I'd said, tears threatening to explode out of me.

"Just find me a gorgeous country girl who speaks perfect English with a French accent," he'd said, and I laughed. He certainly knew how to break emotional tension with his candor.

I looked, once again, at my miserable cup of tea in my quiet café in Chinon. *How did I end up here?* I thought. When I'd first arrived in Paris, I wasn't sure I'd last one year, and now here I was, living on a goat farm in country France.

Then my thoughts turned to Serge. My rock. At least he seemed happy with our new life. Thank God *he* was fully embracing this change of pace.

A kerfuffle at the door interrupted my daydreaming about Serge. I watched as a man lugging multiple bags flung himself onto a seat. He was wrapped up against the weather and as he slowly began to peel off layers, I realized he was the very same man I'd seen working at the café when we'd first visited Chinon. He was hard to mistake, with his clean-shaven face, rural-swank outfit, and swept back, wavy hair. He pulled off a burgundy knit jumper and pushed up his dark-rimmed glasses.

He ordered an Americano and began to unload books onto the small round table in a clumsy fashion. As his coffee arrived, he knocked a hardcover onto the floor, causing a rather loud bang. He seemed oblivious to the outside world as he opened a notebook and began scribbling quickly with one hand while grasping for his cup with the other.

I ordered another tea from the still unfriendly waiter, which made the man stop what he was doing and look over at me. I half smiled at him, wondering if he recognized me from when we'd been here in the autumn, before continuing with my work. I couldn't help noticing he'd stopped writing and was now staring out the window, with the occasional glance over to my table. I checked my reflection in the screen of my phone to make sure I didn't have dirt on my face or in my hair—I did live in the country now—but all was well.

Draining his cup, the man walked up to the bar and asked for another coffee, diverting via me on his way back.

"*Excusez-moi, Madame, mais êtes-vous Américaine?*"

Am I American? I thought. *Is it so obvious that I'm not French?*

"*Australienne,*" I said proudly. "*Et vous?*" I asked, although I was sure that, with his presumptuousness, he had to be French.

"Oh, I'm English," he said, sounding now unmistakably British.

"Ah, I didn't notice you had an accent," I said.

"And yet the locals never fail to mention it," he said with a chuckle. "Mind if I join you briefly?" he asked. I looked over to his belongings, still strewn over his table.

"Please do. I was just finishing up." I motioned with my hand to the empty chair facing me and shut my laptop. I was intrigued. "I'm Ella, by the way."

"Charles," he said quickly and I was reminded of the multiple visits I'd made to Serge's *fromagerie* before I'd even learned his name. "But people call me Chuck. Except the French, they refuse to call me anything but Charles. But then, have you tried to pronounce 'Chuck' with a French accent? Quite absurd, really. But who cares about me? Tell me what you're working on. There normally aren't too many new faces in town over winter," he explained warmly. I guess he didn't remember seeing me across the square.

"I work for a food app in Paris," I said. "I've actually just moved here."

"Fabulous news!" he said. "This town is as quiet as a dead mouse."

I ignored his odd choice of simile and asked, somewhat desperately, if he also lived in town.

"Sort of," he said. "I'm what you could call a drop-in local. I spend a few months here and a few months there. But I'm here for a good stint at the moment," he continued.

Could Chuck be my first country friend? I wondered. Now, sitting opposite him, I figured he had to be around my age, or slightly older.

"And how did you end up in Chinon?" I asked, still curious as to what he was doing in this tiny town.

"Well, my grandmama left me a little land and an old house when she passed away."

I offered my condolences before asking the question I was most nervous about the answer to: "So, do you like living here?"

"It has its moments. I like the quiet. The countryside is beautiful." I pictured him walking down country lanes with a hunting dog, wearing wellingtons and carrying a large walking stick. "But it can be a little dull," he continued.

"Ah," I said. "That was what I was most worried about."

"Well, compared to Paris, things move slowly here. But I find that it's a nice contrast to the city. Allows for a little more headspace to think and ponder. I've never done well in captivity," he said. I wanted to laugh but wasn't sure if he was making a joke. "And what brings you to Chinon?" he asked.

Even though I'd only just met Chuck, his willingness to open up made me feel completely at ease. And it seemed so natural to be chatting to another English-speaker that my own backstory just sort of slipped out. I told Chuck about how I'd fled Melbourne to set up a new life in Paris, how I'd met Serge, and how he'd somehow convinced me that moving to a goat farm was a romantic idea. The only thing I couldn't bring myself to mention was the pregnancy. I wasn't ready for that to define me yet, and soon enough the belly would simply speak for itself.

Chuck looked out the window and said dreamily: "An escape to the country. How idyllic."

"I guess," I said, unenthusiastically.

"You're not thrilled by the concept?" he asked.

I should have probably sugar-coated how I felt about leaving Paris, but I was sick of pretending.

"I just want to be back there. Back among the people, the shops, the cafés! It's so quiet out here, I don't know how anybody copes," I said, unable to hold anything back.

"You'll find your place and your people out here," he said. "And maybe you'll even come to appreciate the slower pace of life. Do make sure you check out the local market, too, because when in doubt about life in France, I've found all you need to do is fill your stomach with good food and wine, and your heart will follow."

Chuck's outlook was comforting and as I spoke with him, I felt my shoulders soften.

"But enough about me. Tell me what you're working on?" I asked.

"I'm working on a novel," he said.

"So, you're a writer," I said. "Have you published anything I might have heard of?"

"Probably not. I've had a few poems and short stories in literary journals, but I wouldn't recommend them. And I won't bore you with the details."

I didn't even know the names of any literary journals.

"So, what's your novel about?" I asked.

"It's all rather experimental, really, so you'll have to excuse me if I seem a little scattered. It's a multigenerational family saga that I'm writing from quite a few perspectives. I must admit I may have bitten off more than I can chew." He looked relieved to have gotten this off his chest.

"How long have you been working on it?" I asked.

"Ten years," he said, and I struggled to hide my shock.

"But only during the colder seasons," he rushed to say. "In summer, I try to head back to London and enjoy the few months of the year there when it doesn't rain."

I looked out the window and wondered if the weather in London was really any worse than here in Chinon. "Sounds like you've got life sorted," I said.

"At least on the outside," he replied.

We kept chatting, and Chuck told me about his philanthropy work in London, in particular how he was affiliated with some of the small art festivals and galleries. He didn't tell me in as many words, but I understood that he wasn't short of a penny, and I assumed his bank account was full of old money. He was surprisingly unpretentious and very matter-of-fact about what he did. He was, in fact, rather charming. "Anyway, I should let you get back to it," he said, grabbing his coffee cup and making to leave.

"So, you're in town for a while longer?" I asked, hoping to not sound too eager.

"I am. You'll find me working here most days. Stop by for a coffee, or a dismal cup of tea," he said, looking at the gray liquid in my cup.

He haphazardly shoved his books into a leather carryall and left the café. *What were the chances of meeting such a friendly English-speaker on my trip into town? Perhaps country living has something going for it yet.*

I couldn't wait to tell Serge about my new acquaintance. But wait I'd have to. He took hours at the farm supplies store and, by the time he picked me up, I was too cold and exhausted to even bother explaining how I'd met an interesting English author in Chinon.

Thinking about my situation as we drove home through the mist, I decided that I'd have to sort out my driver's license quickly. I was used to being free to go wherever I wanted in Paris, and I didn't want that to change just because I was pregnant and living in rural France. And perhaps now I had something, or rather someone, worth driving to.

Chapter

12

A FEW DAYS LATER WE were back in the car, heading to the Chinon hospital for my first trimester ultrasound. I'd been anticipating the appointment for days, looking forward to seeing how much our baby had grown beyond the speck it had been at the dating scan.

And I'd been looking forward to getting an updated photo.

Dampening my excitement was our tardiness. We were running late to the appointment because Serge had, once again, prioritized looking after the goats over looking after his pregnant girlfriend. Yes, I understood that if they weren't milked they'd get engorged, but would a few hours really matter that much? In the short time we'd been on the farm, I seemed to have slipped right down the priorities list. This was a big day for me and baby, and I wished Serge would take it more seriously.

"Shall I just leave you at the entrance?" he asked me as we approached the hospital.

"What?" I half yelled. "Why?"

"I mean, I will park the car and then come in," he said.

I apprehensively agreed and told him to hurry.

Once inside, I was quickly ushered into the ultrasound room and given a gown to change into. I'd never known a hospital to be so efficient. *Why now? Hurry up, Serge!*

And then the technician returned and she was squirting goo on my stomach and rolling the ultrasound wand over my tiny bump.

She enthusiastically pointed out body parts, but the whole while I was distracted, thinking about the fact that Serge was missing this. *He should be here*, I kept repeating in my head.

"Nothing to worry about, this happens a lot," the technician told me in French, interrupting my thoughts.

"What happens a lot?" I asked, lost and suddenly afraid.

"I can't find the heartbeat," she said.

"You what?"

"It's very normal."

"But I've already heard it once," I said, my own heart jumping into my mouth.

Where the hell is Serge?

"We'll just check with the internal camera," she said, and then asked me to remove my underwear.

"Oh," I said, devastated to be revisiting the dildo cam.

Seconds later, a quick and strong "thump, thump, thump" played out of the monitor.

Thank God, I thought, feeling like I could breathe normally again.

After a few more measurements, the technician instructed me to get dressed and assured me that everything looked perfect before leaving the room. As I was pulling on my clothes, Serge burst through the door.

"Did I miss it?" he asked, looking at me.

"You did. But everything is fine," I said, fighting back tears. "Apparently, we can pick up the report and some pictures at reception."

"I'm so sorry, Ella," he said. "I got a phone call that I needed to take."

"A phone call? Who was it?"

"It was from a potential new supplier. He thinks he might be able to get my cheese stocked at Galeries Lafayette Gourmet."

Although getting stocked in this Parisian department store's food hall would be a big step for Serge, was it really worth missing the ultrasound? Couldn't he have called back later today?

"It doesn't matter. It's fine," I said. "I just wish you could have been here with me. I didn't really know what was going on."

"Oh, Ella," he said, trying to hug me. I shrugged him off and told him we needed to vacate the room.

In the car, Serge asked me if everything was OK. I was having trouble processing how I'd felt when the technician couldn't find the heartbeat. The thought of not having this baby in my life, even though momentary, had been terrifying. But most of all, going through that brief but confronting moment without Serge had made me feel very alone. It was scary enough dealing with all this pregnancy stuff in French, and then on the one occasion that I really could have used my French partner by my side, he was on an "important phone call."

"Everything went fine," I said eventually.

"And you are OK?" he asked.

"I'm OK. Pretty tired, actually." And I was tired. For perhaps the first time since moving to the country, I was looking forward to getting back to the farmhouse.

When we got home, Serge pulled off his shoes and reached for his work boots.

"Where are you going now?" I asked desperately.

"I need to go package up the cheese for a delivery," he said.

"Seriously?" I asked. "I was hoping we could spend some time together. I've hardly seen you since we moved here."

"It needs to happen this afternoon, but I will be back before dinner."

I watched him leave, fighting back tears.

I sat down to do some work, although I was distracted. I wandered around the house looking for something else to do and ended up in the "nursery." Seeing the state of the room, I couldn't hold in my emotions any longer. My tears burst forth with gusto. *We're not ready to have a baby! What the hell were we thinking?*

The nursery was a mess, and while I could tolerate the reality of Serge and me living somewhere ugly, I wanted our baby to live in a precious world of beauty and wonder. I ran my hand across the tatty floral wallpaper, stopping my fingers over a bubble. I pricked it with my nail, managing to rip a small hole in it. I pressed it down, but it popped out again, warped from years of sticking out. Feeling frustrated, I gave the paper a little tug.

The next thing I knew, I'd ripped the majority of one sheet off the wall. And it felt good. I was motivated by anger, frustrated with Serge for having missed the ultrasound and pissed off that he'd deserted me as soon as we'd got home. *Screw this mess of a house*, I said to myself as I ripped away. *I don't need a man by my side for everything*, I reinforced under my breath.

I kept going, panting from the exertion, until the room was an eyesore of bare, shabby walls and paper on the floor. It felt wonderfully cathartic.

⁓

Later, my anger having subsided, I donned my wellingtons and went to find Serge to try to explain my "progress" on the nursery before he saw it in person. He had promised to lead the renovations, and I couldn't help but wonder if I'd jumped the gun a little. *But what does he expect if he's never around?* I told myself.

When I found him, he was immersed in some troubles of his own, fixing a fence. It didn't escape my notice that while I was busy pulling things apart, he was putting them back together.

Since we'd arrived on the farm, one of the first things that I'd learned about goats is that they love to escape. Any gaps in fences, any low-lying wire, any slight incline on either side of the barrier, and it's game on. The slightest whiff of freedom and they're off. They could be bounding off to the abattoir down the road, and that wouldn't matter because the thrill was in the escape. Or that's at least what it seemed like. As a result, Serge always seemed to be fixing fences. If they were my goats, I'd just let them go.

"Hey," I said.

"Can you hold this?" he asked immediately.

I held on to the wire as instructed and asked him how things were going.

"I don't know how they keep getting out. Maybe they have a pair of scissors to cut the wire."

"You mean wire-cutters?" I asked.

"Sure," he said, looking despondent.

"Is everything OK, Serge?" I asked.

"*Mais oui. Bien sûr.*" He smiled, but I could tell it was forced.

There was something he wasn't telling me. I considered pushing him on the topic, but I hoped he'd open up when he was ready.

"How is your work? Are you making progress?" he asked out of the blue. I was surprised he was even worrying about my work when he had so much to do on the farm. I contemplated just saying that things were going well, but my wallpaper-ripping extravaganza had left me feeling dramatic.

"It sucks. Well, this week has sucked. No matter how long I sit and stare at my laptop, I'm just not managing to get anything done. Perhaps it's because I'm surrounded by things that need fixing, or moving, or burning . . .," I said, gearing up to mention the nursery.

"Right," said Serge, although it was one of those responses that made me feel like he wasn't really listening. *Why did he ask if he doesn't care about my answer?*

I continued. "I miss having an office with colleagues. It's so lonely just staring out at the countryside. I miss feeling like I'm part of a team working toward something. I miss getting jacked up on coffee and buzzing through work." I filled Serge's sustained silence with a messy, verbal assault on his ears.

Eventually, he responded by saying, "It will take time for things to settle down here," although it sounded more like he was reminding himself of this fact. And then he added: "Besides, you are pregnant. You need to slow down."

"Slow down? God, if I slow down any more I'll topple over. If anything, I need to speed up."

Serge looked at me, exasperated. I could see he was tired, too. Perhaps he needed a break from the farm as much as I did. Although farmers didn't really get a break, which was another fact I'd learned when the goats didn't get the memo last Sunday and ended up mowing our neighbor's paddock.

"Why don't you just call Michel and ask him to come and help you? I'm sure he'd be very willing," I suggested. "He probably misses the farm anyway. At least you could get some tips on where to let the animals graze, or how to stop them from knocking down all the fences."

"I don't want to bother him, Ella. He's retired now. I should let him enjoy some peace. He worked *so* hard for so many years."

The way Serge said *"so* hard" made him sound like he'd been farming his whole life. His stubbornness about doing everything himself didn't bode well. I wondered how long he'd have to battle it out on his own out here before acknowledging that perhaps he needed some help, or at least some guidance. By now he must have realized that farming didn't necessarily run in the family.

A few nails and plenty of hammering later, the fence was fixed. It wasn't the smoothest job I'd ever seen, but it was done.

"Shall we go out for dinner?" I suggested. "I'm not sure I can face another night at home."

"I was thinking exactly the same thing," Serge said, and I smiled, hoping this was the start of us getting back in sync.

⌒

Serge showered, dressed, and, for perhaps the first time that week, smelled delicious. I nestled into his neck to breathe in his aftershave, and the smell of figs and spices felt warm and famil-iar. He smelled so good that I almost stripped him naked, but then I remembered that we had plans and composed myself. We were going out for dinner. In town. It was the most excited I'd been all week. I'd even squeezed into a black dress and put on some heels. After wearing tracksuit pants and one of Serge's woolen jumpers all week, it was fun to get dressed up.

We arrived at the restaurant at 7:45 p.m., and it was dead. Not a soul. Granted it was early, but I thought that maybe because we were in the country and it was the middle of winter, people might eat a little earlier. True to French form, the restaurant started filling up shortly after we'd arrived, but there certainly wasn't the buzz I'd been expecting for a Friday night.

"What can I get you to drink?" a gruff waiter asked, looking around impatiently.

Serge ordered a bottle of wine *à la ficelle*, or "measured with string," which meant that he was given a full bottle of wine and would only pay for what he drank. The waiter went to fill my glass. I said a polite "*Non, merci*," and he seemed offended. Taken aback, I told him that I was pregnant, and he looked at me with a sort of disdain before shrugging, filling Serge's glass and whisking away my own.

"I guess I'll just drink water," I joked to Serge.

"Ella, you can have a little glass of wine. It won't hurt."

"No," I said. "Even the French recommend you don't drink during pregnancy now."

"But a few sips isn't really drinking, is it?"

"Of course, it is. Didn't you read the article I sent you about alcohol during pregnancy?" I asked.

Serge stalled, and I realized that he hadn't even bothered opening the email. He told me I should just do what I thought was best.

So, I drank water, and we ate terrine out of a large communal dish, followed by lamb stew—the food was delicious, the potatoes particularly divine.

I tried, again, to get Serge to open up about how things were going on the farm, but he wouldn't say much, opting to maintain his stoic positivity.

In turn, he shifted the focus off his job and onto mine by suggesting ways to make it easier for me to work at home.

"Before we worry too much about my office space, though, Serge, shouldn't we get onto the kitchen and bathroom renovations? At least paint the nursery."

"Ella, there is something I think we should discuss," he said after a moment's pause. I sat up in my chair. I felt both nervous and intrigued. Important discussions over dinner now tended to give me the heebie-jeebies, but perhaps Serge was finally about to tell me what was on his mind.

"Mmm," I prompted, not wanting to break his flow.

"I'm not sure we'll be able to renovate the kitchen and bathroom immediately," he said.

"Huh? Is that why you've been avoiding discussing the renovations? Can't we afford it? I thought we had plenty of money set aside."

"Our cash is just a little tied up at the moment," he said.

"Oh, no. Not the Paris apartment again?" I asked, fearing the oncoming disagreement.

"No, because of the farm. I've had to replace one of the milking machine attachments. It was very expensive."

"Oh," I said. Having seen Michel's impeccable machinery, I found it hard to imagine any of it needed replacing so soon. I wondered if the "good workman" wasn't just blaming his tools.

"So, what's the plan then?" I asked.

"We should be able to get the money back soon, but it's just taking a while for things to get established."

"What do you mean?" I asked.

"Sales are down," he said quietly.

"Really?"

"People out here are very resistant to change. The locals were very fond of Michel," he said.

"Well, can't we come up with a way to sell more? Can't Fanny help? What happened with the department store?" I asked. While I'd anticipated Serge might struggle as a farmer, I never thought he'd actually struggle to sell cheese.

"I'm working on it. And everyone is doing their best," he said. "But in the country, things can take time. You can't force people to buy something they don't want."

I thought back to the discussion Serge and I had had before I'd agreed to move. If I told him I wanted to leave now, would that even be possible given that our money was now tied up in some milking machine? I wondered how much cheese he would need to sell in order to get back on top of things.

"How long before you're back in the black?" I asked.

"Not long, Bella," he said. "A couple months, perhaps."

"Well, maybe the house renovations aren't necessary anyway, especially if things might not work out on the farm," I said.

"You're not enjoying it?" he asked. He seemed to take my comment as me telling him I was ready to leave.

"Well . . .," I paused.

"So maybe you'd prefer to be back in Paris?" he asked.

Does he sound relieved?

"We're still getting set up, I guess," I said, noncommittally. I didn't want to crush Serge's dream of bringing up a family here; but if he wasn't happy, then I was ready to drop everything and go immediately.

"*Bon*," he said, with an expression I couldn't read.

I tried to remember if I'd ever had a more confusing conversation with Serge but was interrupted by the waiter asking us if we wanted dessert.

To my relief, Serge suggested we share a *tarte tatin*. I adored the fact that he was always willing to go halves.

"So, what color do you want to paint the baby's room?" he asked rather cunningly after the waiter disappeared, knowing that it was a topic close to my heart. The one good thing about having a house in the country meant that the baby could have their own room, which meant I could have fun imagining what it would look like. And after Serge had seen my wallpaper-removal technique, I assumed he was keen to make the room more presentable.

"Are you sure we have enough money for paint?" I asked, only half joking.

"For paint? Of course," he said.

Driving home that night, I felt like a lot had gone unsaid at dinner. What was clear was that we wouldn't be doing any big renovations immediately. But perhaps none of that mattered, because I felt like Serge had hinted at going back to Paris. Or was I reading too much into things?

Chapter
13

I **SPENT THE NEXT DAY** preoccupied with thoughts of Serge not being able to sell cheese. Every time I'd try to do some work, I'd get distracted trying to come up with a plan to help. I toyed with the idea of calling Fanny (who, to this day, had never once shown any willingness to help me, despite my multiple attempts to win her over) or maybe getting Clotilde to ask Gaston to write an article for his paper's food column on Serge's venture (too awkward to even contemplate further). These were the only two people I knew who might be able to help promote Serge's cheese, and I didn't have a good relationship with either of them. *Shit*, I thought, wishing there was something I could do. The afternoon flew by as I researched the best ways to sell cheese and to establish a brand.

Later that afternoon, Tim called.

"Ella, I've got some news," he said in a tone that immediately made me nervous.

"What's up?" I asked.

"I have to cut back your hours."

Tim had never been one to beat around the bush.

"Oh," I murmured, my heart beating loudly in my ears. "Did something happen?" I couldn't help but think about how little work I'd done since Serge and I had moved. Was I being fired?

"Not really," he said. "It's just that I've found someone local who can take up the slack. It'll be easier with this person in the office. I know it's perhaps not ideal . . ."

"Right," I said, desperately trying to figure out a way to convince Tim that I needed this job.

"But I can keep giving you occasional freelance jobs if you're interested," he said, as though this would be a good consolation. "And that way you can keep your work visa."

"OK, yep," I told him, tears welling in my eyes.

"And soon you'll have your hands full with the baby anyway," he added.

"Not for a few months," I said.

"It'll come around quicker than you think, or want."

"I guess," I said. My mind was spinning, trying to come to terms with what was going on.

"Anyway," Tim said. "How's life in the country? Are you guys loving it?"

The sudden switch to small talk threw me. "Serge is warming to it, I guess. What's the adjustment period from cheese guy to farmer?"

"Probably not that different from you getting used to the country."

"So, interminable," I suggested, attempting a laugh despite wanting to cry.

"At least you're still sleeping through the night," he said. "Wait until you start questioning all your life decisions when you're severely sleep-deprived. Enjoy the pregnancy while you can. Babies are much easier in than out."

Hanging up, I felt numb. Almost as easily as I'd got the job with Tim, I'd lost it. Yes, I realized that things hadn't been going particularly well, but I would have found my feet eventually. I was devastated that I could be replaced so easily.

On top of wondering what I was going to do with myself now, my biggest concern was worrying about how Serge would take the news. I wasn't bringing in a lot of cash but it was a dependable income, and with cheese sales being down, it was probably an important contribution.

I decided not to tell him right away, until I'd figured out another way to make money. He had enough going on down on the farm. He didn't need to worry about me, too.

What else can go wrong at the moment? I wondered.

⌒

The following week, my panic at having lost my job and at having zero new work prospects on the horizon had to be put on hold. Clotilde and Chris were both scheduled to visit, and I'd promised to show them a good time.

Clotilde arrived in her father's convertible, armed with treats from Paris. Spying a bag of pastries from my favorite bakery, Du Pain et des Idées, I said to her, "You do know we have bakeries out here, right?"

"But do they have the *sacristain*?" she asked.

The *sacristain* was my favorite pastry. I'd previously firmly been a croissant—regular, almond, or chocolate—for breakfast kind of girl, but the *sacristain* changed all that. The baton-shaped combination of puff pastry, almond, and vanilla was delicious and the perfect shape and size for dipping into coffee. I was thoroughly converted, and now it took the flakiest of flaky-looking croissants to woo me back. I'd yet to find a better example of the *sacristain* than the one from this bakery by the Canal Saint-Martin.

"I have more goodies in the trunk, too." She smiled.

"So, did you finally get a job with Uber Eats?" I asked.

"Very funny," she said as I took her inside.

I walked her through the house, telling her that we'd decided to hold off on renovating for a while.

"It actually looks much better than I remember," she said.

I watched her closely, trying to figure out if she was just being generous.

"Seriously," she said, noticing my look. "Your furniture works surprisingly well in here. And it's much cleaner now. Sort of has a retro-chic look about it, too."

I looked at the kitchen and squinted, wondering if Clotilde needed an eye test. Perhaps I'd just started imagining it to be worse than it actually was?

"Are you just saying that because we haven't started the renovations?" I asked.

"Not at all," she confirmed. "It's a good thing; at least you don't need to rush."

Even if Clotilde was just being nice, it was good to know the farmhouse wasn't a complete disaster.

"Coffee or tea?" I asked.

We sat, and Clotilde pulled out a box of meringues from Aux Merveilleux de Fred. The little parcels of whipped-cream-filled meringues were as light as air while still managing to burst with the flavor of coffee, chocolate, or cherry. As I bit into one, it dissolved on my tongue, and I was taken back to the time when Clotilde had first introduced me to them and we'd eaten an entire box while lying in the park near our apartment.

Full of sugar, I suggested we head into town for a spot of shopping, but Clotilde had a better idea. "We'll go to my favorite castle. Perhaps you could get some inspiration for the remodeling," she joked. "Besides, you can't live in the Loire and not know *les châteaux*."

We arrived at Château de Villandry after a quick drive. The approach from town was nothing short of spectacular. We walked around the perfectly manicured gardens—which looked more like large-scale artworks—admiring the impeccable lines of hedges and the artistic use of vegetables in the garden beds. Clotilde was right—being surrounded by such beauty was inspiring. I felt a kind of peace as we walked through the castle grounds, imagining a very different kind of life.

Clotilde interrupted my thoughts of joining a royal family somewhere and started grilling me on what had been going on. She must have sensed that there was something on my mind.

"So, how is everything out here, Ella? Are you terribly bored yet? How's work?"

"I'm actually winding down my hours at Food To Go Go. Tim is going to keep me on the books, but more on an occasional freelance basis."

"What does that mean?" she asked.

"No confirmed paycheck each month," I said.

"Damn. So, what's your plan?"

"Well, I've been mulling things over," I said, feeling things out as I spoke.

"And?" she asked.

"The way I see it is that I have two options. I could look for a job in town—"

"Mmm, something in tourism perhaps," she suggested, cutting me off.

"Or . . . I was thinking I could help Serge on the farm," I said.

"On the farm?" she repeated, seemingly as surprised at the idea as I was.

"Sort of," I confirmed. "But more in a sales and marketing capacity."

"OK," she said, clearly trying to keep up.

"I'm hoping to get the cheese-tasting room up and running. You know where we tasted Michel's cheese that first day we visited the farm," I said. "Well, the other day I had a vision of me standing behind the bar, wearing a cute little apron and serving cheese, and it got me thinking."

It felt weird expressing my plans aloud. Even though it wasn't a particularly wild idea, I would be taking a risk—and committing myself to actually staying on the farm.

"Tell me more," she said.

"Well, I figured I could help Serge actually sell some cheese, help get his name out there. It'd be sort of like running a *fromagerie*, so Serge would be able to lend a hand with the set-up. And then I could work there."

"OK," she said.

"Well, what do you think? Is it a terrible idea?" I asked.

"No, not terrible. I'm just wondering what kind of market you'd have out here for something like that."

"I still need to run the whole idea by Serge, anyway. And if he's not keen, perhaps I could just help him with the goats while I look for something more suitable."

She chuckled and took my arm in hers. "Ella, I think one day on the farm will be enough for you to realize that you're not destined to be a farmer."

Clotilde helped me figure out a way to gently introduce the idea of the cheese-tasting room to Serge. She'd convinced me that a coercive approach would be more effective than a bombardment.

"Especially if he's got a lot going on at the moment," she'd said after I'd explained to her that Serge often worked from sunrise to sunset. "Best to go in slowly so he doesn't just dismiss it as being too much work. Perhaps join him on the farm for a few days and then magically 'stumble' on the idea. Make him feel like it's a joint venture."

It was a good plan, of course. Clotilde had a knack for being right.

"Don't you have work to do?" Serge asked when I suggested I could help him feed the goats after Clotilde had gone back to Paris.

"Actually, Tim has asked me to work on specific projects for a while, so it looks like I'll have some more free time now," I said, figuring I could explain the financial implications of this when I pitched the cheese-room idea to him.

I thought he'd ask more questions but he just looked relieved.

My intentions to help Serge, however, went out the window when Cecile tried to attack me. Things had been going relatively well all morning. I'd managed to move a few wheelbarrows of feed for the kids and had even attempted a pat. This last move, however, had been a mistake, something I only realized when Cecile—a rather large goat with one lazy eye—decided to intervene, and chased me almost the entire way back to the house.

I rushed inside, looking over my shoulder to make sure she wasn't about to barge through the door. If ever I needed a sign that I shouldn't be a farmer, Cecile had just given it to me.

Serge came in shortly after.

"Ella, where did you go?" he asked.

I quickly ushered him in and shut the door. "Serge, thank God you're back. Cecile is loose. She nearly attacked me. I think she might have rabies or something. I'm pretty sure I saw her foaming at the mouth."

"Really? When I saw her she looked fine. She's back behind the fence now. She actually went back in very obligingly. She really is one of my favorites."

"Well, not mine," I said.

"Shall we go back together?" he asked.

"Perhaps I should stay here and make us some lunch," I said, my heart still beating quickly.

Serge only needed to look at me to realize I was traumatized. He nodded his agreement and gave me a reassuring hug.

Perhaps I can find another way to convince Serge that the cheese-tasting room is a good idea, I thought while busying myself in the kitchen.

Cooking turned out to be the ultimate distraction from my other concerns. It was meditative and warm. It kept me both physically and mentally occupied. And neither Serge, nor the *bébé*, complained about the outcome.

I needed to find recipes and go shopping, all before even starting to prepare and cook. If it wasn't market day, I'd have to head to the supermarket for supplies, which always felt like a mission. Country supermarkets—or *les grandes surfaces*—didn't bear much resemblance to the ones I'd frequented in Paris. They were huge warehouses with equally large parking lots, and felt big and cold. Everyone used trolleys and stocked up on things like long-life milk and six-packs of water. The selection of products was overwhelming, and I missed the careful curating that made the delis and *épiceries* of Paris so perfect. But still, the collection of cheese was enormous, so I couldn't really complain.

Cooking filled hours of my day, and I seemed to have the wonderful ability to choose recipes that would take a long time to prepare. Serge had a Paul Bocuse cookbook from the seventies that was wildly decadent and complicated, but provided me with an opportunity to test both my French and my skills in the kitchen. And it served as great fodder for my Instagram feed. While last year had been all about cheese in its natural state, this year would be all about dishes that incorporated cheese.

Building on my reasoning that everyone is happy after eating well, I planned to tell Serge about my plans for the cheese room eventually, over a lavish dinner. But the nights went by and the moment never felt right, and then Chris was due to visit, so I put it off a little longer.

⌒

Chris arrived and brought with him a breath of Paris air that I didn't even realize I'd been desperate for. And he was thrilled to be out of the city, exclaiming that even the journey had been refreshing. Serge and I picked him up at the train, took him back to our house, and gave him the tour. He loved the place.

Later, with Serge back looking after his goats, Chris drove us into town. We headed to my usual café, the only one I'd found with decent Wi-Fi.

"Now, sorry to be the bearer of bad news, but from what I've seen, you won't get a decent flat white out here," I told him.

Opting for a glass of Chinon wine instead, Chris asked me how I was holding up.

"It's been an adjustment," I told him.

"No kidding," he said. "Even Paris can be hard to get used to. I can only imagine being out here in the backwaters."

"There are certain things I do like. The local market is amazing. Serge keeps telling me how delicious the wine is. Goat cheese is rife. This town is *gorgeous*. I guess I'm just missing my creature comforts—my Haussmann apartment, my favorite barista . . ."

"Who wouldn't miss me?" he asked.

I punched him in the arm. He was only joking but he actually wasn't wrong. It felt indulgent to admit that I was missing coffee, but it was more than that. I was missing café culture. Hanging out in a friendly space with friendly people. Having a meeting point.

"And how's work?" he asked, bringing me back from Paris where my mind had wandered off to.

I guessed Tim hadn't mentioned anything to Chris. I started to explain the situation as I had done with Clotilde.

"So, what are you doing all day?" he asked, interrupting.

"Well, I've taken to cooking, which fills in a surprising amount of time."

"Have you been checking out the area? Visiting other towns?"

"Not really," I admitted. "A little bit while Clotilde was here."

"Ella. It sounds like what you need is a break from the farm. Being pregnant doesn't mean you're housebound," he said.

"No, but I'm certainly less fun."

"You probably *have* less fun, but that doesn't make *you* less fun. What else is there to do around here?"

"There's plenty of wine," I joked.

"Yes! Let's go to a winery and try some wine," he said quickly.

I pointed at my stomach.

"Ella, you're mad—a winery is probably the one place in the world where it is acceptable to spit out wine."

I actually hadn't considered that. "OK, let's do it," I said.

⌒

It was that time of year when most of the wineries were either quiet or closed for tastings, but we found a beautiful vineyard just outside of Chinon that was open.

Chris enthusiastically tried every wine on offer, while I was more reserved, trying only a couple and making sure to spit the samples out.

Walking through the spindly vines—Chris jolly from the tasting—I explained my idea for the cheese room to him.

"Like a café?" he asked.

"No, more like somewhere you can go and try—and then buy—the cheese, and perhaps sit down for some simple food. Like a wine-tasting room, but for cheese."

"I like it," he said.

"Yeah?" I asked, relieved.

"But why not just throw a coffee machine in the corner, too?" he suggested.

"I guess I could," I said, thinking it over for a minute. It would certainly manage to kill two birds with one stone. It'd make good coffee available in the country and it'd probably bring in more business. "It's a good idea," I admitted.

"You'd need a barista, though," he added quickly, obviously remembering how bad I was at making coffee.

"You?" I suggested.

"Move here?"

"Yep!"

"No way, Ella. I've hardly seen anyone under forty here— there's certainly not enough action for my liking. But I could help you get things off the ground. Are you serious about it?"

"Well, I'm not sure about the café aspect, but I want to do something to help Serge sell his cheese. And really, I don't have much else going on."

"And what about all that?" he said, pointing at my belly.

"You underestimate the power of a pregnant woman," I told him with a grin. "And a bored one at that."

"You'll need a proper plan then," he said.

We spent the afternoon figuring out a business proposal and a budget for the cheese room. I told Chris we wouldn't have much disposable money, and he reassured me that he had the contacts to help me do things affordably. "Besides," he said, "you've got amazing second-hand markets in this area. I'm sure you could set up something really fun while sticking to this budget."

After Chris's visit, the idea of starting a café/cheese room in the middle of nowhere had officially become my new dream. It even made me cool slightly on the idea of immediately moving back to Paris. I'd begun to realize that I couldn't fit my old city life into this new country setting, and in order to create a life for myself here, I needed to acclimatize to the surroundings. For perhaps the first time since we'd arrived on the farm, I was excited to see how things might evolve.

Serge must have noticed my change in disposition, too, because even though he was still constantly busy, he seemed happier than he had been in a while.

He'd taken the news of me cutting back my hours at Food To Go Go surprisingly well. When I'd explained that Tim had found someone in Paris to replace me, and that I'd just be doing occasional freelance jobs, he didn't seem too bothered. Perhaps he felt guilty for making me leave the Paris office in the first place. Or perhaps his money troubles were sorting themselves out, and he didn't need to rely on my income anymore.

It probably would have been a good time to pitch the café/cheese room to Serge but, following Chris's advice, I wanted to do a little more research—and investigation into the state of our finances—before doing so.

Serge was a numbers guy. I had to make sure what I'd budgeted wasn't too far out of reach before sharing it with him. I was already worried he'd think it was mad to take on this project, what with our eventual house renovations and the baby on the way, but as Serge once said, why walk when you can run?

Chapter

14

AFTER THE BUZZ OF CLOTILDE'S and Chris's visits, the house felt desperately quiet, and with Serge still spending most daylight hours on the farm, my boredom returned quickly. I decided to drive myself into town to do our weekly shopping. I was no closer to getting my French license, but in the end I'd thought bugger it, figuring my Australian license and a little foreigner charm would probably do the trick if I ever got pulled over by any country cops.

The Chinon market was easily one of the best things I'd found since arriving in the countryside, with the buzz of the shoppers and stallholders taking over the streets of town. I'd amble along the busy, cobbled lanes, sampling little tasters as I went. I'd spend minutes inspecting the pieces of fruit that were cut open and put on display for all to judge their worth. I'd fill my basket with seasonal produce.

In general, market shopping in France was a very laid-back affair. You were never rushed, and therefore it was expected that you'd never rush anyone. And while it wasn't unheard of to queue for close to twenty minutes to buy fish from the fishmonger, as soon as you reached the front of the line, you were

VICTORIA BROWNLEE

120

treated like royalty. You could ask for recommendations, for cooking advice, even about the water temperature of the sea that a certain fish was fished out of. I'd learned more about seafood from market shopping in France than I think I'd ever learned in Australia, a country surrounded by water.

Shortly after arriving at the market that morning, I ran into Marie, who was weighed down by a huge basket of apples and pears. She put down her shopping and kissed me hello. After exchanging some pleasantries, she asked how I was enjoying life in the country. I think she was still baffled at the idea of anyone choosing to live in an apartment above, below, and next door to strangers.

"It's mostly going well. I'm finding plenty to keep busy," I exaggerated.

"I know the feeling," she replied.

"Oh? Is the B&B busy at the moment?" I asked.

"Oh, no, a few bookings, but it's manageable. I'm spending most of my time at the moment in the kitchen baking."

Just as I was imagining her and Jacques eating their weight in baked goods, she explained that she baked tarts for a café in town. The enormous basket of fruit made a lot more sense in that context.

"That's a brilliant side gig," I said.

"It brings in some more money and keeps me busy. I wasn't brought up to sit around idly."

I envied Marie's down-to-earth approach. *I could really do with a dose of her get-it-done attitude in my country living plan*, I thought, as we said goodbye.

I stopped by the *fromagerie* on wheels to pick up my standard selection of hard cheeses—Comté, Emmental, and Gruyère—

and was surprised to see a row of Serge's wrapped goat cheeses. I didn't know he'd gotten his cheese stocked at the market. I beamed with pride.

"Is it good?" I asked in French, motioning to the goat cheese, hoping to do a bit of sleuthing for Serge.

"*Comme ci, comme ça,*" he replied.

Huh? The cheese is only so-so?

After everyone had raved about farmer Michel's cheese, why was this guy saying that Serge's was average? *Oh, God, is Serge making bad cheese? Is this the real reason why it's not selling?*

"Is that right?" I asked.

"There's been a change in ownership," he said, as though that explained everything. "It's just not the same."

When I'd asked Serge if I could sample his first batch of cheese, he'd told me quite strongly that I should continue to avoid eating unpasteurized varieties. I regretted not having sneaked a small taste and quickly ran through the likelihood of a bad batch. Yes, Serge had never farmed nor made cheese before; but he had immaculate taste and he certainly wouldn't try to sell something that was below par. Or . . . did he need to sell it? I guess what else would he do with the stuff he'd already produced? And what did this mean for my cheese room?

I pushed on with my market shopping, but I was distracted by my interaction with the cheese guy, and I ended up with a rather random assortment of vegetables. I'd settled on a very handsome and very heavy pumpkin, some pears, onions, carrots, and potatoes. Looking at my haul, I felt a little dismayed, wondering what I was going to cook.

Then, on my way to the butcher, I spotted Chuck working in the café. I automatically ran my hand over my hair, hoping I didn't look too dishevelled, and then tapped on the window and waved. It took him a moment to look up and I panicked, wondering if he was ignoring me. But he raised his hand, obviously finishing writing a sentence, and then waved me inside.

"Chuck, what a surprise. I haven't seen you recently," I said. I didn't take off my coat out of fear of having to explain my growing bump.

"I had to zip back to London for an event. Did I miss anything?" he asked.

I looked around at the near-empty café and laughed.

"So, what's for dinner?" he asked, looking in my basket.

Is he angling for an invite? I wondered momentarily before awkwardly asking him if he'd like to join us. I wasn't sure how Serge would feel about a surprise dinner guest, but I knew I was keen to spend more time with Chuck.

My offer was met with an equally awkward answer. "Oh, um, sorry, I didn't mean to just invite myself to dinner," he said.

"Oh, it's really no problem. You're very welcome," I rushed on. "Anyway, I've been brushing up on my cooking, and it seems I'm still learning about portion control."

"Then I'd be honored," he said seriously.

"Great, well, it'll be pretty casual. It won't be the most glamorous meal," I said, trying to keep expectations in check. "And our house is in a bit of a state." I stopped myself from making any more excuses in case it was starting to sound like I was retracting the invitation.

"I'm sure it'll be perfect," he said encouragingly.

"Would you like to bring someone, perhaps? A girlfriend? A boyfriend?" I offered. I didn't really know anything about Chuck's personal life.

"Will it spoil your plans if I join you solo?" he asked, not giving anything away.

"Of course not," I reassured him before rushing off to continue my shopping.

I went to the butcher for some chicken and my daily dose of friendly service. Visiting him reminded me of when I first arrived in Paris and used to visit Serge to be guided through the world of French cheese. Although the butcher was around sixty and wasn't any threat to my current relationship, he'd taken a shine to me, and his smile when I walked through his door brightened my day. And his advice on cooking meat had so far played a big part in my success in the kitchen.

I headed home with a long to-do list buzzing around my head. On top of cooking an unintentional comfort-food-inspired menu, I wanted to clean the kitchen and the living and dining area, and try to hide some of the clutter.

I also wanted to unpack some books to avoid looking completely illiterate in front of Chuck—although I wasn't sure my selection of memoirs on travel and a few trashy romance novels was going to win me many points. Serge did, however, have a solid collection of French books, but their covers were all so identical and boring that I'd never even bothered opening them when they'd lined the shelves of his Paris apartment.

"Serge, what kind of books are these?" I asked later as I was pulling them out of boxes.

"Oh, there are many different genres. A lot of police and crime novels. I also enjoy a good political biography."

"Hmm," I said, wondering what Chuck would make of this, which reminded me: I should probably tell Serge about our dinner guest.

"Oh, I almost forgot. I ran into Chuck earlier today, you know, that English guy I met. He's just back from a trip to London. Anyway, I ended up buying too many ingredients so I invited him over for dinner. I hope that's OK."

"*Parfait*, it'll be nice for you to have an English-speaking friend here," Serge said generously. "I'll dig out some wine."

"And some of your cheese?" I suggested, trying to gauge his reaction.

"I'll see what I can find, but I think most of it is packed already," he said.

"By the way, why don't you have a stall at the market?" I asked.

"I hope to eventually," he said.

"But why not now?"

"Don't rush me, Ella," he said sharply, making me wonder if my pregnancy hormones were contagious.

He went off to the cellar, and I was left to question whether there'd been some truth behind the cheese vendor's comments. *Why else doesn't he want to show off his creations?*

———

Chuck arrived in a beat-up Renault that evening. I watched him out the kitchen window as he walked up to the door, flowers in hand.

"For my lovely host," he said when I opened the door. "You look wonderful."

I blushed. I hardly even took off my coat these days, so I guess I'd made a little bit more of an effort when getting dressed tonight. I was wearing black jeans—elastic-waisted, of course— and a red top, which was perhaps a little too low-cut considering I was now sporting a more generous bust thanks to the pregnancy hormones.

"Welcome, welcome," I said, ushering him in.

I'd done an OK job of making our house look a little more charming. Thank God it was winter and the sun had set hours ago, meaning that a little flickering candlelight went a long way to soften the look and feel of the farmhouse. I just had to keep Chuck out of the kitchen, where, unfortunately, I'd been relying on the fluorescent light bulbs to finish dinner.

"This is Serge," I said, introducing the two.

"I'm Chuck," he said, and then paused. "But you can call me Charles if you like." I couldn't help a little laugh, remembering what Chuck had said about the French finding it hard to pronounce his name.

Serge looked relieved. "*Bonsoir*, Charles. Welcome to our home," he said, extending his hand.

As we all sat in the living room, I realized I felt nervous. I was desperate for tonight to go well, for Chuck to become a friend to me and Serge rather than just an acquaintance of mine. I took a deep breath.

"So, you're enjoying the country life?" Chuck asked Serge, who was busying himself serving a couple of glasses of whiskey.

"*Oui, c'est magnifique*," Serge replied, looking up; however, his delivery of the word "magnificent" felt very flat. "And it will be so much better for the little one," he continued, handing a glass to our guest and sitting down. Chuck looked confused.

Merde, *I forgot Chuck still doesn't know*. Clearly my bump wasn't as visible as it felt.

"Ah, yes," I chipped in. "I'm pregnant. Ta da!" *Oh, dear God, shut me up*, I thought as we fell into an uncomfortable silence.

Chuck looked at me carefully; his expression was hard to read. His eyes creased slightly and his shoulders seemed to slump.

Does he seem surprised or just ambivalent? And why do I care?

"We've moved here to escape the city life and bring our baby up among the trees," Serge continued. At least he had a way of making our escape to the country sound poetic.

"It's not too much of a change then?" Chuck asked.

I looked expectantly at Serge, wondering how he might respond.

"Well, it is certainly not like Paris," he said and then chuckled. "But it has always been a dream of mine to have a family in the country."

Before I could get any more clues on how Serge felt about our move, he asked Chuck what he was doing in Chinon.

"I'm a writer," he said with conviction, before adding, "Well, at the very least, a tortured artist."

Serge looked to me for help deciphering what this meant. I quickly explained to him that Chuck was writing literary fiction, and that this process involved a certain amount of torment and heartbreak. It wasn't like writing romance novels, I told him, figuring that writing anything less than a literary masterpiece had to be easy.

"And how is the farming business?" Chuck asked.

Again, I carefully watched Serge's reaction, hoping he'd perhaps be more honest with Chuck than he had been with me until this point.

"*Ça va, ça va,*" Serge replied, either evading the question or wanting to keep the small talk light. "But enough about business. Shall we eat?"

Dinner itself was a veritable success. The food—despite my concerns that the menu lacked finesse—was delicious and, maybe due to the freezing temperatures outside, it was well received. We started with a hearty onion soup topped with a cheese-laden crouton, followed by a rich coq au vin with a buttery potato mash and roast pumpkin.

Serge organized the cheese plate and presented a selection of pasteurized varieties that he claimed were all pregnancy-friendly. The absence of his own cheese among the selection seemed to confirm my earlier suspicions.

For dessert, I took inspiration from Marie and made a pear tart. The flavor of the fruit was deep and the taste was sweet, almost like candy. And the pastry, which I'd made with local butter, was thick but not heavy, soaking up the pear juice and the sugar that I'd used to glaze the top of the tart.

Over tea and coffee, Chuck and I fell into a lengthy discussion about the TV shows we used to watch as kids. As we were laughing about one in particular that had encouraged us to do large-scale, and very messy, artworks, I realized Serge's attention had drifted, and he was staring off into space. I tried to bring him into the conversation but he continued to seem distracted. I decided that he must be tired, so I started to clear the table.

Chuck gracefully took the hint.

"Do you mind if I call a cab?" he asked. "I've probably had one too many drinks to drive myself."

I was about to offer to drop him off, seeing as I hadn't been drinking, but Serge had already dialed the number.

Later, Serge asked me what the deal was with Chuck's writing. I explained again his ambitious, multigenerational, multiperspective project.

"Seems a little pretentious to me," Serge said.

"Serge, that's because you're a farmer now," I replied.

"What is that supposed to mean?" he asked, his voice catching slightly.

"I was just ribbing you, Serge. I adore your new rugged ways," I said, giving him a hug and dragging him off to our room. Thankfully he let my comment slide.

⁓

But, in bed that night, I mulled over the fact that I was now dating—and having a child with—a farmer. In France of all places. Serge had been an integral part of my first year in Paris, but I couldn't ever have predicted we'd end up here.

When Billie had convinced me to try going out with a different kind of man, was this what she'd had in mind? I snuck out of bed to call her.

"Hey, Billie. It's just me. Do you have time to talk?" I asked.

"Yep, what's up?"

"Why does something have to be 'up'?" I said incredulously, stalling so as not to immediately bombard her with my question.

"No reason . . .," she said, playing along.

"Well . . . seeing as you asked, I have a few follow-up questions on something we talked about a while back."

"Oh, dear," Billie said.

"It's just that I'm worried I misunderstood what you meant when you told me to date different types of guys. Did I rush into things with Serge?"

"Ella, you can't be thinking like this now. You're having a baby together."

"I know, but it's just—"

"Nope." She cut me off. "This is a very unproductive line of questioning. Are you not enjoying your country château?"

I looked around the living room unenthusiastically.

"Just a few adjustment issues, I guess," I said.

"Talk me through them," she said.

I outlined some of my concerns about our escape to the country—the isolation, the state of the house, my doubts about Serge's farming capabilities—and as I was finishing the list, I heard the bedroom door. I panicked.

"Serge?" I called out. "Shit, Billie, I better run. Thanks for the chat."

I went back into the bedroom and saw Serge getting back under the covers. Merde! *How much did he hear?*

"You OK, Serge?" I whispered.

"*Oui*, Bella. Come back to bed."

I apprehensively slid back into bed and risked slipping my arm around him. He didn't throw it off, which seemed like a positive sign, but as I lay there I replayed my entire conversation with Billie, trying to remember exactly what I'd said. The words "Did I rush into things with Serge?" contributed intensely to the growing feeling of nausea in my stomach.

Chapter

15

I **WOKE TO FIND THE** spot in bed next to me empty. *Shoot!* I got up to look for Serge but, instead, found a note from him on the kitchen bench telling me he'd gone to the bakery. *Is he hiding from me? Running away?* It wasn't the first time I'd feared he'd leave me under the guise of buying a baguette.

I made myself a cup of tea and sat staring out the window into our barren, unstructured winter garden. *Next step in the Ella domestication/country-fication project will have to be gardening,* I said to myself with a sigh, wondering at the same time if the word "country-fication" actually existed.

Serge's blue Citroën appeared in the driveway a little later, and I couldn't help but let out a long exhale. At least he'd come back. I turned on the coffee machine for him and got out some of Marie's raspberry jam (probably my favorite upside of country living—delicious organic jam, hand-delivered, for free, in exchange for a coffee and a chat).

"*Bonjour,* Ella," he said rather solemnly, laying down a baguette and a bag of croissants.

"Serge, are you OK? I missed my morning cuddles," I said to him.

"Everything is fine," he said. "And with you?"

I looked at him carefully, watching for a hint of anger or disappointment that would indicate that he'd heard my conversation with Billie last night, but he gave nothing away.

"I guess. Just missing home a little at the moment. I think because it's so cold," I rattled on. "I actually called Billie last night for a gossip."

"Oh, yes?"

"Mmm, no real news."

Serge nodded. "Is that right?"

"Yep, all the same, boring as usual in Melbourne."

Our conversation felt stilted but I could also have been reading too much into things. Perhaps he hadn't overheard my phone call at all.

The coffee machine noisily came to a halt, interrupting the silence.

"Well, I'm glad everything is going well for your friend," he said after a long pause. *Was that a pointed comment?* I wondered. I don't think he'd ever referred to Billie as "my friend" before. Perhaps she was now in his bad books.

"So, what shall we do today?" I asked, trying to lighten the mood. "Perhaps we should visit some castles for gardening inspiration."

The previous weekend, we'd tried to recreate one of our favorite Parisian activities, and it had been a bit of a disaster. It had been a relatively sunny and warm day, considering it was winter, so I'd set up a picnic rug on the recently mowed grass and scrambled around the kitchen to try to organize a semi-respectable picnic.

But by the time Serge had come back from the farm, I'd already eaten the majority of the food. He'd joined me on the rug to finish off my leftovers.

"Ella, this is nice," he'd said.

"Sorry I ate most of it already," I'd told him.

"No worries, you're eating for two."

"Sure am," I'd said, even though I knew that the tiny life inside me didn't actually need half a baguette and almost an entire block of Comté.

I'd hugged Serge and had been about to tell him how nice it was to do something we used to do in Paris, how perhaps not every aspect of life had to change even though we were now living in the country. But then I'd gotten a waft of goat manure. I'd asked Serge to check his shoes. Culprit discovered. Vibe ruined. The sun had gone behind a cloud, and it had immediately gotten cold. I'd suggested we head inside, and that had been that.

So, this weekend I wanted to improve on the experience. But Serge wasn't up for attempting to do something fun. "I need to work, Ella," he said. He already sounded exhausted.

"Nooo! We should go and explore."

"I can't stop working just because you have," he said bluntly.

I was momentarily speechless. He continued. "I'm having issues with another milking machine, so I'll need to juggle the line to make sure all the goats get milked."

"How about I help? I can milk a goat," I said with confidence.

"You can?" He looked at me with raised eyebrows. I guessed my earlier efforts with the animals hadn't gone unnoticed.

"Of course. Well, I've milked cows plenty of times. It can't be that different," I told him. And sure, by "milked cows," I meant I had milked one cow, and by "plenty of times," I meant once at a school camp.

"Great. Shall we go start, then?" Serge asked.

"No time like the present," I told him, stuffing half a croissant into my mouth, while thinking to myself, *This should be interesting.*

Down in the milking shed, my freezing hands were soon squeezing the life out of a poor goat's teats. I felt quite proud watching the tiny squirts of milk shooting into the bucket—until I looked over at how efficiently the machines were doing the same job. I considered coming clean to Serge about my incompetence, but he seemed happy enough with how things were going, so I decided to persevere.

I managed to build some momentum and was actually quite enjoying myself when suddenly my hand cramped, causing me to clamp the teat, causing the goat to start, causing *me* to start, causing my foot to knock over the bucket.

"*Merde!*" I screamed.

"Ella, what happened?" he asked, rushing over.

I burst into tears. The tension from earlier that morning, plus my inability to milk a goat—plus an irrational fear that by being unable to milk a goat, I would be unable to feed my own baby—had officially gotten to me.

"Serge, I can't do this, I'm sorry. I hate these damn goats."

"So do I, sometimes," he said wearily.

"You do?" I asked, feeling like he finally might open up to me.

"Of course, I hate them at times," he said, straightening himself. "But farming isn't meant to be easy."

"No, but is it meant to be miserable?" I asked.

He ignored my question. "And don't you worry about the milk. We've got plenty more. It was more important that the goats don't get engorged." He put his arm around me and wiped the tears from my cheeks.

It wasn't the confession of Serge hating farm life that I'd been hoping for, but it was a glimpse into his current frustrations. I shouldn't forget that his life had changed pretty dramatically, too.

We both agreed that my time would be better spent cooking (again), so I walked back up to the house, wondering how much longer Serge would endure managing the farm on his own, and at what point he might consider that he needed help beyond what his farming-incompetent girlfriend was able to offer.

When I got back to the house, I was surprised to find Chuck sitting on one of the rickety chairs out front. He must have come to pick up his car. Just the sight of him was a welcome distraction from my thoughts.

"It's a nice pond," he said, when I got closer. "Perhaps you could get some ducks."

"Good idea! And where does one buy ducks?" I asked.

"I'll look into it for you. A housewarming and welcome-to-the-country gift," he said, making me smile for what felt like the first time that morning. With Chuck I felt relaxed and calm, like the pre-farm version of myself.

"Why don't you come in for a cup of tea?" I said, happy at the prospect of some company.

"Yes, I'm as parched as an Australian camel in the outback."

In the warmth of the house, with a cup of peppermint tea in my hands, I told Chuck about the disastrous morning I'd had. As I got into the story, I couldn't help letting a few leftover tears escape.

"Ella, hasn't anyone ever told you not to cry over spilled milk?" he said, a little stiffly but with a chuckle.

I smiled. "It's a little more complicated than the milk, though. Let me explain."

I went on to tell Chuck that I felt Serge was out of his depth on the farm. I told him about my conversation with the cheesemonger in Chinon, and that sales were down. I explained how any money we'd set aside to renovate was now being used to fix farm machinery. I'm not sure that I meant to open up to him so fully, but his gentle encouragement made it all too easy.

"It seems like you're harboring a lot of resentment for this move," he said.

"Part of me, yes, but then I did willingly agree to it. And recently, I've sort of come around to the idea of staying."

"Well, that's good news, at least for me," he said.

"I've had a few ideas on how we can make things work on the farm, but every time I try to talk to Serge about them, he just changes the topic or claims that he's got things under control."

"So, it's more a relationship issue than a farm issue," he said, at which point Serge walked in.

I shelved Chuck's comment for later.

"Charles, nice to see you again," Serge said, stomping over to the couch in his work boots. They shook hands.

"Anyone for more tea?" I asked.

"I should probably be going, sorry," Chuck replied. "I've got some writing I need to finish this afternoon, and I'm already running rather behind."

"Thanks for stopping by," I said, and then more quietly, "And sorry for chewing your ear off."

"And thank you both for dinner last night. I'll have to pay you back in the New Year," he said with a wide smile, before leaving Serge, me, and a weird vibe hanging over the house.

"So, what did you end up cooking?" Serge asked.

Shit, I thought. The only thing I'd made since coming up from the farm had been pots of tea.

"It's a surprise. Go jump in the shower, and it'll be ready soon," I said, thinking I could sneak a frozen quiche out of its box and shove it in the oven.

Serge watched Chuck's car drive off and then went to the bathroom. I got the feeling that he wasn't as into our new friend as I was. But friends, let alone English-speaking friends, weren't easy to come by in the country, and I certainly wasn't going to let this one go.

The next morning, things at the farmhouse went from being a tad awkward to completely awful when I checked the post. Bills, bills, spam, and a handwritten letter addressed to Serge.

Huh? I thought, flipping it over to see if there was a return address. *No . . .*

I slipped it into the pocket of my maternity jeans and walked back to the house. Serge was out on the farm, again, so I was alone with the letter and my thoughts—which proved to be a terrible combination. I was sure that if Serge had been there to open it in front of me and tell me who it was from, there wouldn't have been an issue, but the longer I was left alone, the more intrigued I became.

After ten seemingly endless minutes, I suddenly realized where I'd seen the handwriting before: on the letter from Françoise.

It can't be, I thought. *How did she even get Serge's new address?*

Before I knew what I was doing, I'd slipped my finger into the envelope.

"Oh, I thought it was for me," I practiced aloud to myself. *Sounds convincing enough*, I decided.

I ripped it open. My eyes dropped to the end of the letter. It was indeed from Françoise. I felt the blood rush to my face.

Serge

I heard from Marie that you have returned to the Loire. It's so nice not to think of you stuck in Paris. The country suits you so much better.

I'm begging, will you please call me? I really need to speak to you about Clovis.

With love, Françoise

I took a breath. What on earth could Françoise want to speak to Serge about now? And if her news is so important, why can't she just pick up the phone like a normal person? And who the hell is Clovis?

My mind flew to imagining Françoise begging Serge to reconsider their divorce. *Does she still love him?*

I heard Serge taking off his shoes outside and scrunched the letter back into my pocket. I'd figure out what to do about all this later. I got up and rushed into the kitchen and began flinging stuff out of the fridge.

"*Bonjour*," Serge said, wrapping his arms around me. "How are my babies?"

"We're good," I said, jolting out of his grip. "I'm just in the middle of making some lunch. You hungry?"

"Always. I just have to call Jacques about some deliveries he is going to help me with."

"Off you go, then," I instructed. The letter felt like it was burning a hole in my pants, and it was making me twitchy.

I lit the stove, and as my gaze rested momentarily on the flame, I wondered if I should just burn the evidence. Then I thought about what I would want Françoise to do if our roles were reversed. I paused, immobilized by panic.

As I lit one corner of the paper, I immediately regretted it. I tried to blow out the flame, but by the time I had, the letter was half gone. *Shit, shit, shit. What now, Ella?*

Serge walked back into the kitchen and asked me if everything was OK. I threw the letter into the sink and told him I'd set my recipe on fire. As he bumbled over to try to fix it, I shooed him away.

"It's fine. I've got it."

He walked off, looking confused at my intense reaction to a burned recipe, and I continued to cook lunch so as not to arouse any more suspicion.

Now, I'd just need to figure out how I could explain the opening—and partial destruction—of my boyfriend's mail. *Ugh. What a mess!*

Convincing Serge that we needed to open the cheese-tasting room looked like it would have to wait until the New Year. Before committing to such a big project in the country, I needed to get to the bottom of this whole Françoise—and now Clovis—debacle.

Chapter 16

WHEN CHRISTMAS EVE ARRIVED, I was all over the place emotionally. On the one hand, I was still excited at the prospect of opening the cheese-tasting room; on the other, I wasn't even sure if Serge and I would make it through the festive season. We hadn't spoken about the burned letter; I'd decided never to mention it, although the thought of the contents still hung over my head like a dark cloud.

On a more positive note, I was in that gorgeous stage of pregnancy that up until recently I thought people had been lying about—the glowing phase. I felt strong and beautiful.

In the lead-up to Christmas, I'd cooked a feast. Enough food for at least six people, which when laid out on the dining table looked completely excessive for just Serge and me.

"Wow," said Serge when he saw it.

"I know, right? What a spread," I said, taking a little bow.

"Somewhat excessive, *non*?" he said quietly.

"Serge, I'll never forget the day you told me there was 'no such thing as too much holiday cheese.' It was a life highlight for me. Since then, I've applied the decadence theory to all festive food groups."

He looked at me thoughtfully, as if trying to figure out the best way to reason with a pregnant woman at Christmas. He hugged me and said, "Let's sit, then."

So, we sat and ate and laughed. It reminded me of my first Christmas in France, somehow only a year earlier, although it felt like a lot longer ago than that now. I remember I'd been horrified when Mum and Ray had invited Serge, who was still firmly just my cheesemonger at that point, to join us for dinner. If only I could have known that dinner would end up being a turning point in our relationship.

"Can you believe this time last year we weren't even dating?" I asked him, as I was serving the Yule log and the rather unnecessary—and very dense—Christmas pudding and custard.

"It's hard to imagine a time before you, Bella," he replied.

Swoon. Perhaps the romance isn't dead yet, I reassured myself.

"But seriously, though, talk about moving fast. Last Christmas I was just starting to fall for you. Now we're living in the French countryside, and we've got a baby on the way. It's almost hard to believe, when you think about it."

"Almost," he agreed.

I was on the brink of asking Serge if he'd heard from Françoise recently when Mum called on video chat.

"Ella, darling, happy Christmas. And *Joyeux Noël* to Serge," she said, popping up on my phone screen. Since coming to terms with me staying in France for the foreseeable future, she'd started learning some French. It was sweet. And the prospect of a new baby had gone a long way toward helping Mum forgive me for not coming to her wedding. She'd since informed me that we'd be able to celebrate together in France while she and Ray were on their honeymoon, which sounded like a good, if maybe overly intimate, compromise.

When I saw her face, tears threatened to explode out of me, but I held them back. As we were wishing her a happy Christmas, Ray's smiling face popped up in the background. They were in the garden drinking their morning coffee and eating mince pies. I felt disastrously homesick. To be sitting outside on Christmas morning in the Australian summer sun felt like a dream.

"Ella, let me show you the flowers that have just come out," Mum said, racing through the garden, causing the video image to freeze. I looked desperately at Serge, as if he'd be able to fix the connection.

"Mum, go sit down, you keep freezing," I ordered.

"Ella, don't be like that. It's Christmas. Is pregnancy making you moody?"

Ugh! Mothers can be so annoying. I must remember not to turn into an annoying mother myself.

"I'm just desperate to chat with you both. The flowers can wait," I attempted, and she begrudgingly obliged.

We spoke until Mum needed to put her own turkey in the oven. My desire to be there, rather than in freezing Chinon, was so intense that it created a ball of anxiety in my stomach.

"Enjoy your Christmas lunch," I said, after she told me for the third time she really needed to go.

"And happy Christmas, my love. I didn't bother sending a gift, but we'll give some money to charity for you. And thanks for the apron you sent. You really shouldn't have. We're too old for gifts now."

"Never too old for a little love from the other side of the world," I said pointedly.

"I missed that, sorry, love. The connection seems to have gone again. Talk soon," she said, and then disappeared.

"Feel better?" asked Serge.

My tears finally made their anticipated debut. I sat and blubbered for quite some time. And then, just when I thought I was fresh out of tears, another round arrived. *Maybe I'm more hormonal than I realized.*

Serge disappeared into the bedroom, then returned with one hand behind his back. "I was going to wait to give you this in the morning," he said.

I looked up expectantly.

"But it seems like you need a little Christmas cheer," he continued.

My heart started racing as I wondered what surprise Serge had up his sleeve.

He handed me an envelope and said, "Two train tickets to Paris, a few nights in a hotel, and a prearranged dinner with Clotilde and Jean."

"When?" I squealed in excitement.

"We leave tomorrow."

I looked at Serge with relief. This was just what I needed: a dose of my favorite city, time with my dear French friend, and a break from the cold and gloomy countryside. I hugged him hard and raced off to pack my bags. My mood had immediately lifted.

I'm going home! I thought, delighted to realize that Paris still felt like "home" in my mind.

Chapter
17

THE NEXT FEW DAYS LOOKED set to be as magical as I'd hoped. Paris was cold, but it didn't feel as cold as Chinon, and there were so many cafés and cosy restaurants to visit when my toes got numb that the weather wasn't going to stop me from having a good time.

Serge had booked us into a hotel in the Marais, and we walked our old neighborhood nostalgically, stopping in to visit friends from the stores around Serge's old *fromagerie* and going to see Fanny to pick up cheese.

Clotilde and Papa Jean were well in the festive spirit when we arrived for dinner, and Jean had cooked up quite the Christmas feast. Gaston apparently had a better offer, which thankfully meant that I didn't have to submit to the awkwardness of seeing him again, especially now that I was pregnant.

As Jean and Serge were in the kitchen discussing—at length—the *jus* for the roast goose, I got to catch up with Clotilde. She filled me in on life in Paris and downplayed how well the modeling was going.

"And how about you, any developments on the cheese room?" she asked.

"Well, I've decided to add a coffee machine," I said.

"But have you spoken to Serge?" she pressed.

"Not yet," I admitted.

"What on earth are you waiting for? It's been weeks."

"Well, I guess part of me still wonders if it's a good idea for me to commit to living out there. Regardless of whether Serge is into the idea, I'll be nervous. If he agrees, it'll mean we'll spend longer in the country. If he doesn't, it'll mean I have to figure out what the hell I'm going to do with my life. Other than baby, of course," I said, rubbing my belly.

"Hmm," she said.

"And then there's the question of the cheese itself," I added.

"What's wrong with the cheese?" she asked.

"Well, Serge has been very guarded about it. I get the feeling he's not entirely happy with what he's produced so far—"

"Ella, you've got to speak with him," she interrupted. "About the cheese, but more important about the cheese room. Even if you do decide to leave the country and sell after you've set everything up, it'll be a good asset for the farm. It would probably help attract potential buyers, too."

"That's a good point," I said.

"But you're not going to get far if you don't talk to Serge about it soon," she said.

I was on the brink of telling Clotilde the other reasons I hadn't pitched the cheese-room idea to Serge yet—because of whatever was going on with his ex-wife, and because of the state of our finances—when Papa Jean called us to the table. "We'll talk more later," I whispered to her as we sat down.

And then we feasted. Jean's spread was decadent beyond measure. We ate figs stuffed with *foie gras* before carving the goose, which was accompanied by shredded Brussels sprouts and roast potatoes, crisp from the heavy-handed addition of salted butter. Cheese followed, with a comically large slice of Comté that Jean insisted on being reserved for me and *bébé*.

After dinner, we ate sugared chestnuts and drank tea while anticipating what the next year would bring. By this point, everyone—except me—was rosy-cheeked from the bottles of wine that had already been consumed. Jean and Clotilde argued jovially about his possible retirement, with Clotilde protesting that he couldn't retire because it would make us all seem too old.

"And you two? Any additional plans for the farm?" Clotilde asked, giving me a little wink.

Serge looked at me. "I hope to keep making cheese," he said.

"Maybe Ella has some ideas," she suggested.

"Ella?" Serge said, looking at me.

"Oh, I've just been thinking about how we could bring in some more business," I said, trying to maintain a casual tone.

"Ella, don't be bashful. Why don't you tell Serge your plan?" Clotilde prompted.

"Yes, Ella, perhaps you should," he said.

"It's really nothing important," I added, reaching across and rubbing Serge's arm. "At least, it's not something that can't wait until next year."

I gave Clotilde's leg a little kick under the table and shot her a loaded look, trying to convey that now really wasn't the time. Things on the farm were already tense enough and I didn't want Serge to think I'd been plotting behind his back.

"Let's dance!" Clotilde said, getting the message, as she jumped up and grabbed Jean's hand. "It's our Christmas tradition."

"We've never danced at Christmas before," Jean began to protest, before giving in to the whims of his daughter.

I grabbed Serge's hand and pulled him up and we danced around the dining table. It was Christmas, after all, and discussions about our future could be dealt with later.

The next morning, we woke late and snuggled. Being in Paris felt so natural, spending time with people we loved in a city we (or at least I) adored. But I think we both realized we couldn't keep pretending that we lived here. We'd be heading back to the farm shortly and our future was waiting for us.

I still wasn't overly keen on talking to Serge about the cheese room yet, but Clotilde was right—I had to bring it up with him eventually.

"So, Serge. Shall we talk about last night?" I asked.

"What about it?" he asked. *Perhaps he was too tipsy to remember my friend's less-than-subtle questions about my plans for next year.*

"Well, I've been thinking a lot about how we can make things work in Chinon," I pushed on. "Anyway, I stumbled on the idea of getting the cheese room up and running, maybe even turning it into a little café."

"Shouldn't you be slowing down with work rather than taking on something new like this?"

"Serge, we've spoken about this. I don't want to slow down," I said. "Besides, I can't sit around doing nothing next year. I'll go mad."

"You should think of the baby," he said.

"That's what I am doing. This project will be good for the farm. It'll be good for the future. Serge, I've planned it all out.

I've even written up a budget, back at the farmhouse. What have we got to lose?"

"Well, for starters, we might lose more money. Also, I think you remember that one of your conditions for moving to the farm was that we could leave at any time. If we start this cheese room, you will be tied to staying there."

Huh? I thought. Previously, he would have been thrilled at the prospect of us staying on the farm.

I had a sudden realization.

"Serge, be honest with me, do you even want to stay in the country? Because I feel like you shut down every idea I have to help or improve things."

He went silent for a moment.

And this was when the real conversation, the conversation I'd been trying to initiate for weeks, finally started.

Like me, Serge had been struggling to adjust to country living and find his feet. Unlike me, Serge had been hiding it—albeit poorly at times—bottling up his anxiety, which had led us to this moment and to the frustrating disagreement that followed. We spoke at length about how difficult Serge was finding running the farm, about how sales had been slow, and about how he was increasingly worried about money.

"I just feel so much pressure to get everything ready and for everything to be perfect, but things move so slowly in the country. It's almost impossible to get help, and even when it's an option, I can't afford it. That's why I've been working all hours," he said.

I nodded, remembering the list of demands I'd placed on him prior to the move and feeling guilty for having contributed to his workload.

"And I do want to renovate," he continued. "Especially the nursery, but before then I need to get on top of things on the farm. I need to start bringing in some money before we can start spending it."

"Why didn't you just tell me what was going on?" I asked.

"Because you never wanted to move in the first place," he said. "I wanted to give you the perfect country life. I didn't want you to worry."

"I'm sorry you felt like you couldn't speak to me about it. Perhaps I could have helped. Maybe I still can," I suggested.

I wanted to talk more about the cheese room, about the potential benefits it could bring, but decided it was a step too far for Serge considering his current preoccupations.

I rubbed my stomach as a way of apologizing to our little growing baby for the unnecessary stress and uncertainty.

"You do remember the whole reason behind us moving here was so we could spend more time together as a family," I said.

"Ella, things have happened beyond my control."

I considered asking about his cheese production but I got the feeling that Serge's issues ran deeper than that. He seemed dissatisfied with life on the farm and with life as a farmer.

"So, what do you want to do, Serge?" I asked. "We need to find a way to make things work on the farm, otherwise what's the point of all this?"

"I do not know," he said. He had a look on his face that seemed like a mix of exhaustion and worry.

I started to feel sorry for him. "There's no shame in admitting that it might not be what you want anymore," I said.

I briefly considered suggesting we move back to Paris, but didn't want to push Serge to this conclusion, especially as he seemed to be dancing around it anyway. *But if we leave the farm, what about the cheese room?* I asked myself. Even though it was still just an idea at this point, it was an idea I'd become rather attached to.

Serge just nodded.

I felt like we were at a stalemate. Serge was struggling to run the farm but didn't seem to want to accept any help or change anything. I felt like I had solutions to some of his problems, but that they were falling on deaf ears. And then there was my own confusion over whether I actually wanted to stay on the farm. I hadn't imagined ever getting to this point, and I really couldn't figure out why I was bothering to convince Serge that we could make things work. But something inside told me I needed to.

Before the discussion went any further, I had to get my own feelings in line.

"Serge, I have a suggestion," I told him. "Why don't we both go away for an hour and think about what we want to achieve next year individually, and then come back together to see how we can make it happen?"

"Ella, this is smart," he said. I blushed. It wasn't often I could be considered the reasonable one.

"Do you want to go out or shall I?" he asked.

"I'll go. Baby is asking for a hot chocolate."

Serge kissed me hard, and it felt like both an apology and a plea.

⁓

As soon as I was outside, I called Mum.

"Hi, Lovie," said Ray's voice.

I rolled my eyes. As much as I liked my stepfather-to-be, his voice wasn't the one I needed to hear right now.

"Hi, Ray. How was the rest of your Christmas?"

"Too much Chrissy pud," he said, and I could tell he was patting his stomach. Another eye-roll escaped me.

"Sorry to rush you, Ray, but is Mum around? I really need to speak to her."

"Afraid she's just popped down to the shops," he replied.

"Shit," I said, my voice cracking.

"Has something happened?" he asked, concern in his voice.

I paused. I didn't really want to get into any of this with Ray. But in the absence of Mum, and with an hour deadline to figure out a workable solution with the father of my unborn child, he'd have to do.

"Well . . .," I said, taking a breath before launching into a rapid-fire explanation of our current situation, detailing Serge's struggles to settle into life as a farmer, my desire to open a cheese room, and then the overriding questions: Should we just move back to Paris? Was that even enough anymore? Should I just move back to Australia, either with or without Serge?

"Slow down, Lovie," Ray said. "First, tell me some more about the farm issues."

So, I told him all about Serge's struggles with the cheese and the lack of sales, which ended up with me complaining about the man himself. "I get glimpses of the old Serge, but now they're interspersed with this more vacant, more stressed version of himself."

"It's a big change you've both gone through," he said and paused. "Maybe Serge just needs time to iron out the kinks. He's gone from owning a cheese shop in Paris to actually making the stuff. Big ask, I say."

"But what should we do? Should we leave the farm? Should I leave Serge? Could I even raise this baby alone?"

"Let's not get ahead of ourselves," he replied calmly. He'd swung into problem-solving mode, and while I appreciated his slow and methodical approach, I was on a deadline.

"But I don't have forever, Ray," I protested. "Serge and I need to figure out what we're going to do. And I'd really like to be settled somewhere before the baby arrives."

"Why don't I see if we can change our tickets? Come over to France a little earlier and help out with things. I'm sure your mum would love to see you, too."

"I guess that could help, but it's a lot to ask," I said.

"Nothing too big for our little girl," Ray said, and I smiled. "I'll call you back after talking to your mum. Hoo-roo."

"Bye," I replied.

I sat down in a café and ordered a hot chocolate. My mind was racing, so I pulled out paper and a pen and tried to etch out a bit of a plan for how Serge and I could work things out on the farm. Ray had given me hope, and now I was oscillating between excitement and fear. From experience, I knew that it was possible for both emotions to exist simultaneously, but in general, one eventually became more prominent than the other—I just hoped it'd be the former.

And then Gaston walked into the café. I'd only seen him once since I'd busted him for cheating on me, and then I'd avoided actually talking to him.

We saw each other at the same time, and both of us had a moment where we looked for a way to escape the interaction. But the café was desperately quiet and acknowledging each other seemed inevitable. He walked over briskly, leaned down to kiss both my cheeks, and wished me a happy Christmas.

He sat and we chatted for a few minutes, with both of us clearly eager to go our separate ways but neither of us wanting to appear rude. It was definitely long enough to convince me that I'd made the right decision leaving him behind. He either didn't notice I was pregnant, or perhaps chose not to acknowledge it, speaking only of himself.

"I mean, it's exhausting, all those dinners," he said. "The other day I drank a two-thousand-euro bottle of Bordeaux, and by that point in the meal I was too drunk to even really taste it."

"Have you thought about a career change?" I suggested, knowing full well that he'd never give up his champagne lifestyle.

"And then there's the travel . . .," he continued, clearly ignoring me.

What did I ever see in this man? I asked myself.

After I rather dramatically checked the time—even though my watch battery had stopped working a few weeks prior, and I still hadn't found anywhere to get it replaced—I motioned for the bill.

As I stood up, Gaston finally noticed my belly, and I saw his jaw drop. I could tell he was desperate to ask more—perhaps for a second while he calculated how long we'd been separated, he even wondered if he was the father—but I wasn't going to indulge him.

I simply shrugged, smiled, and walked off.

Serge seemed happier when I got back to the hotel, as if a weight had been lifted from his shoulders.

"How'd it go?" I asked, getting straight to the point. "Any closer to knowing what you'd like to do?"

He nodded.

"Well? You go first," I said.

"No, you," he insisted.

"Same time?" I suggested and he nodded.

"I think I'm done," Serge said, just as I blurted out, "I think we should stay."

· PART ·

Three

SPRING

Chapter

18

SERGE AND I LOOKED AT each other in astonishment. The seconds after he'd told me that he was done seemed to last for an eternity.

I ran through what he meant in my mind. *Did he mean done with the farm? Or done with me? Oh God!* I started having flashbacks to Melbourne, to when Paul told me he was leaving me to go and find himself. Was Serge about to do a Paul? My heart started beating uncontrollably fast.

I suddenly couldn't believe I'd been trying to find a way to help Serge succeed when he was planning to leave me. I'd never thought it was possible for things between us to end in the same way as they had with Paul, especially now that I was pregnant.

This time I decided not to dance around the subject.

"Do you want to break up?" I asked.

"Ella," he said before pausing and looking me deep in the eyes. "Of course I do not want to break up. I mean that I think I'm done on the farm."

"Oh," I said, and paused a moment, trying to figure out how I felt. Only weeks earlier this would have been my ideal outcome, but now, spending a few days in Paris had reinforced my desire to get back to our whole country-living experiment and work things out.

"Serge, we've only been on the farm a month. Where do you want to go? Back to Paris? I thought you didn't want to have a baby in the city," I said, my voice laced with a panic I barely recognized. I took a breath.

"I don't know," he said, tears welling in his eyes. It was the first time I'd ever seen Serge come close to crying. "I just cannot get things right. My father would be so disappointed. I am a disaster on the farm. I don't want to waste any more of your time living out there."

"You're not a disaster, Serge," I said, although I wasn't 100 percent convinced that this was true. "You're learning the ropes. We're only just getting started on the farm. These things take time. You're the one who convinced me of that."

"But the cheese, it's no good," he told me.

It seemed he was finally ready to admit it. "What happened?" I asked.

"I have no idea. It was too acidic, not enough salt. The weather was so cold and wet, perhaps that messed with the aging process. Or the goats were eating the bad grass. I did everything like Michel showed me. I don't understand where I went wrong."

"Serge, forget about all that for a minute: If you could make good cheese, would you want to stay on the farm?" I asked.

He nodded. "I love the farm. I just do not love the farming."

"Well," I started. "If you want to stay, then you just have to find a way to make the business side of things work."

He mulled this over before saying, "But before now, you didn't want to live on the farm. I thought you would be happy to move back to Paris."

He was right; I had wanted to move back. But now, I didn't want us to quit so soon. Serge was just doubting himself. He'd told me repeatedly that he didn't want to raise a child in Paris. Now, he was backing out because he'd got cold feet. I wanted to try making things right. And on a more selfish note, I had a cheese room-cum-café I wanted to open. *And* a friendship with Chuck that was worth pursuing. Perhaps surprisingly, there were still things I wanted to do in the tiny town of Chinon.

After a few moments, I said, "Well, I guess life in the Loire has started to win me over. Besides, you can't just give up on the farm, especially if the only thing stopping you is some bad batches of cheese. I think you need to get Michel back to help you."

"I shouldn't need help," he said.

"There's no shame in getting somebody to give you some pointers. Everyone needs help when they're doing something new. Look how much help you offered me when I moved to Paris. By teaching me about cheese, you taught me about French culture and history. And then you taught me about love. I wouldn't still be here if it weren't for you."

Serge looked at me, still teary-eyed, but now with a hint of hope.

"You don't think it is weak that I need help?"

"Nope. And if you think I'm not going to need help with the cheese room, you're crazy. I'm going to need *so* much help. But we'll discuss that later. What else do you need to get things back on track with the farm?"

"I'll call Michel when we get home."

"Oh, and I just found out that Ray and Mum might be changing their tickets to arrive earlier than planned," I added casually, not wanting Serge to think I'd orchestrated for them to come early because we needed them. "So we'll have some extra hands on deck. It'll all be fine, Serge. Let's just stick it out until you get a good batch of cheese and then we can re-evaluate." I still couldn't believe I was now the one convincing Serge to stay on the farm. *What has gotten into me?*

He hugged me.

I felt like we'd cleared the air about our issues on the farm, and it was a relief. While the question of Françoise still hung quietly over my head, I wasn't ready to mention her. Not now that Serge and I had just made up. We sat quietly, wrapped in each other's arms, for a long time before heading to our old local wine bar for dinner.

We ate baskets of bread with a rich olive tapenade, a creamy fish pie, and far too much truffle ham with thinly sliced Gruyère. For dessert, we shared a dark chocolate and raspberry tart, and Serge let me steal a few sips of his espresso. It felt good to be out in Paris with Serge, and I felt optimistic about the New Year. Spring was just around the corner, and reinforcements were on the way. I was feeling positive.

$\sim$

When we returned to the farmhouse, Serge and I both had a renewed sense of energy. We "celebrated" New Year's Eve by staying home, eating hearty winter food and drinking lots of tea. We made resolutions and plans to get things back on track, including our relationship, which had suffered from the pressure of the move, the pregnancy, and all that had gone unsaid as we'd both struggled to settle into our new life away from Paris.

As soon as the public holidays were over, Serge called Michel and invited him over to the farm for lunch. Perhaps the least surprising thing to come out of their meeting was that Michel was rather bored in his retirement and the prospect of helping Serge perked him up immensely. He was already full of stories and tips. And Serge's openness to lean on him and finally accept some help seemed to be a relief for all of us.

Knowing that Serge was safe in Michel's hands, I opened my laptop to do some research on the cheese room. No sooner had I set myself up than my phone rang.

"*Bonjour*," I said.

"*Bonjour, ma fille.*"

"Oh, hey Mum. What's up?" I asked.

"Well, I was speaking with Ray, and he filled me in on your little chat."

"Actually quite an important chat, but continue . . ."

"Yes, yes. Well, we've changed our tickets. We'll arrive early March. Is that OK?" she asked.

"Sounds perfect," I said. I wasn't sure I'd ever been so relieved at the prospect of seeing Mum.

"We couldn't let you have a breakdown and leave our Serge now, could we?" she said.

Our Serge? I sighed. Some things would never change.

"You'll be able to help me set up the nursery," I said, changing the topic.

"About that. I've got a few little bits you could have. I fished out some of your baby clothes. They're in surprisingly good condition. I'll bring them over, yes?"

"I didn't know you'd kept any of that," I said.

"Well, I wasn't sure if I'd ever need to pull them out of storage, but there we go. They're clean and packed."

I couldn't resist smiling. I was looking forward to sharing this time with Mum.

"I can't wait to see you guys," I told her. "It's awfully quiet here."

"You still haven't made any friends?" she asked.

"Well, I met this one English guy. He's an author. Although he doesn't live here full-time," I rattled on. "He's working on the most fascinating project—"

She interrupted me. "Easy, Ella. Don't go complicating things by spending too much time with another man."

"Oh Mum, don't be ridiculous," I said, laughing.

"Well, in my day—" she started to say, but another call came in and I told her I had to run.

"*Bonjour*," I said again.

"Ella. Chuck here."

Speak of the devil! I thought.

"Why, hello! Happy New Year. How was London?"

"Oh, fine. Good. I'm back now, though. I want to keep working on the novel. I made a resolution to finish it this year."

"Nice. You think it's doable?" I asked.

"Who knows! Really, all I can do now is press on," he said.

I laughed. I felt like "All I can do now is press on" was my current motto for everything in life.

I'd *press on* to make a life in the country.

Press on to have a baby.

Press on to open a café—

"Anyway," Chuck said, interrupting my thoughts. "The reason I'm calling is to see if you can come help me choose a color to paint a couple of my rooms. I've decided it's time to start giving my house a bit of a refresh, and I don't really know where to begin. Would you mind terribly?"

"Would I mind? I love choosing paint colors. I'll be over in a flash."

Chuck gave me his address, and I left a note for Serge letting him know I was heading out.

"I'm off to help decorate my friend's house," I sang to myself cheerily.

The New Year was off to a good start. Things were looking up for Serge and the farm, I was back working on my plans for the cheese room, *and* I had the beginnings of a social life.

As I drove over to Chuck's, I remembered Mum's "back in my day" comment and chuckled. Soon enough, she'd get a sense of how lonely it could be in the French countryside and would understand why I was keen to pursue any offer of friendship.

Chapter

19

DRIVING OVER TO CHUCK'S, I tried to imagine what his grandmother's house would look like. While I knew his family had money, it was hard to picture him living anywhere too imposing. Since meeting him, I'd always felt that he seemed too artistic—and scatterbrained—for too much grandeur, envisaging him in a loft, or perhaps an attic, tapping away on a typewriter, wearing three woolen jumpers because he'd forgotten to pay his heating bill.

When I arrived at the striking wrought iron gates, I had to double-check the address. I turned off the radio and drove the long driveway in silence, admiring the huge park. I couldn't help imagining what it would feel like if this were my garden, so much so that I could hear Mum's voice in my head saying, "Easy, Ella."

And then I saw it.

Chuck's modest inheritance was, in fact, a rather spectacular château. It was compact, but only compared to some of the neighboring castles in the region.

Wow!

But, as I got closer, I started to see the cracks. One in particular along the front wall made me wonder how sturdy the whole property was. I counted at least sixteen windows at the front of the house, many of them missing shutters, a few even missing pieces of glass. The château in its current state looked like it was letting out a deep, guttural groan. It looked exhausted.

But, despite the dishevelled façade, the building was still elegant—an old soul who still had the potential to get back to a version of its youth if only the cycle of neglect could be broken. *What a project!* I felt a little twinge of jealousy.

I spotted Chuck waiting for me on the stone steps leading up to the front door and he welcomed me warmly. "*Bienvenue* to my humble abode."

"Chuck, this place is very grand," I said, still shocked at how much he'd downplayed his "house."

"Well, you know, it's a little embarrassing inheriting a château. Especially when I can't even afford to maintain it properly."

"That doesn't matter. Will you give me a tour?" I asked, desperate to find out what else Chuck might have glossed over.

We started with the rooms he actually lived in, which made up only a small percentage of the house. The interiors, like the exteriors, were beautiful but run-down. The furniture, all wood and pretty upholstery, was either covered in tatty sheets or was showing signs of being unloved. It was sad to see such a lovely place suffering from abandonment. But for Chuck, I guessed, it was more of a holiday house. And I knew that inheriting property in France came at a cost, which meant that neglect was common. Running and ensuring the upkeep of a château was expensive. The heating costs alone were too much for some.

Chuck's outlook on the whole thing seemed very relaxed. As we walked through, he mentioned all the odd jobs he was planning to do, pointing at buckets and telling me he was waiting for the rain to stop, and picking up random building materials that his builder had apparently left behind. Mostly, I got the feeling that Chuck enjoyed living the down-and-out life of an artist in this huge house.

"Eventually, my success will speak for itself," he told me. "And for now, the château is a good reminder of the work I still have to do. It'll all get an overhaul as soon as I'm published."

"So why paint now?" I asked.

"A good question," he said, leading me into the two rooms where he said he spent most of his time: a cute sitting room with large windows overlooking the park outside, and a tiny adjoining bedroom, with an ornate four-poster bed and requisite velvet frills.

His living areas certainly didn't scream rich Englishman in France, but the effect was rather cosy, which I assumed wasn't necessarily easy to achieve in a château. After admiring the old bed, I noticed the piles of paper on the floor and the tattered walls.

"So," he said, giving me a nod, "I was having a particularly bad writing day when I remembered you telling me about your wallpaper-ripping catharsis. And with you at the forefront of my mind, I hunted for a peeling corner. The rest is history."

I laughed. "Chuck, how could you? I was ripping off eighties wallpaper. You were probably ripping off something of value."

"But it felt so good," he said sheepishly.

I smiled. "Don't worry. I get it." I looked at a leftover piece of wallpaper on the ground. It was thick and textured, with an embossed floral motif. *Such a pity*, I thought.

"I knew you would understand," he said.

As we began clearing the room, we talked in more detail about Chuck's plans for the château. It was a long-term project that involved both interior and exterior work, but apparently no major structural changes—I didn't dare bring up the cracks. He was planning on restoring most of the current furniture, except for his two main rooms, where he preferred to buy some new pieces. Compared to what Serge and I were hoping to take on, it sounded like a huge project. But then again, Chuck had been working on the same novel for years; I didn't have him down as a rush-job kind of guy.

"And how's the novel coming along?" I asked.

"It's going well, but also terribly. I'm stuck on my eighth perspective. And my third generation . . . Or is it the fourth generation? I don't know anymore. There's been quite the argument between two lovers. I don't know how it's going to pan out," he said, looking out the window wistfully.

"You don't have a plan for the plot?" I asked, surprised.

"Of course, I do. I just haven't gotten around to writing it down. It's all up here," he said, tapping his head.

I laughed. From what I understood of Chuck's novel, it seemed elaborately complicated, and I struggled to understand how he could continue without a written plan. I imagined his château renovations would unfurl in a similarly chaotic manner.

"And how was your Christmas break?" he asked.

"Enlightening," I told him.

"That's not an answer I was expecting. How so?"

I told him about the surprise trip to Paris, and then about Serge's and my plan to make things work on the farm. I also told him in detail about my idea for the cheese room and café.

"That's brilliant," he said. "After all these years, I'll finally have a writing spot with decent coffee! When do you think you'll open?"

"Slight hiccup—I still need to properly pitch the idea to Serge."

"Why do you need a pitch for Serge? He's not into it?" he asked, sounding surprised.

"No, it's not that. We just had a few other issues we needed to sort out before getting to it," I said.

I was downplaying the situation to Chuck, but there were so many variables that could stop the cheese room going ahead. Would we even stay on the farm long enough to see it open? Would the cheese be worth selling? Would Françoise swoop in and ruin everything?

Mostly I was worried about the financial aspect. Yes, it would involve a small start-up investment, but I'd been cautious with my budget and figured it wouldn't be a huge stretch. I just needed to convince Serge that it would benefit the farm in general. And us. And me.

"Well, if you need help—financial or otherwise—let me know," Chuck said.

"Seriously?" I asked, thinking this could be the solution to any possible money concerns.

"As a deer in headlights," he said.

I thanked him and assured him that I would, although I wasn't sure how I'd ever convince Serge to accept a loan from Chuck.

"So, let's see these paint samples then," I said, trying to change the subject.

Chuck got out a color chart and showed me which ones he was thinking about.

"And are you keeping the bed?" I asked, reaching up to inspect the velvet ruffles on the canopy.

"I hope not. It's terribly uncomfortable," he said.

I sat on it. "Hard to disagree with that."

He sat next to me and sighed. "There's just so much work to do. So many things to replace."

I wondered if Chuck had anybody else who could help him. *Why is he asking me for advice? Surely there must be someone more suited to the job.* Still, I couldn't help but feel flattered he'd come to me.

"Well, I think a version of white should do the trick. Then you're not going to be bogged down by finding furniture or decoration to match. A blank slate," I said.

He patted my leg. "Smart thinking, Ella."

We sat in silence for a second as his hand lingered. It felt warm but out of place. I hoped my involuntary quiver wasn't as noticeable as it felt.

"And how about your sitting room?" I asked, leaping up and walking toward the other room. "You may as well paint them both at the same time."

"Oh, yes, of course," he said, following me into the adjoining room. "I've already got a little plan in my head for that space. But first, let's have tea."

I agreed.

With cups in hand, Chuck talked me through how he hoped to set up the sitting room, but by then I was finding it hard to concentrate and my heart was still racing from the leg touch. Although it was hard to admit, part of me wished that I hadn't been so quick to jump up. The idea of being desirable, even now while I was pregnant, was flattering. But I shut down those thoughts quickly. I was probably just being overly sensitive because of my raging hormones. Besides, I was sure Chuck would agree that our relationship was platonic. *After all, why would he make a move on a pregnant woman?*

Feeling conflicted, I decided I should probably head back to the farmhouse.

"You're off so soon?" he asked.

"Duty calls. Serge is cooking dinner and I want to talk to him about the cheese room tonight." *And I've somehow already been here for two hours*, I thought, but didn't voice aloud.

With Chuck, time seemed to fly. What I'd intended to be a quick trip had turned into hours of chatting. I'm not sure which one of us had enjoyed the distraction more.

"Well, do feel free to pop around any time, now that you know where to find me," he said.

"And let me know if you need a hand pulling off any more wallpaper," I said with a laugh.

Later that night, as I was snacking on some Comté in the kitchen, I heard a message come through on my phone. It was from Chuck.

Ella, thanks again for all of your advice today. I'll repay the favor when you're ready to start work on the café. Chuck x

Serge looked over at me from the stove, where he was stirring a pot of beef stew. He seemed happy to be cooking me dinner for once, humming along as he moved about the kitchen. His day had obviously gone well.

"Who was that from?" he asked, gesturing to the phone that was still in my hand.

"Oh, just Clotilde," I said.

Why the hell did I just lie?

I felt immediately guilty. Even though I'd justified the leg touch as a nonevent, the memory of it was still fresh in my mind and alive in my stomach. I guess I was worried that I might start blushing if I mentioned Chuck. And I certainly didn't want Serge to get the wrong idea.

"How is she?" Serge asked. "What did she do to give you that big smile on your face?"

"Nothing much. She was just telling me how she fell over on a photo shoot and bruised her ego," I said, wincing as the story flowed out of my mouth.

Serge laughed and came over to kiss me on the head. I put my phone face down on the bench. *What's gotten into me?* I thought. Perhaps all the fresh air had finally gone to my head.

Over dinner, I pitched the cheese room and café idea properly to Serge, explaining that the focus would be on his produce but that we'd also serve good coffee and some simple country-style food.

He nodded, and I took this as my cue to keep going.

"I think it'll help on so many levels. It'll bring in extra income. It'll help people get to know your cheese. It'll bring *us* closer together." I thought about Serge and his father setting up the Paris *fromagerie* and how it had helped rekindle their relationship. "And even if we do decide to leave the farm eventually, it should increase the resale value dramatically," I added.

I waited, holding my breath for Serge's reaction. I knew the idea wasn't a total shock to him, seeing as we'd briefly discussed it over Christmas in Paris, but I don't think he'd realized how serious I was about it. It had been a while since I'd wanted to take on a project that was so different. The last time I'd done something this foreign was when I'd moved to Paris. I'd felt the same apprehension then as I was feeling now.

"I love it," he said. "It'll be a wonderful way to help." I looked at him with a mix of gratitude and relief. But then he addressed the—pregnant—elephant in the room. "But what about the baby?" he asked.

"What about it?" I asked, as I pulled out the budget and the design and marketing plans I'd prepared.

Serge must have seen the determination in my eyes and thankfully decided not to bring up the idea of me slowing down again. After all, growing this tiny human was one of the most natural things in the world.

"Let's talk numbers then," he said. I couldn't help but grin a little.

I talked him through the budget and as soon as I was finished, he asked me straight up: "How are you going to fund it?"

"I figured we'd have enough money for at least the basics," I stalled. "And if we need more, I could always ask Mum and Ray for a loan." I was ad-libbing. I also remembered Chuck's offer to help out, but I didn't want to bring that up with Serge just yet.

Regardless of the eventual source, I was sure I could come up with some extra cash.

"Absolutely not," he said. "I will not take money from your mother."

"Leave that to me, Serge. Let it be my problem."

He eventually agreed to let me look after securing the additional funding.

Having cleared that hurdle, I asked Serge if he had any more feedback.

"Not feedback, but a suggestion. I still think you'll need to allocate more money," he said.

"Oh?" I asked, looking back over the budget pages.

"The sums look good," he said. "But there are a few things you're forgetting. A few French things that maybe you don't know about."

I let out a generous exhale. *Of course, there are French things I don't know about.* If I needed a reminder that I was doing something well out of my comfort zone, in a different country, I could trust the French to make that apparent.

"What should I add to the list?" I asked, trying to maintain my composure.

"You'll need a license. Then insurance, registration, and you'll probably need permits. I don't know everything that will be required, though. I've only set up a store, and in France, that doesn't qualify me to open a café."

"Seriously?" I asked.

"You'll probably want to hire a lawyer. A specialist, so we don't end up getting fined."

"Fined?" I asked.

"Yes, if the authorities have it in for you, you will get fined. You must have seen it on the news."

I looked away, thinking about how that sounded like exactly the type of news segment I'd roll my eyes at or at least stop listening to. I'd already had a taste of what dealing with French administration was like when I'd applied for my work visa and it resulted in a pile of paperwork, multiple tellings-off, and hours waiting in lines at the visa office. None of which I wanted to repeat. But the cheese room . . . *Ugh! Why are the most appealing projects always the hardest?*

"Will you help me find a lawyer?" I asked.

"Of course. We'll ask around. Perhaps Marie and Jacques know somebody," he said, and I cheered up slightly.

"And you'll do my taxes?" I asked.

"That I can help you with," he said.

"Good, OK," I said, feeling like we were getting somewhere.

"Because in France there are many taxes," he continued.

Ugh! I thought again; the prospect of giving away even more of our potential earnings was an unpleasant one.

"But you think it could work? Will it help?" I asked, and Serge shrugged that quintessential French shrug. It didn't instill much confidence.

"Let me do some sums of my own, and I will tell you how many coffees and how much cheese you will need to sell to make this little venture profitable."

"Deal," I said.

"So, what will you call it? Maybe 'Ella's'? Or 'Ella and the Goats'?" he suggested, chuckling, obviously trying to lighten the mood.

"I haven't even gotten that far," I admitted.

I'd been expecting Serge to come up with greater opposition to my proposal. But now he came to mention it, the idea of having a business named after me in this regional part of France was exhilarating—if terrifying. *How did I, a haphazard Melbourne girl, end up trying to start a business in the French countryside?* Origin story aside, the name would have to wait. Serge and I needed to talk more about logistics and make a plan to get things in order.

"You're so brave, Ella," he said.

"I am?"

"Of course. There are so many French people who wouldn't even dare open a business. And here you are, willing to battle *l'administration française* after having lived here for only a short time."

"That's me," I said, feeling the blood drain from my face as I wondered if perhaps I'd taken on more than I'd realized. "I love a challenge."

We went to bed but I couldn't sleep. All the talk of lawyers and taxes reinforced the fact that I was completely green when it came to setting up a business. As I weighed the pros and cons of opening the cheese room, I wondered if it was too late to go back to the idea of just working alongside Serge on the farm.

But could I really be happy knowing that I'd pulled out of this opportunity because I was scared of a little administrative work? Besides, I needed a new focus, and I needed to make myself useful here with Serge. I wanted this farm to succeed. It was time to fully make the leap.

Chapter

20

SOME WEEKS LATER, WHEN I was knee-deep in orchestrating the cheese-room fit-out—and when I was on the brink of telling Serge that I was far too pregnant and exhausted to finish the job—Mum and Ray arrived. It was a beautiful, sunny morning when Serge and I met them at the train station, and I was overwhelmed with joy when I saw them walking toward us.

I welcomed them both into my arms, relieved to have *their* very able arms here to help lift, move, and decorate. Serge and I had both been working long hours in the lead-up to their arrival so they wouldn't think we'd left everything to them.

Michel was now helping Serge a few mornings a week, and Serge had been taking full advantage of his knowledge and guidance, which meant we would often only get to work on the cheese room late in the evening. All we'd really had time to do was to patch the walls and paint them, and to renovate the toilets.

Ray and Serge hugged warmly while Mum inspected my belly.

"It's good to see you guys," I said, tearing up.

"Pregnancy hormones?" Mum suggested, to which I shrugged.

"Can't I just be happy to see my parents?" I asked.

Ray looked at me, beaming. I wouldn't go as far as to call him Dad, but I'd now come to consider him a parent. After all, it wasn't just anyone who would bring forward a flight to France to come and help a pregnant, soon-to-be-stepdaughter open a cheese room while being put up in a run-down farmhouse.

We drove back to the farm chatting about their flight and the train trip out here. They'd been to the restaurant car on the train and were buzzing from the little bottles of wine they'd ordered while zipping through the countryside.

"It's a very civilized way to travel," Mum chipped in.

"Especially at this hour of the day," I added with a laugh.

Arriving at our house, I gave Mum and Ray the grand tour, first showing them to the guest room, which we'd furnished sparsely the weekend before their arrival. I'd added a few rugs to cover the worst of the old chipped floorboards for now, but eventually they'd need replacing.

Thankfully, Mum and Ray didn't even look at the floor, preferring to admire the view of the garden. Ray couldn't resist telling me that it would be perfect for this and that type of plant.

"The garden will have to wait," I said, punching Ray's arm in what I hoped was a loving gesture. "Moving on." I shooed my parents out the door. I was fully aware that I was being bossy, but I had a firm idea of the things I needed help with, and the garden wasn't high on that list. To emphasize that point, I opened the door to the nursery, which had turned into a bit of a dumping ground for odds and ends.

"This is where your baby will sleep?" Mum asked, a look of horror on her face.

"Well, obviously it's not finished," I said.

She gasped. "And what if *my* grandchild comes early?"

"*My* child would prefer to arrive on time," I told her. And while I obviously had zero control over this, I'd already had a quiet word with *bébé* asking if he/she wouldn't mind staying put at least until the nursery was finished.

"We'll work on this room first," Mum said, determinedly.

After we'd finished the speedy house tour, we headed out to see the goats and the cheese room. The farm was bright with the beauty of early spring. The grass looked fresh and dewy, wildflowers had popped up in the fields, and the trees were looking less naked, little green leaves breaking away from the starkness of the bare branches.

I could tell Ray was already enjoying being outside; he was commenting on the goats, the equipment, and the set-up. Mum mostly remained quiet, until we got to the cheese room. Over the phone, I'd explained as best as I could my idea for the space but all she'd told me was that she'd prefer to wait and see it in person. She couldn't visualize it without being there. I felt oddly desperate for her approval.

"So, I'm thinking the coffee machine here," I started out once we were inside. "Then over here, tables and chairs will line the windows, with big outdoor picnic tables just outside here. Eventually I'll put in one of those concertina doors so it becomes an indoor/outdoor space, but until then, people will have to use the door."

Mum and Ray paced around the empty room, footsteps echoing loudly as I waited for their assessment. Silence.

"And then over here," I continued, "I'll have the cheese cabinet, and I'll do cheese platters, cheese quiches, and a cheesecake. We'll mostly use Serge's cheese and some local ones, helping to show off the region. And then we'll also do takeaway cheese sales. And perhaps even jams and desserts once we've really got things up and running. And scones. I've been craving scones like crazy recently, so I'd like to add them to the menu."

Mum was first to comment. "So what will you do with the baby?"

"We'll just make it work, won't we, Serge?" I said, with an almost pleading look over to him.

"Of course, and there will be help if needed," Serge rushed to add. "A good friend of mine, Marie, has offered to assist in the early days once the baby arrives. She's quite the cook, too."

"And besides, we'll only be open Thursday through Sunday, so there'll be three days a week for everything else."

"Ella, babies are hard work," Mum said.

"I don't need a lecture on this, Mum. We'll figure it out. And if not, we'll just shut up shop, or hire someone permanently," I told her, brushing my hands together in an attempt to end the discussion. "Anyway, come see the toilets," I said proudly.

The renovation we'd done in the bathrooms reinforced how great our house could look if we ever had enough money to renovate properly. We'd gone for white-tiled minimalism, with gold fittings and big porcelain sinks. The cubicles were clean, bright, and, most important, practical. I showed Mum and Ray the "before" picture from my phone and received nods of approval.

"It looks like something from one of those renovation rescue shows you'd see on the telly," Ray said. "Bloody good job, too," he added, inspecting the grouting.

"Thanks, Ray. It's amazing what you can pick up on YouTube," I told him.

"You did this yourself?" he asked.

"Hah, not really. But I did assist the tiling guy. Got a free French lesson out of it, too. These guys get paid pretty damn handsomely so I figured he wouldn't mind."

"Quite nice," was all Mum said, but this comment was enough to tell me that she thought I'd done a good job.

"Anyway, you guys must be hungry," I said. "Let's go back up to the house."

We sat down at the table to have lunch and, before I knew it, Mum had a pen and paper in her hands and was crafting a tight schedule of things to do to get the nursery looking less like a death trap, and the cheese room finished before Easter.

"So, you don't just want to do the house renovations at the same time?" Mum asked. "It'd probably be easier that way."

"No, no," I rushed to say. I hadn't had the chance to tell Mum the ins and outs of our financial situation, and I didn't really want to do so in front of Serge.

Since I'd very quietly, and hesitatingly, accepted Chuck's offer of a loan a few weeks prior, I felt like I was spinning a few different plates in the air. I needed to be careful who knew what. I could only imagine how disappointed Serge would be if he found out Chuck was the man behind my brand new, and much adored, coffee machine.

"I mean, we'll paint the nursery and furnish it, but that's it," I said to Mum firmly. I could justify accepting Chuck's financial assistance when it came to the cheese room, but there was no way I was going to spend any of his money fixing up our house.

Mum nodded and, to my relief, didn't pursue the topic any further.

After we finished compiling the to-do list, I realized that we had our work cut out for us, but thankfully Mum and Ray's energy renewed ours. And after a good lunch, coffee, and a homemade chocolate tart, we all got to work.

"How are things between you and Serge?" Mum asked, after the men had gone back down to the farm.

"They're good," I said. "We've just been so busy. Honestly, it's been kind of stressful."

"I noticed things were a little tense."

"You did?" I asked, surprised.

I changed the subject and while Mum twittered on about her rose bushes, I replayed the morning's events, trying to figure out what had given her the impression something was off. Yes, Serge and I hadn't been communicating like we used to, but I didn't think that things had been "tense." Even when Mum eventually moved on to talking about her plum tree, I was still none the wiser.

Chapter

21

WITH EACH SPRING DAY THAT passed, there were a few extra minutes of daylight, which suited us perfectly, because progress in the cheese room was slow and our to-do list was long.

Perhaps unsurprisingly, the nursery was quickly finished. From the get-go, Mum had been determined that it was the priority, and despite my efforts to tell her that the *bébé* wouldn't mind if the walls didn't match the bed sheets, she was taking her grandmothering duties very, very seriously.

And she'd taken to life in France surprisingly well. She navigated the country roads like a pro and managed to accomplish tasks that I'd been putting off since arriving here. After finishing her work in the nursery, she'd moved on to the cheese-room renovations, coordinating deliveries of new appliances and bossing around workmen in her rudimentary but very practical French. Seeing what she was capable of simultaneously impressed and stressed me. I wondered if she'd always been so efficient and perhaps I just hadn't realized it. *Does that mothering gene surface when the baby does?* I wondered. *Perhaps it'll skip a generation, and I'm destined to always rely on Mum for help.* I couldn't help but feel a little inept in her shadow.

Gradually, though, things in the cheese room were slowly taking shape. Theoretically, all that we needed in order to open was the oven and more furniture, which I still needed to hunt down either on second-hand sites or at the local trash-and-treasure markets. While we were close, I couldn't shake the feeling that something wasn't quite right.

"It's just a little cold," Mum said one afternoon while Ray was installing the dishwasher, and I was sitting in the sun taking a tea break.

"Turn up the heater, then," I said, annoyed at the prospect of standing up.

"Not physically cold, just, you know, cold. Not very inviting. For a café, it's a little stark."

I felt hurt.

"But it's not finished yet," I told her.

"I don't know if an oven will necessarily change that," she said.

"Just you wait," I told her. "It's meant to be a clean space, nothing too frou-frou. It's not an English tea shop; it's more of a café, or rather a hybrid French–Australian cheese-tasting room and café all in one. It defies categorization, really," I explained, feeling like my pitch was getting more confused with time.

"Well, I'm just saying that it could do with a little something extra," she said matter-of-factly.

I looked around and wondered if she had a point. "I've still got some decorating to do," I told her. And although I hadn't planned anything in detail, I figured a quick hunt around Instagram would be enough to give me some ideas to cosy things up a little.

"And when will the cheese cabinet arrive?" she asked.

Oh shit!

I'd totally forgotten about the cheese cabinet. Serge had offered to order it for me but I told him I'd take care of it.

"It should be here any day now," I lied, panicking. I wondered if I could blame this slipup on "baby brain."

"Good. You wouldn't want Serge to think you've forgotten him," she said.

"Hah," I laughed uncomfortably, pulling out my phone to find out where I could order a damn cheese cabinet to be delivered in the next few days. I'd been so focused on the café side that I'd completely forgotten the point of this whole venture was to help sell Serge's cheese. *How could I have been so thoughtless?*

"And perhaps a couch or two in the corner against those walls would be nice," Mum added, still pacing around.

"Mum, stop. I've got this," I told her, adding "find some damn couches" to my to-do list.

She looked at her watch and reminded me it was time to get to the doctor.

"Ah, shoot, I totally forgot," I said, wondering if anything else important had slipped my mind.

"That's why I'm here, darling. To make sure you don't lose your head in all this."

In the doctor's waiting room, I had one of those "What on earth am I doing here?" moments. I had to be the only patient in the room under sixty, and Mum and I were definitely the only ones without walking canes.

"So, tell me about your doctor," Mum said, looking around skeptically.

"He's fine," I told her. "A little old, perhaps. Anyway, he just gets me through the monthly checks. He won't be at the delivery. I'll just have a midwife, and a doctor on call if I need one."

When it had come to choosing a GP, Serge had mildly insisted we meet with his family's old doctor, Doctor Gerard. I'd blindly agreed, as I didn't really mind whom I saw. What I hadn't realized was that Serge's old family doctor was extraordinarily, well, old.

When I first met him and shook his hand, I could feel him shaking and figured he must have been at least eighty. *How is he still practicing?* I'd wondered. His office looked like it'd been untouched in decades, and I didn't even see a computer. The bookshelves, however, were lined with medical books, which instilled some confidence, although I didn't dare look at when they'd been published.

Age aside he was delightfully sweet, and after our first appointment, I hadn't had the heart to find somebody else. Besides, women had been growing babies for much longer than even Doctor Gerard had been around.

"And is it normal for French partners not to attend these appointments?" Mum asked, reminding me that Serge wasn't by my side.

"Of course not. French men are generally very supportive. Serge just has a lot going on right now," I said in his defense. I wasn't sure why I was sticking up for him, though. After reassuring me multiple times that he would come, he'd pulled out at the last minute because Cecile the goat had apparently gone missing. It'd taken a lot of deep breathing during the drive over to stop myself from bursting into tears.

And now the lump in my throat was back.

Thankfully, we were called in shortly after.

"Good news," Doctor Gerard said in French after we'd sat down.

I looked at him, feeling nervous. "What do you mean?" I asked.

"We've got a new ultrasound machine," he said, rubbing his hands together.

Mum looked to me to see whether she'd understood correctly. "I'll get to see the baby?" she asked, rubbing her own hands together with glee.

"*Le bébé*, yes!" he said excitedly.

"Oh, great," I said flatly, devastated that Serge was going to miss *another* opportunity to see his child growing. Now that Mum was here, he seemed to have happily handed over the role of looking after me to her. He was working even longer hours, and when I did see him our interactions were efficient and practical—mostly discussing what we'd done in the cheese room and what was left to do.

"Shall we do the ultrasound first, then?" Doctor Gerard asked. "Get to the more boring bits after."

I wasn't sure how comfortable I was with Doctor Gerard referring to a medical discussion as "boring," but I, too, was eager to see the baby.

Seconds into the scan, and just as I was about to tell him we were keeping the sex a secret, he blurted out, "*Oh là là. Elle est grande, votre fille!*"

"*Elle?* It's a girl?" Mum echoed, squealing. "What brilliant news!"

"We weren't planning on finding out the sex," I told Doctor Gerard, crestfallen.

"Why on earth not?" he asked. "How will you know what color clothes to buy? Not knowing is very unpractical."

I shrugged. It seemed the concept of gender neutrality was lost on my old doc.

"So, you're certain?" I asked him. "About the sex."

"Mostly, yes. I guess we will know for sure in a couple of months," he said, laughing. "Anyway, all looks good as far as I can tell."

The remainder of the appointment passed in a blur as I was consumed by excitement about having a baby girl.

As we walked out, Mum said, "Serge is definitely going to regret not coming now."

Although she didn't mean anything by it, her words stung.

I couldn't help but wonder what else Serge might end up regretting if he continued to remain so absent.

Chapter

22

IT WAS THE NIGHT OF the village spring party, and I think we were all excited to be getting out of our work clothes and into something a little prettier. Although things had been a little tense between Serge and me following my doctor's appointment, I wanted to put my frustrations aside for the evening and have some fun. I needed to remember what life was like before we'd gotten so busy.

Seeing Serge walk out of our bedroom in a white linen shirt and dark pants, I felt something deep in my stomach that for once wasn't our baby girl kicking me. When I'd told him about the doctor's gender-reveal slipup during the scan, he'd been overjoyed. I don't think he'd stopped smiling since.

"It's nice to see you out of your farm clothes for once," I said.

"And you," he replied, spinning me around.

Mum and Ray joined us in the living room, both giggling, seemingly riding high on the same emotions as we were. We piled into Serge's Citroën. The four of us squeezed into the car, heads bopping along to a Françoise Hardy song, must have looked like quite the comical French cliché.

The fête was in full swing by the time we arrived. Serge had told me about these village parties, but I'd had trouble believing him when he'd explained that nearly everyone would be there, with long dinner tables set up and huge vats of incredible-smelling food bubbling away on makeshift stoves. It was the kind of French occasion that had to be seen to be believed.

There was a rag-tag band playing in the corner of the tent and a small dance floor set up in front of them. A few kids were spinning around and laughing. Mum smiled and looked at me as if to ask, "Is this for real?" and I just looked back and nodded. A real sense of community filled the air and, with summer around the corner, it seemed as though my countryside compatriots were ready to celebrate.

Mum dashed off confidently to the bar to get everyone drinks while Serge, Ray, and I chatted with Jacques and Marie. Moments later, she was back, balancing a tray filled with glasses.

"Ella, I just had the strangest conversation," she whispered to me. "I was ordering drinks in French and, from my accent alone, the man next to me guessed I was from Melbourne. Isn't that bizarre!"

I wonder if she just met Chuck? I thought.

"This is him, now," she said quietly, confirming my hypothesis. I couldn't help but smile. I loved the idea of him messing with her.

"Chuck! I didn't realize you were coming tonight," I said, leaning in to kiss him hello.

"Wouldn't miss it for the world," he replied with a grin, and then whispered in my ear: "Great material at these village parties. Always a drama or two that could make for a fun subplot."

Mum looked confused. "You two already know each other?" she asked.

"Mum, this is Chuck," I said. "We met just after Serge and I moved here. He's the Englishman I told you about."

"Oh, right," Mum said, although I couldn't tell from her expression if she remembered the brief conversation we'd had about Chuck that ended with her telling me not to spend too much time with other men.

"And Chuck, this is my mother and her fiancé, Ray."

"So, you didn't really guess where I was from, then?" Mum asked, seemingly embarrassed at having been so gullible.

"No, your French is actually very good. Ella mentioned you were coming to help with the café, so when I saw you all come in, I put two and two together," he said, shooting me a wink. I laughed.

Mum then proceeded to interrogate Chuck on his life and how he managed living between France and England. If I weren't already with Serge, I would have worried that she was trying to set me up with him.

With Mum monopolizing the conversation, I took the opportunity to go to the bar and get another glass of juice. I'd gotten the feeling we wouldn't be eating for a while, and I needed some energy.

"So, *he's* the one who's taken over Michel's old place?" I overheard a lady say in a very animated voice to her companion. My ears pricked up and I snuck a glance at the couple. They were well-dressed, looked to be in their fifties, and if they weren't gossiping about Serge, I would have thought that they seemed quite likable.

"*Oh, oui*," the man replied. "And I hear it's not going well. A friend tried the first batch of cheese since the takeover and told me it's gone downhill."

"Is that right?" the lady asked, nodding along, encouraging him to continue.

"The new owner apparently had to beg Michel to come back to help him," he added.

"Hah!" she laughed. "These city people never last long out here."

Clearly they don't know Serge, I thought. *Or me!*

I walked back to our group, eyeballing everyone and wondering if they, too, thought of Serge and me as "outsiders." Mostly, I was worried for Serge. I was used to feeling like the odd one out in France, but this was meant to be his home, his people.

Thankfully it seemed as though word hadn't spread too far, because Serge seemed happier than ever, deep in conversation with Michel and Jacques, probably discussing something to do with the farm. He laughed heartily. It was the most engaged I'd seen him in weeks. Perhaps these past few weeks hanging out with only English-speakers had been frustrating for him. Serge's English was so good, I often forgot that he wasn't a native speaker and that conversing in a different language was tiring for him. If I had to speak in French all the time, I probably would have been out the door a long time ago.

I left Serge to enjoy himself and went to relieve Chuck of any further interrogation from Mum. When he saw me, a look of relief crossed his face.

"So, how are the renovations going, Chuck?" I interrupted Mum.

"Splendid," he said. "I added a bath to the bedroom, under the window. I just need to get it hooked up to the plumbing."

Oh, dear, I thought, trying to figure out how a bath in Chuck's room could be anything other than a decorating disaster.

"Meanwhile," he continued, "I've been using it as a writing space."

"Using what as a writing space?" I asked.

"The bath, without the water. I've added some cushions and it's actually rather cosy."

I laughed so hard, I started wheezing. I'm not sure what it was about the image of Chuck writing on a laptop in the bath that set me off, but once I started, I couldn't stop. And it appeared to be contagious, because after an unintentional snort from me, Chuck was off and away, too.

Mum looked at us both like we'd gone mad.

"I just don't understand what's so funny," she said seriously.

"I guess it's hard to picture unless you've seen Chuck's bedroom," I said, still laughing.

Mum looked at me, this time so seriously that it stopped my giggles in their tracks, and we were plunged into an awkward silence.

"Where's Ray gone?" I asked eventually, hoping she might go off and find him.

"He's just over there. You know Ray, making friends everywhere he goes," she said.

"Watch out," Chuck said to Mum. "He's talking to Franck, the most persuasive real-estate agent in Chinon. Come and I'll introduce you; he's a good laugh."

Franck was a jolly-looking moustached man, rosy-cheeked and clutching a Ricard. I got the impression it wasn't his first drink of the evening.

"*Bonsoir, Mesdames, Monsieur,*" he said as we joined him and Ray. *Definitely French.*

"*Alors*, Charles, have you thought anymore about my proposition?" Franck asked.

"You're selling?" I asked Chuck, feeling slightly panicked. *Is this the real reason for the renovations? Am I about to lose my only friend out here?*

"Oh, no," Chuck assured me. "At least not by choice. Franck's trying to sell my place from under my feet."

Franck laughed off Chuck's comments before turning back to Ray and bringing Mum into their conversation, asking them what they were doing in France and how long they planned to stay.

"So, you must be in the market for a little property here," I heard him say. "A summer château, perhaps?"

"Oh no," I heard Mum reply. "We're happy staying with Ella."

Chuck jokingly shot me an apologetic look, and I giggled.

"Chuck, while I have you alone," I said to him. "I just wanted to say thanks again for your help with the café. I should be able to pay you back shortly after we open."

"Anything for a decent cup of coffee in this town," he said with a grin. "But seriously, don't mention it again."

I smiled. I'd never been great at accepting help, and Chuck didn't seem great at being thanked for helping. Not discussing the loan any further seemed like the best outcome for the both of us.

"Now, shall we go sit down?" I asked. "It looks like they're getting ready to serve dinner."

"Yes, let's get a spot overlooking the dance floor. It should be good entertainment," Chuck suggested.

I tried to find Serge in the crowd, thinking I should probably sit with him. When I did, however, he looked like he was still having a good time with Jacques, so I left him to it. Besides, this was the kind of event that needed careful deconstructing from the sidelines, and I got the feeling that Chuck was just the man for the job.

~

As the entrées went out, I eyed the plates of oysters and the glasses of Muscadet enviously, but more than made up for my sacrifice when it came time for the pig roast. All around me, cheeks got rosy from the flowing bottles of Chinon, and then the dancing began. Hair got let down and shoes got kicked off. From my vantage point with Chuck, I was finding everything both wonderful and hilarious.

And then I ran into Mum in the toilets.

"Ella, thank God I can get you alone for a minute."

"Why? Is everything OK?" I asked.

"You tell me," she said. "What's going on between you and Chuck?"

"Huh? Nothing's going on. Chuck's a friend. One of my only friends out here."

"Are you sure he doesn't have other designs?" she asked.

"Seriously? With a pregnant woman?" I wondered if Mum had perhaps had one too many glasses of wine, but the look on her face told me that she meant business.

"I saw the way he winked at you. And the way you laugh at his jokes. You really shouldn't be leading him on. And right under Serge's nose."

Oh. My. God! I thought. Typical Mum, always sticking *her* nose where it didn't belong.

"Mum, please don't get involved in this. I'm more than capable of having a platonic relationship with a man."

"That's how many relationships start out," she said.

"And sometimes, that's how they continue," I said.

"Darling, I know it's normal when you're going through a stressful period to look for distractions outside your home, but I don't think you understand the implications. Or how it looks for a pregnant woman to be spending her time with a man who is not the father."

"So, what would you rather I do? Spend all my time alone? Or with you?" I asked. "And what about when you go back to Australia?"

"Well, maybe it's time you started to think about moving back, too," she said.

"What about Serge? And the café?" I asked. "Should I just drop all that and come back?"

A lady walked into the bathroom, which put a halt to our conversation. I was relieved and frustrated—happy to get away from what had turned into a futile discussion about a platonic relationship and annoyed that it had happened in the first place.

"Well, perhaps you should just consider it. I can talk to Serge if you like," Mum suggested as we walked out.

"You will do no such thing, Mum," I whispered angrily.

I went back to sit with Chuck, but while I'd been gone he seemed to have entered into an animated discussion with Ray about the country property market. I was left to think over what Mum had said, with her comment about moving home to Australia playing on my mind.

Eventually I saw Jacques and Marie leaving, which was when Serge came to find me. He sat down.

"I've hardly seen you all night," he said.

He sounded disappointed, although I couldn't figure out why. It wasn't a huge party; if he'd wanted to find me, he wouldn't have had to look far.

"Serge, would you ever leave France?" I asked.

"*Oh là!* What's brought this on?" he asked.

"I've just been thinking about it. Do you think you would?"

"I don't think I could leave France, no," he said. "Look around us. It's my home."

Since we'd started dating, Serge and I had never really spoken at length about where we'd spend the rest of our lives. After my near-decade with my ex, Paul, I hadn't wanted to think about anything too long-term because it just stopped me from enjoying the present. And then there had been Paris to fall in love with, and then the baby and the farm to focus on. I'd just assumed that if I were ever desperate to return to Australia, Serge would follow me. But perhaps this wasn't the case.

"Do we need to decide this now?" he asked.

"No, of course not. It's just——" I started saying.

"Good," he interrupted. "Then shall we dance? You're too beautiful not to be on that floor."

As he twirled me around in time to the music, I laughed on the outside but on the inside I couldn't help feeling a little trapped. I knew I'd been the one who had chosen to come to France and even to move to the countryside, but I hadn't ever considered that it would be a life sentence.

For the first time since leaving Australia, I felt like my future depended on a man, and that scared me.

Chapter

23

AFTER A COUPLE OF WEEKS of spring rain, the sun came out, just in time for the soft launch of Ella and the Goats—the café name still a work in progress for want of Serge, me, Mum, and Ray agreeing on a better idea.

It'd been a mad race to the finish line—of course—and, with a last-minute burst water pipe slowing our progress, we'd worked late into the night to get everything done. The result, thankfully, exceeded expectations. We'd found two perfect brown leather couches, and I'd sourced some huge vintage posters to add pops of color to the walls. The cheese cabinet had arrived just in time—after more than a few phone calls to ensure the express delivery—and Serge had carefully filled it with a selection of his cheeses.

I stared out at the empty car park, which Ray had landscaped beautifully, creating a line of shrubs that he promised would soon grow into a hedge. I was proud of what we'd managed to create but I still wasn't sure how it would resonate with a French crowd. I felt both nervous and excited to find out.

With the early-morning fog lifting and rays of sunshine streaming through the windows, it finally felt like we were ready to go. I arranged the scones and tarts, and set up a sample cheese-tasting plate for some promotional pictures. As a finishing touch, I placed the congratulatory bouquet of wildflowers that Serge had picked for me that morning next to the coffee machine. He came over and wrapped his arms around me.

"Congratulations, Ella. You did it!" he said.

All we needed now were customers, or at least some friends, to come and help fill the space.

Thankfully, Chris was catching the train from Paris with Clotilde to be with me in time for the opening. To my surprise—and perhaps Clotilde's—Chris had recently decided to take a break from pursuing French women, having had his heart broken "more times than was worth counting," in his own melodramatic words. He was focusing on himself for a while, which also worked in my favor because he was able and willing to teach me to make coffee. Clotilde, as always, was just excited to be involved in an activity that was away from cameras and catwalks. While I didn't have many friends out here in the French countryside, my friends from Paris managed to take up the slack.

After I gave them a quick tour, we got to work—Chris on my coffee-making skills and Clotilde on our social media presence. She promoted the cheese room as a destination for Parisians looking for good coffee and good vibes outside of the city. As she went outside to take photos of our goats to highlight the farm-to-table aspect, I double-checked if Chris's romantic feelings toward her, which were as strong as a pungent slice of Munster when I was still living in Paris, were also on pause.

"Ella, I will always love Clotilde. But now is not the moment," he told me.

"Have things really been that bad?" I asked, and he nodded gravely.

"I've decided I need to wait for the right person. Perhaps the female version of Serge," he said.

"I'm sure she'd be magnificent," I joked. "But seriously, nobody is ever perfect."

"Trouble in paradise?" he asked.

"Not so much trouble, just some roadblocks," I said.

"Well, Ella, what did you expect? You haven't done things the easy way," he replied.

And Chris was right. Serge and my honeymoon period had been hacked into like a wheel of Camembert at a party. After a few months of uneventful bliss, we'd been placed under an increasing amount of pressure, from the unexpected pregnancy and the move to the farm to starting a business. It had been an intense period. *Perhaps I should cut Serge more slack*, I thought.

A dozen trial coffees later, and after a few decaf versions for me, we still didn't have any customers beyond Marie and Jacques, who had arrived at eleven o'clock and had been slowly sipping two espressos in an attempt to fill out the tables until lunchtime. Although we'd distributed flyers telling people in Chinon about the "grand opening," they were obviously holding out on stopping by.

I thought back to the conversation I'd overheard at the village party and wondered if people weren't coming because they continued to think of Serge and me as outsiders. But I wasn't about to let some hesitant locals cramp my style. If all went well, the cheese room would become a destination. People would travel to come and visit us, and we wouldn't need to rely on our more small-minded neighbors. And for now, at least there were enough of us to make it look like we were having a relatively busy day to anyone who drove past. *Everything will be fine*, I kept repeating to myself, although as the minutes ticked by, my nerves intensified.

In true French style, some customers arrived for lunch at midday on the dot. Two women in their late sixties looked around, mouths agape, at the cabinets and the imposing coffee machine. I quickly stepped in to explain the concept of the cheese room, something that should have been obvious but, in country France, was actually quite original.

"It's a melange of a cheese-tasting room and an Australian-style café," I told the pair. "We also have cheese tarts, salads, or maybe dessert if you prefer something sweet. And coffee, of course. *Good* coffee," I clarified, smiling, although perhaps the nuance was lost through my French.

"And do you have a lunch *formule*?" one of the women croaked.

Merde! I thought. *How could I have not thought to have a* for-*mule? The French love their entrée—main or main—dessert combo.*

"Of course we do. It's fifteen euros for main—dessert," I ad-libbed.

"Quite reasonable," they said, nodding, and went to sit down.

I looked on desperately as the women ate goat cheese tarts with lettuce from Ray's makeshift garden, followed by a peach cobbler. When they initially refused an espresso, I told them it was on the house to celebrate our opening. They begrudgingly agreed.

"I'll be up all night," one said grumpily as I dropped the cups off at their table.

"I'll probably have heartburn all afternoon," said the other.

The coffee was met with stern approval.

"*Très bon*," one said, as the other murmured either enjoyment or disdain; it was hard to tell.

Once the ladies had gone, I rubbed my hands together and looked at Serge.

"Not bad for our first lunch," I said.

"You think?" he asked.

"Well, it's not a very big village. Word will spread," I reassured him.

"And they liked the goat cheese in the tart?"

Crap. I'd actually forgotten to ask.

"They said they enjoyed everything," I replied.

Serge forced a smile, but I could tell he was disappointed at the lack of customers.

"Good things take time, Serge," I reminded him, but I, too, felt his disappointment.

"I'm just relieved we didn't get a proper loan from the bank," he said.

I still hadn't told Serge about the money Chuck had contributed, and until now, I'd hoped he simply hadn't noticed.

"Huh?" I asked.

"It's much easier knowing we have some flexibility in our repayments."

"Right . . .," I said, nervously. *Is this conversation about to get ugly?*

"Well, it was very generous of your mum," he said.

"Mum?" I said, before retreating back. "Of course, Mum. Yes, it was generous. But let's not worry about all that now," I went on, trying to buy myself some time to figure out what was going on. "I'll make you a coffee."

Over the sound of grinding beans, I furiously tried to figure out how Serge came to think that Mum had lent us money.

Other than the conversation we'd had very early on about me securing extra funding, had I said anything that would lead him to believe she was behind the loan? *Did Mum mention something?* Regardless of how he came to the conclusion, now that he knew about the extra money I'd spent, it was probably time for me to come clean.

I went to talk to Mum, but before I could even broach the subject, we were hit by a surprise afternoon rush. People had obviously caught wind of the "English" girl opening up a "tea shop," and they piled in for tea and scones. It wasn't quite the market I was after, but by that point, I wasn't going to turn anyone away. Perhaps the "outsider" angle was just what I needed.

I rushed Mum into the kitchen to make another batch of scones as I prepared yet another pot of English Breakfast tea. I stared longingly at the coffee machine and gave it a consolatory rub while Serge stood futilely behind his cheese counter.

"Ella, coffee order," Chris called out some time later.

Finally, I thought, heading over to the machine. *All is not lost.*

"From someone French?" I asked.

"Not sure," he replied. "He's over there if you want to find out."

I spotted the enormous bunch of flowers before I saw the man who was behind them.

"Chuck, hello," I said, after I'd glimpsed his face over the foliage.

"Congratulations, Ella! What an achievement," he said, hugging me. I stole a glance at Serge to see how he reacted to Chuck's flowers, but he was busy rearranging the cheese cabinet for what felt like the tenth time that afternoon.

"Thanks, Chuck. Although it's been a bit of a disaster," I said honestly. "Only two customers for lunch, and now we seem to be running some kind of English tea shop. We've already sold out of scones."

"Hmm," he replied. "I wouldn't have minded one."

"How about some peach cobbler instead?" I suggested.

"Perfect."

I made Chuck a flat white and then went to sit down with him. It felt good to rest my legs. I was determined not to let my belly slow me down but I had to acknowledge that it was tiring me out.

"So, what's the news in the world outside of this place?" I asked.

"Same old," he replied. "Except with the addition of a roof leak."

"Oh, no. Perhaps you could use the bathtub to catch the water," I suggested.

We both laughed, causing Serge to look over. I motioned for him to join us but he either didn't notice the invitation or chose to ignore it. I turned back to Chuck.

"And what's going on with your book?" I asked.

Chuck launched into his current plot dilemma, asking me for advice. It was a relief to jump into his fictional world and its problems so I could forget about my own for a few minutes.

Mum brought out a fresh tray of scones and spotted me sitting with Chuck. She came over to say hello to him, standing behind me and resting her hands on my shoulders. As she chatted away happily, I felt relieved that she now seemed to have accepted him as one of my friends.

"Well, I best get back to it," she said. "You too, Ella, chop-chop."

"Yep, I'll be with you in a minute," I said.

Before walking away, she leaned over and whispered in my ear. "You should be helping Serge. People will get the wrong idea."

I got back to work.

⌒

We shut the café to customers around five o'clock. It had been a long day, and to thank everyone for coming and lending a hand, I'd bought a six-pack of local sparkling wine. I set down glasses and got everyone onto the couches.

Chuck, who had tried nearly everything on the menu by this point, made to leave but I insisted he stay. I ushered him into a spot next to Clotilde, hoping they might flirt a little and get Mum off my back.

I began blushing before I began talking.

"I just wanted to say thank you to everyone for your help. I only came up with the idea of starting this place a few months ago," I said, laughing because, while I could sound casual now, I knew how much work had gone into setting it up. "But since then, it's been all I can think of, and without your help I certainly couldn't have got everything ready in time."

I could have gone on, but Serge got up to relieve me from my embarrassment. "So, we should all raise a glass to Ella—for her crazy dreams and her capacity to follow through on them. It's one of your most admirable qualities, *ma belle*," he said, turning to me.

I blushed harder, finally taking a moment to acknowledge how wonderful it felt to have survived day one of owning a business in France.

But then Serge added, "And thank you to Ella's mum for her financial assistance. It wouldn't have been possible without her help. So, cheers!"

Merde! I still hadn't spoken to Mum.

I shot her a look that said "I'll explain later," and then glanced over at Chuck to see he'd gone a deep shade of red. I smiled, but Serge seemed to have noticed all of the looks darting around the group and suddenly seemed uneasy. What should have been a joyful moment had suddenly turned complicated.

While Serge was packing away his cheese, I pulled Mum into the kitchen and told her about the mix-up.

"So, he must have realized I got some additional funding and then assumed it was from you. I was going to tell him earlier today, but then we got so busy this afternoon."

"Ella, you should have told him as soon as Charles had offered," she said sternly.

"I know, but it's complicated. And the money seriously helped at a time when I was rather desperate."

"You could have come to me," she said.

"But you've already done so much," I replied. "Besides, Chuck offered so willingly, and he made accepting very easy."

"And you're sure his intentions are honorable?"

"Oh, Mum, stop! I just need you not to mention anything to Serge."

"You're entering dangerous territory, Ella," she said. "But if this is what you want . . ."

"It is. Thanks, Mum. I'll tell him everything soon enough."

Thankfully, Serge didn't bring up the loan again for the rest of the evening. I'd finally managed to convince myself I was just being paranoid about it until later, when we were alone in our room.

"Did I do the wrong thing by thanking your mum for helping fund the cheese room?" he asked. "She seemed upset when I mentioned it."

I'd been trying to figure out the best way to tell Serge about Chuck's financial assistance since his speech earlier that evening. I still wanted to come clean but I got the feeling Serge wouldn't take the news well. And I certainly didn't want him to feel like he couldn't support his own farm and business, especially when things had gotten off to such a rough start.

"Of course, you didn't do the wrong thing," I said to Serge. "Mum was just embarrassed. I don't even know if she'd spoken about it in concrete terms with Ray."

"Oh," Serge said, and then he apologized.

"It's totally fine," I said. "Already forgotten."

Despite my exhaustion, I couldn't sleep. I felt dreadful. Not only had I lied to Serge, but now I'd also implicated Mum. I wasn't sure what to do. I knew I'd be able to pay off Chuck's loan quickly enough; I just had to hope that Serge wouldn't find out the truth before I did.

Chapter
24

A FEW WEEKS LATER, THE cheese room had unofficially and unwittingly turned into an English tearoom. The takings were good, so I didn't dare complain, but if I'd known how much English Breakfast tea I would be serving, I wouldn't have spent so much money on a coffee machine. Some kind of industrial scone machine, on the other hand, would have been a good investment.

Also frustrating was the fact that those early days hadn't actually resulted in as many cheese sales as I'd hoped. Still at a loss as to why, I'd had Clotilde taste-test the cheese behind Serge's back.

"I mean, it's OK," she'd said. "But it's just not quite the same as Michel's."

"And?" I'd asked.

"Well, maybe people expect things to stay the same," she'd hypothesized.

"But, does it taste bad?" I'd asked, still fearing the worst.

"Of course, it's not bad. Serge wouldn't sell bad cheese."

"That's what I thought."

"It's just different; Michel's cheese tasted very traditional. Serge's cheese is fresher. Younger."

"Cooler?" I'd asked.

"Is cheese ever that cool?"

"For me, it can be," I'd said.

"Maybe he needs to modernize his offerings a little. Differentiate himself completely from Michel. Make something new and exciting," she'd suggested.

I'd been relieved to confirm that Serge's cheese was at least edible, but I still couldn't figure out why people were coming in for tea and scones and not his produce. More than once, Serge had made a comment about how much time he'd spent helping get the cheese room ready, and how that time would have been better spent with the goats.

I tried to not engage with his negativity because I felt like we just needed to give things time. The concept of tasting and then buying cheese direct from the farm was solid. People would come around to it eventually. And the novelty of an English tearoom would wear off at some point.

I'd also made a plan to incorporate even more cheese into the food menu—hello, cheese scones!—to further drive sales and get the word out about Serge's *fromage*.

But now I'd be doing everything myself. With my Parisian friends back in the capital, and Mum and Ray back in Australia, I was about to go into my first week of managing the cheese room alone.

At least I won't have time to get lonely, I consoled myself.

Mum and Ray had offered to extend their stay, but I'd figured that I'd have to rip off the Band-Aid eventually. This was my project, and I needed to either make it work on my own or find a permanent solution to keep things running. I also wanted to spend some quality time with Serge before the baby arrived.

We didn't have long until the two of us became three, and I hoped to make the most of it.

That said, for the first few days after our guests had gone, we'd pretty much spent any moment that we weren't working collapsed on the couch watching TV. It'd been a busy time, and I tried not to worry about our lack of intimacy, figuring that we had our whole lives to spend together; but Serge did seem distant. When I asked him if everything was OK, he'd just say that he was tired.

We'll get into the swing of things eventually, I kept telling myself.

Back in the cheese room, I was staring at a calendar while another batch of scones baked. The weeks since we'd opened had passed remarkably quickly, and now I feared that the remaining time before my due date would zip by in a similar fashion. There was still so much to do.

Marie had very willingly agreed to manage things while I was in hospital, and I needed to make sure everything was running perfectly before then. I was already starting to feel a little anxious. And I kept thinking about how we could drum up more business. Clotilde's social media posts had created a little buzz, but I knew that would die out quickly. *Perhaps I should just embrace the faux-English vibes and dress up like the Mad Hatter? Or perhaps I am just going a little mad myself.*

"Morning, Ella," said a familiar voice, breaking my reverie.

"Oh, hey, Chuck," I said, grateful for some company to distract me from my current thoughts. "Coffee?" I didn't even offer Chuck the option of tea as he was one of the very few people who ordered coffee, and I needed to keep the dream alive that my coffee machine would one day pay for itself.

He'd come in every day since I'd opened, in a show of support. At times he'd been the only customer, but his good humor had stopped me from stressing about the lulls.

"A flat white, if you don't mind," he said. "I wasn't going to come in today because I didn't sleep last night, but the lure of coffee was too great."

"I understand completely," I said.

"But I should apologize: I'm not pretty when I haven't slept," he said, smoothing back his hair.

"I'm not pretty when I'm pregnant but that doesn't stop me," I deflected.

"What are you talking about? You're gorgeous," he said.

I laughed off the compliment, but it made me stand a little taller.

"Fancy a scone?" I suggested. "They're just about out of the oven."

"Brilliant," he said, pulling out a notebook and a pen.

Business started picking up, and Chuck and I didn't get a chance to chat again before he had to leave a couple of hours later. On his way out, he ran into Serge, who was coming in to check on the stock in his cheese cabinet. They shook hands quickly, engaged in a brief chat, and went their separate ways.

"He's a little odd," suggested Serge, joining me.

"I guess, but aren't we all?" I replied. "And on the plus side, he's pretty much the only person who comes in here to order coffee," I added.

"I'll have a coffee," Serge said quickly.

"Latte? Flat white?" I asked, cheering up.

"Espresso, please," he said, leaving me to wonder why the French always drank their coffee short and black.

"Coming up," I said. "And guess who sold two of your flower-coated goat cheeses this morning?"

I'd eventually found a way to tactfully suggest to Serge that he could perhaps start modernizing his cheese offerings, and he'd begun making a beautiful little cheese dusted in flower petals. It was delicate, tasted great, and looked gorgeous both in a cheese cabinet and on a cheeseboard. I felt like it was destined to sell well.

"You sold two?" he repeated.

"I did," I said with a smile. "Seems like word is getting out."

"Two is good, but if we're ever going to make a profit, we need to sell a lot more than that," he said seriously.

"Well, it's a good start," I told him, thinking back to Christmas when he'd wanted to leave the farm and move back to Paris. "Give it a few more months and your cheese will be flying off the shelves." I was feeling positive. It was amazing how quickly everything could change.

Later that afternoon, as I was cleaning the café kitchen, I heard the door open and wondered who could be coming in at that hour. I assumed it must have been Serge, perhaps wanting another coffee, so I sang out that I was in the kitchen.

"*Beh, 'ello*," said an unfamiliar woman's voice as she rounded the door. My head whipped around quickly. *Who have I just invited into the kitchen?*

A petite woman was looking directly at me, her perfect brown bob, completely motionless, surrounding her pretty face. She looked somehow familiar, and I wondered if she'd been into the café before.

"I'm sorry," I said in French, "I thought you were someone else. We're actually closed for the day."

"*Où est Serge?*" she asked. Her voice was soft but determined. I prayed that her enquiry had something to do with cheese, or goats, but my gut told me otherwise. The woman in front of me was too carefully put together to be here on farm business.

Merde, I thought, finally realizing where I'd seen her face before.

"I'll just call him for you," I said.

She nodded and went to take a seat.

As I called Serge, I inspected her carefully. She was short and thin, carefully dressed in black jeans and what looked like a silk blouse. Her handbag was black leather, and her shoes the same deep purple as her top. Compared to my ripped maternity jeans and flour-stained apron, she looked like perfection.

My heart was beating hard in my chest.

"Serge, there's a woman here asking to see you," I said, trying to keep my voice level.

"Who is it?" he asked.

"I think it's your ex-wife," I said and hung up.

⟋

Serge walked through the cheese-room door shortly after. I noticed that his face was white as he stood motionless, looking between Françoise and me. He didn't seem to know what to do. I gave him a little smile to try to let him know it was OK that he go to greet her.

After he had, he introduced us. The shock when Serge announced that I was his girlfriend was written all over Françoise's face. While I'd eventually recognized her from her wedding photo, she obviously had no idea about me. Her eyes darted to my round belly, and she inhaled sharply. I looked at the ground uncomfortably, and Serge muttered something unnecessary about the pregnancy. The tension was all a little much for me, and rather than risk saying anything stupid to fill the silence, I took myself into the kitchen and busied myself washing dishes that were already clean.

Serge and Françoise sat down and began a quiet and rather intimate-looking conversation. I tried to give them space, but I couldn't stop myself from keeping an eye on things.

What the hell is she doing here?

From my vantage point, I couldn't hear what they were discussing and the minutes seemed to last hours. *Maybe her surprise visit has something to do with the letters? Maybe she's begging him to take her back?*

My mind was racing.

I messaged Billie. She always knew what to do in uncomfortable situations. I hugged my phone, hoping she'd reply quickly despite the time difference between France and Australia. I nearly jumped out of my skin when she started calling me.

"Billie, what are you doing awake?" I asked. I'd clearly forgotten what it was like to stay up past midnight these days.

"I was on a date. But it was a disaster, so now I'm home working."

"Anyone I know?" I asked.

"No, another idiot. But no matter, plenty more idiots in the sea, right?"

"Oh, Billie, I'm sorry. Do you want to talk about it?" I asked.

"Nope. Now focus, El. Tell me what's going on."

"You don't mind?" I asked.

"It'll be a nice break from my own drama."

I made a mental note to call and find out what was really happening with her love life once this Françoise thing had been sorted, and then I filled her in. It was a quick rundown, because I myself was rather clueless as to what was currently playing out. "So, I don't actually know why she's here," I finished, searching for meaning. "Maybe it has something to do with the letters."

"What letters?" she asked.

I realized that I hadn't told Billie about Serge's pen pal, probably because I myself hadn't wanted to think about what Françoise's attempts to contact Serge had meant for my relationship. But now here she was anyway, dressed to impress, commandeering Serge's attention.

"Well, she's just sent him a few letters," I said. "Asking him to meet up, or to call her. That kind of thing."

"And what does Serge say?" Billie asked.

"I haven't actually asked him about them directly," I said, thinking back to when I'd burned the most recent one.

"Hmm," she said, clearly mulling this all over.

I felt foolish for still not understanding the dynamic between Serge and Françoise.

"So, what's the plan, El?" she asked.

"That's what I was hoping you could tell me," I said.

"Well," she said, and paused a moment. "As soon as they're done, you need to ask Serge what's going on. Tell him that her being on the farm makes you uncomfortable. Find out the truth."

"You're right," I said. "I need to confront the problem head on. Face to face. Really smash it out."

"Ella, I think the expression's 'thrash it out' and that's not quite what I meant. Don't go in too strong. You should still give him the benefit of the doubt. Perhaps it's just something to do with their divorce."

"I guess," I said, thinking that it would be preferable to go down the "smash it out" route instead.

Suddenly, I heard chairs moving out in the café and told Billie I had to go.

"Try to remain calm," she warned as she said farewell.

I walked over to Serge and Françoise. She was leaving. I said a quiet goodbye and tried to maintain eye contact. She gave me a curt smile and a nod, and then walked off, the sound of her heels echoing on the floor as she left.

After she'd gone, I felt nervous. Moments before, I'd been desperate to find out what was going on. Now it was almost as if I didn't want to know. I prolonged the suspense by making a cup of tea. Serge waited for me to come over as my fingers bumbled about the teapot and the mug.

"So?" I asked, finally sitting down.

"So," Serge said.

"Big day," I said.

"Big day," he replied.

"Get to the point, Serge. What was Françoise here for?"

"She's here because Clovis is sick."

"And who is Clovis?" I asked, remembering having seen his name in the letter.

"Her father. She wants to know if I could visit him."

"Oh . . .," I said, surprised that she hadn't been plotting something more sinister.

"He has Alzheimer's."

"Oh, dear," I muttered, suddenly feeling sorry for her.

"Françoise said he's been asking to see me on and off for the past couple of months. She thinks it might help if I go to visit him."

"Of course, you should," I said. "And was that all she wanted?"

"What else could there be?" he asked, making me feel as though it was completely normal for an ex to turn up unannounced.

"She could have come to buy some cheese," I suggested, knowing full well that Françoise was one of the only French people I'd heard of who didn't actually eat *fromage*.

"Well, apparently she has started to eat cheese," he said.

"I knew it!" I replied, wondering what other tricks she had up her sleeve.

"Ella, I am joking. She will never like cheese."

I flicked his hand away as he reached out to grab mine.

"And even if she did," he said, coming over and rubbing my belly, "I have my hands full at the moment. I'm rather smitten with my girls."

His words caressed me like a gooey slice of Camembert nuzzling into a hunk of baguette.

"Despite one of them acting a little crazy at times . . .," he added, ruining the moment.

"So, you'll go see her father?" I asked.

"If you agree," he said.

"And Françoise will stop writing?"

"When did she write?"

"Huh?" I asked, trying to deflect. I could have kicked myself.

"She did mention a letter," he said, looking at me carefully. "I assumed it had never arrived."

"Oh, that's strange. Tell you what, that postman seems a little rogue," I fumbled, feeling my cheeks redden. "What I meant to ask is if she'll stop coming by the farm?"

"Her father lives locally, and she seems to be getting things organized," he said, ignoring my question but thankfully not taking my mention of the letters any further.

It seems like Françoise's cameo role might be destined for a repeat performance, I thought, and then felt immediately guilty. If she was here dealing with her sick father alone, it must have meant that she didn't have any other support. I couldn't even imagine having to do the same thing for Mum.

But still, why does her support have to come in the form of my boyfriend?

Chapter
25

I UNEXPECTEDLY RAN INTO FRANCK, the estate agent, a few days later when I was in the village doing a pregnancy-craving-fuelled pastry run. If I was forced to eat another scone, I was sure I'd give birth to one.

"*Bonjour, Ella. Bonne nouvelle, non?*" he said after kissing me hello and eyeing my rather bulging bag of chocolate croissants.

"Good news? What do you mean?" I asked in French.

"You haven't heard? Your father put in an offer on a house just down the road. It's been accepted."

"*Excusez-moi*, but I think you're mistaken. I don't have a father," I said.

He looked at me like I was crazy for a few long moments.

Oh, shoot, maybe he means Ray . . .

"Ray?" I asked.

"Yes, your papa, *non?*"

"No, well, not really. My soon-to-be-stepfather," I clarified, to which Franck looked baffled, but undeterred.

"Well, he's soon to be the proud owner of a three-bedroom house in Chinon," he soldiered on.

"You're joking, right? Did you set this little prank up with Serge?"

"*Mais non*, I did the paperwork yesterday. It is a very good purchase. A great price."

"But why wouldn't he have told me? Mum certainly hasn't mentioned it."

"This I cannot know, Ella. Perhaps you should ask Ray yourself?" he suggested.

"Oh, I will," I said, walking out of the bakery furiously.

As I drove home, I couldn't wrap my head around the fact that both Serge and Ray had bought surprise houses in the same village in rural France. It was almost like a bad joke.

⁓

"Ella, I have the most wonderful news," Mum told me when I called to ask her about the house.

"I know," I said. "At least I know you have news. I'm just not sure how wonderful it is."

"Ray bought me a holiday house in France!" she squealed. Obviously she was delighted with the turn of events. "He was going to keep it a surprise, but he got your message earlier. Clearly that real-estate agent he's been dealing with has a big mouth. It's a wedding present! Can you believe it?"

"No," I said honestly. As much as I loved Mum and Ray, I still wasn't sure I wanted them living down the road.

"So, I'm thinking we'll spend a few months there this year, and then when Ray retires in a few years, we'll spend half the year in France, and the other half in Australia."

"Mum, I don't even know if we'll still be here in a few years. I don't even know if we'll stay on the farm."

"Oh," she said. "Why not? I've already spoken to Serge, and he confirmed that he doesn't want to move to Australia. And this way we'll get to spend lots of time together. I'll get to spend half a year with my grandchild! It'll make up for the other half when we'll be separated."

"But what if we move back to Paris?" I asked, thinking back to Serge's and my discussion after Christmas.

"But things are going well on the farm, no?" she asked.

"Things are better, but not perfect."

"Nothing is ever perfect," she said.

"So, the deal is already done?" I asked.

"Deposit has been paid. We can move in in a couple of months, in time for the arrival of the little mademoiselle."

"Well, I guess there's no stopping you now," I said, resigning myself to the fact that I'd now spend six months of the year living a few minutes from Mum.

And then I realized that I'd spend six months of the year living a few minutes from Mum—a source of love, support, and kindness. Yes, she'd likely drive me insane, but she'd be here to drive me insane. And she'd be here to help with the cheese room and the baby. *Could this actually be a good thing?* I wondered.

I made a note to email Ray and let him know what a great guy he was. I wondered how he felt about living in France for half the year. I'd have to come up with some interesting gardening projects to keep him occupied. And I'm sure Chuck could do with a gardener. Perhaps he could even start a little gardening business. My mind was suddenly racing with possibilities. A slice of home was coming to my village. I hurried off to find Serge and tell him.

"Oh," was the only thing he said after I'd explained Mum and Ray's plan.

"What 'oh'? What does that mean?"

"Well, we don't even know if we'll stay on the farm," he said.

"I tried to explain that to Mum but she won't be deterred."

"And you're happy about this?" he asked.

"I am. I wasn't too sure to begin with, but the more I think about it, the happier I feel."

"Well, good. And it will be good for the baby to spend time with his grandparents," he said.

"Her grandparents," I said. Given the word "baby" in French was masculine, Serge occasionally mixed up the pronoun. Either that, or he knew something I didn't.

"Yes, that is what I said, *non*?"

"Not quite, but it doesn't matter. Are you sure you don't mind about Mum and Ray?" I asked. I couldn't help wondering if Serge was just being generous. Perhaps he'd thought that by staying in France he'd avoid the "in-laws." But then, if he hadn't understood how headstrong my mother could be when he first met her, he was the one to blame. Regardless, from experience I was sure he'd be happy to have the extra support when the time came.

"It will all be OK, Ella."

"Thank you," I said, and I hugged him for being such an understanding boyfriend. "And I'll be the best gatekeeper. I'll make sure Mum and Ray never impose," I promised, although the likelihood of me keeping my mother in check was slim. *It's the thought that counts*, I told myself.

Serge kissed my head. Surprisingly, it seemed like the prospect of Mum and Ray living around the corner might actually turn out to be a good thing for both of us.

In the weeks that followed, Serge and I settled into a productive period. We both felt the pressure of the baby's due date approaching and wanted to make the most of the time that remained. While I'd hoped the cheese room would bring Serge and me closer together, we mostly worked independently, with me looking after customers and Serge busy with the goats or making cheese. He kept telling me that he was proud of what I'd created, that it would bring a lot of value, but then he would also insist that I couldn't maintain the same devotion to the cheese room going forward, and often spoke about getting Marie to come on board earlier.

I reassured him that, for now, I felt fine, and that if anything changed, we could reassess. Our life was about to go through a pretty dramatic change with the arrival of the baby, and I figured it was best not to plan everything out when there were still so many variables.

And then, just when I'd finally managed to stop worrying about the future, the past came back, once more, to bite me in the arse. It had been a sleepy morning in the café, and I was on my second pot of chamomile tea when Françoise reared her not-so-ugly head. She arrived in a panic.

"Where's Serge?" she demanded in French.

"*Bonjour,*" I said. The French insistence on always saying hello was well drilled into me by this point, and her lack of greeting felt abrupt.

"*Bonjour,*" she said, apologetically. "Can you please help me find Serge?"

"I think he's down in the milking shed," I told her.

"I've already looked there," she said.

How presumptuous to walk around our farm uninvited.

"Did you try calling him?" I asked, knowing full well that Serge had never given her his number.

"Can you call him for me?" she pleaded.

She had more than a couple of hairs out of place; I got the impression she'd had a rough morning.

Over the phone, I told Serge that Françoise had stopped by. Again.

"I'll put her on," I said to him, hoping that they would both hear my begrudging tone. *Better I don't become the intermediary between the two*, I figured.

I passed the phone over and resigned myself to only hearing Françoise's end of the conversation. She then proceeded to speak so quickly and in such blurred French that by the time she'd hung up all I'd understood was that she'd driven directly here, and something about a hospital.

She handed the phone back and went to sit down, calling out to me: "*Un café, s'il vous plaît.*"

I picked my jaw off the ground and then set about making her coffee. I also warmed her up a scone, hoping a little comfort food might soften her up.

Thankfully, Serge appeared five minutes later. After kissing Françoise hello, he explained to me what was going on.

"Clovis, her father, fell over last night in his house. Apparently he is in a lot of pain but will not go to the hospital with the ambulance."

I nodded, trying to figure out how all this related to Serge.

"She doesn't have anyone else to help her," he said. "Do you mind?"

"Mind what?" I asked.

"If I go and assist?"

"Right. And do I have a choice?" I asked.

He looked at me with his big eyes.

"Fine, go," I said, shooing him away.

I saw Françoise gathering up her bag to leave with Serge.

"*Merci*, Ella," she said before leaving. "*Très bon*," she added with a half-smile, motioning to the remains of the scone.

I couldn't decide if she was being genuine or just polite. As I watched them go, I hoped I wouldn't come to regret allowing my boyfriend to go and save the day.

⁓

When the sun started to set and I still hadn't heard anything from Serge, I began to worry. I cleaned the cheese room and locked up for the day, then waddled back to the house. My belly had been weighing me down, and I felt slow and heavy. *It's nice of Serge to help everyone but his pregnant girlfriend*, I thought, my fatigue muddling my emotions.

I collapsed on the couch with a bag of popcorn and scrolled Instagram for pictures of Paris and yearned to be in the city again. It was surprisingly lonely in the farmhouse without Serge, and I couldn't find anything to distract myself with.

He returned home around eleven o'clock that night after I'd gone to bed, and I pretended to be asleep. He slipped into bed and wrapped his arms around me.

"Are you OK, Bella?" he asked quietly.

I murmured that everything was fine and squeezed his hand.

"And you?" I asked.

Serge explained that Françoise's father was now at the hospital.

"She's planning to stay in the area for a while, to pack up his house, and get him settled into a more permanent care facility," he confirmed.

Great, I thought, imagining more interactions with Françoise.

Serge fell asleep quickly, and I was left staring at the wall, trying to undo the knot that had tied itself in my stomach. I was thinking about Serge and the baby and our life out here.

One of the things that had attracted me to Serge in the first place was his kindness. I'd never dated a man who was as selfless and thoughtful as he, and I was beginning to realize that his sweet nature extended beyond me.

I wondered how often he'd make himself available to help others once the baby arrived, and how often I'd be left alone to sort things out by myself. Yes, I could manage the cheese room by myself, and the house if I needed to, but I wasn't sure how I'd cope with a baby added on to all that. *Does Serge even consider me as his priority? Or will the goats, Françoise, and anyone else that comes looking for help always be more important?*

I tried to convince myself that these worries were all in my head, but Françoise's dependency on Serge and his willingness to be there for her still made me nervous.

Chapter

26

THE NEXT WEEK, SERGE AND I met Franck just outside of Chinon to do a walk-through of Mum's new house.

"So, this is Mum and Ray's holiday home," I said, as we parked out front.

It was adorable, almost like a doll's house. Two storeys, plus attics in the roof and a little garage off to one side. Cute burgundy-colored shutters framed the windows, and perfectly symmetrical topiary trees sat on either side of the front door. *How was everyone I knew living in these fabulous country properties and I was living in a beat-up farmhouse?*

The interiors were old-fashioned but in good condition. As I walked around, I figured that the heavy, dark furniture could be replaced with lighter, smaller pieces to give the sensation of more space and make the rooms feel more modern. But in terms of renovation work, not a lot, if anything, would be necessary. *Lucky them!*

"Not like your place," Franck chuckled, as if reading my thoughts.

"Mmm," I said, biting my tongue, thinking about how any

work on our house would now probably only happen after the baby arrived.

"And there's the perfect nursery room upstairs," he added.

"Huh?" I asked, looking to Serge for clarification, but he just shrugged.

"For the baby," Franck said, winking at Serge.

"We have our own nursery," I told him.

"But you'll need time for, how do you say, *le couple*."

I blushed.

"That is what grandparents are for," he added. "How else do second babies get made?"

What the hell? I thought, but figured it was probably easier to just smile and nod. I wondered how dramatically Serge's and my love life was about to change. Things in the bedroom had settled down slightly since I found out I was pregnant, but if what Franck was saying was true, they were about to get a lot worse.

Serge pinched my butt as we walked into the "nursery." With this simple gesture, I decided it was probably best not to start taking love advice from some boozy, old-fashioned French dude.

Overall, the tour was heartening for Mum and Ray—they'd arranged all this from Australia, and I was happy we'd be able to tell them that they'd made a good purchase—and disheartening for me because I found myself wishing Serge and I had bought their cute little house instead of our own.

"It's pretty nice," I said to Serge, once we were back in our car.

"It is a smart investment," he said.

"Do you think they'll like living in Chinon?" I asked.

"I do not know the answer to that," he said seriously. "I think they will like the house. And I hope they will enjoy the

French hospitality. But I understand it is not for everybody. Perhaps they will meet some English people and create a little social life."

"Do you think?" I asked.

"Why not? There are plenty of English people in the region," he assured me.

"So how come I've only met Chuck?" I asked.

"Then perhaps they will make some French friends," he suggested.

"Easier said than done," I said.

"People are very welcoming out here. Perhaps you need to make more of an effort to integrate," he said.

I was momentarily speechless. He obviously hadn't heard what some of the locals had said about his cheese.

"Seriously?" I asked, once I'd found my voice. "What about opening a café? Is that not considered 'making an effort to integrate'?"

"It's a good step."

"And what would you suggest next, then?" I asked.

"Well, so far your only regular customer is English," he replied.

There we go! I thought, finally understanding what Serge was getting at.

"So, do you have a problem with my best customer being English? Or is it because that Englishman is Chuck?" I asked, starting to get worked up.

"That's not what I meant," he said.

"But I think it is."

Serge paused for a minute. It was enough time for me to realize my temples were pounding, and I was furious.

"It's not that I *don't* like Charles," he said.

"Great," I said sharply.

"But have you noticed how he acts around you?"

"No," I said quickly, although my voice wobbled.

"I just don't get a good feeling about him."

"Why? Is it because he owns a château? Because he's rich? Because he's got an interesting life? Because he enjoys my company?"

"Ella——" he started to say.

"Or perhaps you've just been too busy helping Françoise to actually know what's going on with your own girlfriend."

Of course, I knew I'd been harboring some resentment from Serge's recent knight-in-shining-armor moments with Françoise, but I hadn't expected it to come out in a discussion about *my* efforts to integrate into French country life.

In the tense minutes that followed, I wondered if I'd overstepped the mark.

"So, that's it, now you're not talking to me?" I asked.

"Is there anything left to say?"

"I guess not," I replied, suddenly deciding that if he was unwilling to meet me halfway in this discussion, I shouldn't bother either. "Perhaps we just both prefer spending time with other people these days."

"Perhaps we do," he said.

It had been a huge week in the café, and I was already feeling emotionally drained from the news of Ray buying Mum a house in France. How could they have done something so permanent when I didn't even know if I was going to stay on the farm? I didn't even know if Serge and I would still be together by the time they moved in.

My feet were aching, and I'd had an upset stomach for most of the day from eating too many damn croissants. *Typical France!*

Hours later, I was still angry. I also felt guilty: I'd been quick to react, and I'd been defensive, perhaps because I worried that there was actually some truth to what Serge was saying. I wished we could go back and have a more measured discussion. How much could I blame on pregnancy hormones this time?

Assuming Serge was still on the farm—he'd stormed off as soon as we'd arrived home—I sat down on the couch to brood until he got back.

And then I spotted his phone by the door.

That's odd, I thought. *He must have forgotten it.*

I looked at it for some time and then found myself cautiously approaching its general vicinity.

I'll just make sure he hasn't had any cheese orders come through that I might need to deal with, I justified to myself before entering his code, the usual 1111.

I looked at his messages and felt a pang of guilt. Nothing new. All good.

I placed the phone down but then snatched it up again. I couldn't help myself.

I quickly navigated to his recent calls.

"WHAT!?" I shouted as Françoise's name jumped out at me.

I double-checked the time of the call and realized it was from earlier that day. And then I remembered Serge rushing outside while we were looking around Mum and Ray's new house, saying he had some "urgent business" to deal with.

I glanced outside to see if his car was still around. There it was, sitting innocently by the garage. *What's going on?* I wondered.

I contemplated calling the dreaded ex-wife to see if Serge was with her, but as I played out the potential conversation in my head, I decided it wasn't worth the ensuing awkwardness.

Instead I donned my wellingtons and went down to the farm to check whether he was there, hoping I was just overreacting and that I'd find him hanging out with his goats. *You've got one last chance, Serge*, I thought as I braced myself against the wind.

Each step I took reinforced the fact that Serge wasn't anywhere to be found. It felt like he was punishing me for our fight. Or perhaps he just didn't want to see me. I'd been unkind, but did that really warrant this? *I'm pregnant, for God's sake!*

I had a sudden vision of myself walking through a sea of animals with a screaming baby in my arms, looking for Serge. *I can't do this alone*, I thought, starting to panic. A goat eyed me as I walked past, judgment almost visible on its face. I quickened my step.

"What the hell am I even doing here?" I asked myself aloud. All of this was Serge's grand plan for our family and now he'd just upped and disappeared on me. It felt like a terrible sign of things to come.

I grabbed Serge's car keys, not knowing where I was going, but knowing I needed to get away.

I found myself pulling into the driveway of Chuck's château, silently resenting the fact that Serge was right: I only had one friend out here in the country.

"Ella. What a surprise," Chuck said, opening the door in a dressing gown.

"Fancy making a pregnant girl a cup of tea?" I asked.

Chuck laughed and invited me in. He sat me at a rickety stool in the kitchen while he boiled a saucepan of water on the stove.

"No kettle?" I asked.

"No kettle, no problems," he replied.

"I'm not sure that's a thing," I told him.

I guess Chuck is a little eccentric, I said to myself, thinking back to my earlier conversation with Serge.

He shrugged and laughed. "Is it not? Oh, well. So, what brings you here this afternoon, Ella?" he asked.

I felt like I'd just walked into a therapy session.

Come to think of it, I could probably do with a therapy session right now.

"Serge and I had a fight. But that's not why I'm here. I wanted to come say hi, to see how your book was going. Have someone else make me a cup of tea for once." I attempted a laugh, but it came out sounding a little forced.

"Tell me more about this fight then. It's upset you?" he asked.

The truth sort of erupted out of me. "It's just that sometimes I feel like there's such a huge divide between Serge and me. He doesn't seem to understand how hard it's been for me to adapt out here, and the things I have managed to achieve since arriving don't seem to matter to him. And then I don't know what's going on between him and his ex-wife."

"Do you worry about his ex-wife?" he asked.

"Deep down, no, but then again, sometimes I worry that Serge regrets getting involved with a foreigner. I don't know. Does that sound stupid?" I asked.

"Cross-cultural relationships are hard. Exhausting even. There's always a risk that things are being misinterpreted or confused. But that doesn't mean that love across cultures can't exist. It's just that sometimes you have to work harder for it."

Chuck's eloquence threw me. He certainly seemed to be speaking from the heart. I wondered whether this subject touched on a sore spot.

"But is it worth the extra work?" I asked.

"Only you can answer that. And Serge. If you feel like something is worth fighting to save, then fight. And be honest with Serge. Don't be afraid of conflict. Sometimes it can be healthy."

"We've got plenty of conflict at the moment, but at what point do you decide it's not healthy?" I asked.

Chuck shrugged. "I'm not sure I'm the most qualified person to answer that."

"Really? I find that hard to believe," I said.

"My story is water under the bridge. And the bridge collapsed into the Loire River some time ago," he said definitively.

I sensed the need to back off. "I should probably get going," I said, gathering my things. "Thanks for the tea. And sorry for unloading on you."

"Any time. Well, except for the next couple of weeks. I'm heading back to London tonight. Some family business I need to deal with. Just let me know if there's anything I can do," he said.

I was grateful for his advice. There were some things that were best explained, and understood, in your mother tongue.

Perhaps that was Serge's and my biggest problem. Things had been fine in the early days, when our relationship was all picnics, bottles of wine, and cheese plates; but now that we had problems and deadlines and responsibilities, we were having more and more communication breakdowns. There had to be a reason it was easier spending more time with someone who spoke my native language. There was a comfort in conversing freely, which Serge and I seemed to have lost.

How much was I prepared to fight?

⁓

I got back from Chuck's to find Serge sitting at the kitchen table.

"Oh, hi," I said. "I was looking for you. You disappeared."

"So did you," he said. His voice told me he was also still angry.

"I went over to Chuck's," I said.

"Of course you did."

"And what the hell is that supposed to mean?" I asked.

"Well, just as I expected," he said.

"And did you expect I would look everywhere for you only to realize you were off with Françoise?" I asked.

The look on his face confirmed my supposition that they'd been together.

"At least I'm honest about who I'm spending time with," I said.

"Ella, she came by to see if I could help her move some of her father's belongings. I wasn't going to let her suffer alone. Besides, she's my ex-wife. It's finished between us. You, on the other hand, go and spend hours with another man when you think I'm not around to notice."

"So, you do have a problem with me spending time with Chuck?" I accused.

"After we have had a fight, yes," he said.

"And what about you going to help Françoise after we've had a fight? Do you know how that looks?" I realized I was sounding desperate, but if he was going to interrogate me about Chuck, I wanted to clear the air about his ex-wife.

He shook his head. "How does it look?" he asked.

"Well, it looks like you're willing to help everyone but me."

"Ella, it's just that I'm worried about you," he said.

"Well, you've got nothing to worry about. Chuck is a friend. And God knows I need friends at the moment, with everything that's been going on with the farm and the cheese room."

"But is he the same kind of 'friend' I was to you while you were dating Gaston?" he asked. "Don't forget we kissed while the two of you were together."

"That's different," I said defensively to this surprise attack.

"Is it?" he asked. "How?"

"Because Gaston was cheating on me," I said.

"And that makes things OK?" Serge asked.

"It's just different. If you can't understand the fact that I enjoy spending time with an English-speaking friend out here in the middle of nowhere, then we have other issues."

"Ella, I know about the money," he said.

"Oh," I replied.

How had he found out about Chuck's loan for the cheese room?

"I saw his name on your bank statement," he added.

I was momentarily taken aback, trying to figure out if he would have hunted out this information or if he just stumbled upon it. Either way, I knew, I was still in the wrong.

"Serge, I'm so sorry. I was going to tell you but I knew it would complicate things."

"You're right. It has complicated things."

"But I promise you, it was nothing more than a loan. I've actually nearly finished paying it off."

"And were you ever planning on telling me about it? Or did you just want me to continue to look the fool in front of your friends and family? Your idiot French boyfriend who just goes along with everything you do."

"Serge, it wasn't like that."

"Am I not enough anymore now that you have a friend with a big bank balance and a château?" he asked.

Oh, my God. When did Serge turn into the melodramatic one?

"Please don't put words into my mouth," I told him.

"I'm just explaining what I see, Ella," he said stubbornly.

"So why don't I 'explain what I see'? I see a man who's taken on more than he can handle and has forgotten the whole reason that he moved to the country was to create a better life for his baby. You spend hours on the farm all day and barely even check in on how I'm doing or help out in the cheese room. I only started the damn cheese room to help you sell your damn cheese!"

"And as I expected, it hasn't really helped sell more cheese, and it's just made you busy and stressed."

"But it's given me purpose," I shouted. "What the hell would I be doing out here without it? It's not like I get to spend any time with you."

"Maybe you could spend less time with Chuck," he suggested.

"Or maybe you could spend less time being somebody's errand boy," I said. I barely recognized this jealous version of myself, but this fight wasn't just about Françoise—it was about everything that had happened since I'd found out about the pregnancy. It was about all the doubts I was having about whether we'd be good parents, whether I should follow in my mother's footsteps and raise this baby alone, and whether I even wanted to stay in France. I loved Serge but as things stood, there were too many uncertainties.

"Oh, Ella. I'm helping Françoise through a tough time. Wouldn't you do the same?" he asked.

I thought about this. I'd like to think I would, but then knowing my ex-boyfriends it was hard to imagine. But perhaps that was the difference between Serge and me.

"Is she still in love with you?" I asked.

"Of course not," he said. "She just doesn't have anyone else to ask."

"That seems convenient," I said.

The usual kindness on his face was replaced by sadness, and just as quickly turned to anger.

"I'm not the one you need to worry about," he said, finally. "I've always been loyal to you. You, on the other hand . . ."

It was a low blow. I realized that I'd pushed Serge to the breaking point and the result was difficult to stomach. My head was pounding.

"I feel like maybe we don't want the same things anymore," I said to him.

"I agree," he said, and then went to stand up.

Is he about to leave this discussion? I thought furiously. *I don't need to put up with this. I shouldn't put up with this—especially not while pregnant. I'm the one who should be leaving!*

I grabbed the keys to the Citroën and told Serge I was going for a drive to clear my head. I needed some air. I needed some time to think things over.

I kissed him briefly on the cheek and threw on a scarf. I hopped in the car once again without any real idea of where I was heading, until suddenly I knew.

An hour later, I was sitting on the train to Paris. Serge was calling me but I didn't have the headspace to answer. And I knew what he was going to say. That I should come back. That I had to come back and figure things out. But I needed this. I needed some time.

"Is everything OK, Ella?" Chuck said, next to me on the train. "Are you sure this is what you want?"

I turned to him and nodded.

· PART ·

Four

SUMMER

Chapter 27

WHEN WE ARRIVED AT THE station, Chuck and I went our separate ways: me to meet Clotilde, and Chuck to catch the Eurostar to London.

During the train ride into Paris, I'd poured my heart out to him even more than I had earlier that afternoon, and he'd listened patiently, only looking at me like I was deranged once or twice. He'd even suggested that I join him in London for a couple of weeks while I figured things out, but I wasn't ready to give up on France, at least not yet. Besides, I had pretty much weekly hospital appointments from now until my fast-approaching due date. It was probably wise not to be gallivanting off to other countries.

And there was also no way I wanted to give Chuck the wrong idea, as charming as he was. A little harmless flirting had been fun while we'd been getting to know each other, but at the end of the day, as Mum kept reminding me, he wasn't my baby's father, and the last thing I needed was to enter into another love triangle like the one I'd found myself in with Gaston and Serge.

Not that I even needed to worry about Chuck's intentions. After I'd been babbling on about my problems for the majority of the train ride, he told me about *his* ex.

"She was the antithesis of every girl I'd dated growing up," he said.

"How so?" I asked.

"Natalia was Italian. Very Italian. She loved wildly and openly. Being with her was an emotional roller coaster. It sounds clichéd, but I'm not exaggerating when I say that we fought all the time."

"Is that why you broke up?" I asked.

"Well, no. I got used to the arguments. And the make-up sex that followed. And as we lay in bed after fighting for hours or sometimes days, she'd apologize or I would. But as we grew older, the debates became more complicated, more interlaced with innuendos and sarcasm. And as Natalia fought to express her intense feelings in English, her words would become increasingly cruel," he said.

"And so what happened?"

"Well, despite the many disagreements, we were still in love, but at the same time I felt like she hated me. On our way to London one weekend, taking this very train, we got into a major disagreement about the French. I mean, it was stupid because neither of us grew up in France, although I guess I had stronger ties because of Grandmama."

"So, what did you fight about?"

"Why the French were so intent on keeping their train rides silent," he said.

I nodded. I often wondered the same thing myself. "Which side did you stand on?"

"The quiet side, of course. I loved the peaceful train journey, but Natalia wanted to sing and dance her way to Paris."

"That sounds pretty harmless," I suggested.

"Stupid even!" he added. "But that's the thing. It was until it wasn't. At that moment, it was as though all our previous fights had led to this one, and she meant war."

Something about Chuck's story sounded familiar. He continued, "Until that train journey, there seemed to be nothing that could destabilize us to the point where we were no longer worthwhile. But as she got out and raced off into Paris without me, not answering her phone or calling me back, I wondered if we were done."

"And she came back?"

"No, actually. I continued on to London without her. I had a lovely time with my friends, going out and chatting in English. It all felt so easy. And I got chatting to this gorgeous girl from London, who was sweet and mild. Drunkenly thinking about Natalia, I convinced myself that I needed to get away from the drama of our relationship. Like you, I was sick of the misunderstandings that arose from speaking different languages, sick of struggling to communicate properly."

I empathized. "So, you started seeing this new girl?" I asked.

"Sort of. But it never felt right and eventually she kind of drifted away. I mean, Natalia and I had never really broken up. And as lovely as this girl was, I missed that Italian fire."

"And what happened to Natalia?"

"I haven't seen her since that train ride. She sent me a letter, telling me she needed a break, that she was going travelling. She said she'd be in touch when she got back and would come find me. She asked me to wait."

"And?" I probed, on the edge of my seat.

"And that was a year ago. I'm still waiting."

"Why?" I asked incredulously. "Why wait?"

"Well, I haven't remained celibate for that time, but I've stopped myself from falling in love. My heart is hers."

Parts of Chuck's story reminded me of my own when Paul had told me he was going travelling to "find himself." Right before I'd broken up with him, he'd suggested I wait. I couldn't imagine what my life would have been like if I'd stayed in Australia.

I wondered if Chuck needed a similar push to let go. It seemed like he had romanticized the thought of Natalia. To me, she sounded mental.

As I thought about her slipping off into the night in Paris, I suddenly realized that *I* was running away, too, from Serge. *I was Natalia! Oh God, I was Paul!*

I messaged Serge.

My love, I'm sorry we fought. I'm sorry I rushed out. I'm desperate for some time to clear my head before the baby arrives. I know you will understand. I'll be with Clotilde tonight if you need me. We can talk properly when I'm home. I love you, Ella x

I felt immediately better after sending the message. Shortly after, he replied.

I understand, Bella. I am also sorry. Please rest and be careful. Serge

I read his message with relief. My heart rate slowed, and I finally felt able to breathe normally again, although baby was still doing her best to inhibit it. I put aside my immediate thoughts of Serge to see if I could help Chuck figure out his feelings.

"Chuck, have you thought that maybe Natalia has moved on? Or that she's changed since she left, or maybe that you've changed?" I suggested.

"Of course, I've considered it. I'm not daft. But until I find somebody who compares to her, who fights for my affection like she did, I don't see the harm in waiting."

I understood exactly what Chuck was saying. He'd had his heart broken, and he was still licking his wounds. He wasn't actively looking to replace Natalia, but perhaps now he was at the point where he wasn't totally against the idea. The niggling idea I'd had that he was interested in me was all imagined. The way he spoke to me about love was similar to the way I'd speak to Billie or Clotilde about it. I laughed at how ridiculous I'd been to let Mum's concerns get into my head, even if it had just been for a fleeting moment. As I'd promised Serge since the beginning, Chuck was just a friend.

Clotilde bundled me into her arms after I waddled my way to her on the platform. I waved Chuck off and Clotilde shot me a raised eyebrow. When I'd messaged to ask her if I could stay, I hadn't mentioned that Chuck would be on the same train. She looked surprised to see him but didn't let that interfere with the important information she had to relay.

"I've spoken to Serge," she said immediately. "I'm on strict instructions to show you a fun and stress-free time."

"He didn't mention our fight?" I asked.

"No," she said slowly. "He said you had a misunderstanding, that I didn't need to worry. But him telling me that only made me worry. I thought I'd wait to get the unabridged version from you."

I attempted a smile but I was still processing everything that had happened that day. I needed a break from even thinking about it.

"I'll explain everything tomorrow over brunch," I said. "For now, let's go get a drink. I've been starved for nightlife too long!"

"*D'accord*," she said, and ordered an Uber.

Stepping out of Gare Montparnasse, we were swept up into the evening commute, and it felt like I'd returned home. For all the less shiny aspects of Paris—the homelessness, the begging, the dogs using the streets as toilets—something about the city made me feel alive. There was an undercurrent of resistance that Parisians carried around, which I found thrilling. They expected you to fight back. You needed to hold your own in Paris and I'd learned that being meek didn't get you anywhere.

I told Clotilde I'd need to do some shopping the next day for basics—having turned up without any luggage for this unexpected Parisian jaunt—and she just nodded like it was the most normal thing in the world to arrive somewhere without fresh underwear. For that I loved her. The lack of judgment in matters of love and passion was one of my favorite character traits of the French.

Once in the car, I took my scarf off. Clotilde looked at me wide-eyed.

"Holy crap," she said. I would have laughed but I was freaked out by her reaction.

"What's wrong?" I asked.

"You're *so* pregnant."

I looked down, wondering if she was seeing something I wasn't. I guess I'd gotten big in the past few weeks, but I didn't think I was *that* big. I rubbed my stomach.

"I mean, you look like you're on your way to hospital," she continued with a laugh.

"Don't worry, I have at least three or four more weeks of lugging this belly around," I reassured her.

By the time we got to the bar through the rush-hour traffic, *les terraces* were full and finding a seat was hard. I think I'd just forgotten how busy Paris got when the weather was nice. After being jostled about at the bar, getting looks as if to say, "Why is this whale of a girl out on the town?" we finally got a seat outside.

It was a gorgeous evening, and I took a deep breath. *Paris, Paris, Paris!* I sang to myself. But my appreciation was short-lived as a cloud of secondhand smoke gradually enveloped us.

I watched the lady next to us puffing away. Her bright red lipstick-stained cigarette butts sat like a disgusting still life between us. The smell was overpowering, and I wondered if my disgust was pregnancy-related or had something to do with how quickly I'd gotten used to the air in the country. I convinced Clotilde that we should move on.

"A friend is throwing a little party if you'd like to check it out," she suggested.

"Sure," I said quickly.

"I'm not sure what the crowd will be like. And there's a chance Gaston might be there," she admitted.

"Then he'll get to see how gorgeous I look *this* pregnant. Let's go!"

We hopped on a couple of share bikes, despite Clotilde trying to convince me it wasn't safe in my "state." We rode slowly, and I felt wonderfully liberated. I could almost forget everything that had happened in the past eight months and pretend I was the same carefree—although heartbroken—girl who'd arrived in Paris all those months ago. The air flowed through my luscious pregnancy hair like I was in a shampoo commercial. I asked Clotilde if she had any hair modeling leads and for some reason we laughed so hard I nearly wet myself. *Perhaps cobblestones on a bike while pregnant wasn't the smartest idea*, I decided.

When we arrived at the party, Clotilde forced me to sit down. As much as I didn't want to admit it, it was a relief to get off my feet.

"So, tell me everything that has been going on here," I demanded.

"Let me see . . ." She spun a long strand of hair around her finger and looked pensive. "Not much really."

"Seriously?" I asked. "There must be something going on. Have you been into Flat White recently? How's Chris?"

"Well, for starters, he asked me out."

"He did?" I asked, surprised that he'd once again changed his stance on dating Clotilde so suddenly.

"He seemed to sort of do it as a last resort, not really caring whether I agreed to go or not. It was as though he was doing it for old times' sake."

"And what did you say?"

"We went for a drink and it was wonderfully weird, and I think we both decided we were better off as friends."

"Oh," I said, feeling sorry for Chris. After all that build-up, all it took was one drink to shatter his dreams.

"But I think I made it up to him," Clotilde said, to my relief. "I set him up with Julie. You remember, my friend from Bordeaux. Anyway, by all accounts, Julie is smitten. Chris is smitten. It turns out I'm quite the matchmaker."

I smiled. Trust Clotilde to patch things up. "This is all wonderful news," I said. "Now, am I allowed to get up and go to the bathroom?"

As I walked off, I overheard a familiar voice quietly asking someone, "Who brought the cow?" I turned to see who was insulting me and saw Camille, the girl who had been responsible for me splitting up with Gaston when I'd busted them having a *ménage à trois* without me. It wasn't the first time she hadn't recognized me, but I'd sure as hell make sure it would be the last. I walked over to her.

"Oh, Ella, it's just you. *Mon Dieu,* you are *huge!*" she said, adding insult to injury.

"Isn't it wonderful!" I said with a big smile. "My boyfriend, Serge, and I are thrilled."

She looked at me blankly.

"And when are you due?" I asked her, despite the fact she was rail-thin and smoking.

"What do you mean?" she asked.

"You're pregnant, no?" I asked as innocently as I could.

"*Mais non!*" she said, a look of horror on her face.

"Oh, I'm so sorry. I just assumed because, well, you know . . .," I said, and then walked off.

I smiled to myself. I'd never been great at insulting people on the fly, but I hoped this would do the job.

The queue for the toilet was long; however, upon seeing my belly, people gave me concerned looks and let me pass. When I eventually caught a glimpse of my face in the mirror, I saw that my cheeks were a bright shade of red. I'd never felt so out of place.

Despite my best efforts to enjoy myself at the party, I just couldn't get into the swing of things. Eventually, after failing to find something nonalcoholic to drink, I couldn't resist sitting on a seat that looked more decorative than functional. When it groaned under my weight, I got up again and leaned against a wall.

Looking around at the crowd, I realized how much I missed Serge and our cosy little farmhouse. Perhaps the grass wasn't actually greener in Paris.

I made one last effort to join a group of people chatting about travel, but as a joint got passed around I realized I was done.

Although it was always wonderful spending time with Clotilde, it felt wrong being away from Serge. I asked if she'd mind if I went back to the apartment, thinking I could catch an early train home in the morning.

"I'll come with you," she said. "What a dud party."

I looked at her, relieved. I hadn't wanted to seem ungrateful, but I was glad she agreed. I'd spent the past few months dreaming of the Paris scene and feeling like I was missing out. Perhaps one last average party was all I needed to realize that I had grown tired of that life. I was entering a different stage. What I wanted now was to snuggle up on the couch with my boyfriend, who was sadly still a long train ride away.

Chapter
28

I WAS WOKEN LATER BY intense stomach cramps.

"*Merde!*" I said in a low voice. "Shit, damn, shit! It can't be."

I couldn't be 100 percent sure that what I was experiencing was a contraction, but it hurt like hell until suddenly it didn't, and then the feeling returned with a vengeance. I tried to remember the interval times that the midwife had given us in our birth preparation classes but my mind had gone completely blank. I pulled out my phone to google them.

Clotilde must have heard me groaning; she came out to the living room to check if I was OK.

"I think I might be in labor," I said, panicked and disheartened. I should have been telling Serge.

"*Merde!* What do I do?" she asked. She sat on the edge of her foldout couch where I lay sprawled. She rubbed my leg tentatively. "I've never done this before."

"Neither have I," I said, managing a rather pathetic laugh. "But it might not be the real deal. That's why I'm timing."

"Timing what?" she asked.

"Contractions," I said, showing her my phone. "I'm just

waiting to see if they intensify. They shouldn't. It's too early. I'm not due for weeks."

"Should I call Serge?" she asked.

"Not yet, I don't want to worry him unnecessarily."

"Right. Then what should I do? Rub your back?" she asked.

"I'm OK for now, but perhaps I should contact the hospital just in case."

"Which hospital?" she asked.

The cramps started again, quite intensely, and stole my concentration.

"Sorry," I said, after what felt like many minutes but according to my app was only sixty seconds. "What was the question?"

"Which hospital should I call?" Clotilde was holding her phone and waiting patiently.

"It's in Chinon," I said.

"If you're in labor, you probably aren't going to make it home to Chinon," she said seriously.

"But I have to. They have my file."

"Leave it to me," she said.

As I slipped into another haze of painful cramps, I heard Clotilde speaking with the hospital in Chinon and asking them about real labor versus fake labor. She was cool-headed, stopping the conversation only to ask me the timing of my current contractions before relaying them to the person on the other end of the line. A look of concern slowly came over her face before she asked which hospital she should call in Paris. I started to worry. *Oh God, this is it*, I thought. *I've ruined everything by running off to Paris.* I was angry with myself, but there wasn't any time to dwell on it.

"Get your things ready," Clotilde said after hanging up. "It sounds like you might be having this baby tonight."

I groaned.

"Another contraction?" she asked.

"No, I've just really messed everything up with Serge."

"No time to worry about that now," she said in an effort to comfort me. "Let's head to the hospital and get you checked out. You can call him on the way."

I grabbed my handbag.

"I'm ready."

"Right. I forgot you don't have any of your things."

She ordered an Uber and then ran into her room and threw some clothes and toiletries into a bag. Shortly after, we were zipping through the empty streets of Paris. It was eerily peaceful in the early hours, and I found myself appreciating the city in its pre-dawn state despite worrying about everything that was about to happen.

—⁓

"Serge, it's me," I said.

"Ella, are you OK? What's going on?" he asked, sleepily.

"I don't want you to worry," I said, realizing as I did that these words tend to immediately instill some sort of concern. "But," I continued quickly, "I'm just off to the hospital for a quick check."

"You're *what!?*" he yelled, obviously very awake now.

"I've been having some contractions. They might blow over, but Clotilde was worried," I said, giving her an apologetic look. "She's forcing me to go in."

"Should I come now? Which hospital are you going to?" he asked.

I was on the verge of another contraction and didn't want him to hear the strain in my voice.

"Don't worry, Serge. I'll call you back when I know more," I said.

"I'll wait by the phone," he replied. "Do I need to call Michel to help me collect our car from the train station and to look after things on the farm?" He sounded about as anxious as I felt.

"I'll let you know."

We walked into the labor and delivery ward, and it was strangely quiet. I wasn't sure what I'd expected, but from all the hospital dramas I'd watched on TV, I think I'd imagined seeing a woman giving birth in a stairwell while hundreds of people were piled into any available space following a volcano eruption or a bridge collapse or some other unlikely natural phenomenon that was both dramatic and involved a sudden influx of unwell people.

It seemed like I was the only patient bothering to have a baby that night.

We walked up to the reception desk and I suddenly lost all my French words. I panicked, mouth agape, trying to figure out how to say, "I think I'm in labor." Thankfully, Clotilde stepped in and did the explaining. She ran the receptionist through the fact that I was visiting from the country and had been directed here by my doctor in Chinon.

The receptionist asked Clotilde if she was my partner and Clotilde nodded. "It's the only way they'd let me in with you," she whispered afterward.

We were sent up to the delivery floor so I could be checked out. As I lay on the bed, I relaxed somewhat, despite having faced a barrage of questions and an internal exam; I knew that I was in good hands.

"Well, you're certainly in labor," a midwife said in French after my waters broke.

I breathed a quick sigh of relief that I hadn't just wet myself.

"When did you say you were due?" she asked.

"Not for another few weeks."

"Well, you're quite dilated already. Four fingers. We'll get you hooked up to the heart rate monitor and make sure the baby is OK. Then we'll get you the epidural."

All notions of a natural birth had drifted out the window with each contraction that I'd already endured. The thought of things getting worse had sealed the deal for pain management in my mind.

"*Parfait*," I told the midwife, suddenly appreciating the French love of medicalized births.

Clotilde and the midwife talked for a few more minutes while I suffered another mind-melting contraction. I wriggled aimlessly, trying to find some relief, listening to Clotilde ask something about how long we had left. Then the midwife was gone.

"Is everything OK?" I asked Clotilde when the wave of pain had passed.

"Just great, Ella. Don't you worry about a thing. I'm just going to pop outside and give Serge a quick call. Probably best that he sets off now. I'm guessing he won't want to miss the show," she said with a wink.

It suddenly dawned on me that I was going to be leaving Paris with a baby, that I was only hours away from meeting *my* baby. I started to panic. *What if Serge is still angry with me? What if he's just waiting until the baby is born to break it all off? What if, once again, I've ruined—*

Another contraction put a sharp halt to any more open-ended questions. I focused on my breathing while praying that the epidural wasn't far off.

Minutes passed, and outside it started to rain. I wondered if it was a bad omen. It'd been raining when Paul told me he was leaving. My mind wandered back to that night back in Australia, the night I'd thought I would start my family with him. Looking around the French hospital room, I suddenly felt very alone.

Thankfully, Clotilde reappeared before I spiraled too far into a pit of anxiety, and told me that Serge was on the way. I wanted to confirm how long he would take to drive to Paris, but the midwife bustled in and told me it was time to head to the delivery room. I was about to tell her she was mistaken, that we needed to wait for my actual partner. But Clotilde was gathering up her bag and nodding. *Oh God*, I thought. *Here we go!*

The windowless delivery room felt cold. It was bigger than I had imagined and was filled with medical equipment. It was a daunting space. A small crib sat in the corner of the room, symbolizing both an end and a beginning. Every emotion I was feeling was amplified. I wished Serge could be by my side.

The midwife held me still while the epidural was administered and things calmed down slightly. I rested and waited for Serge, praying that he'd arrive in time. I was beginning to get the urge to push, but I resisted as long as possible.

And then the midwife told me it was time.

When I was pregnant, I'd tried to imagine what labor would feel like, but even in my most vivid imagination I hadn't expected it to be so wildly painful. Thank God our memories are flawed and we can forget pain, because what followed over the next hour or so does not bear remembering. And, if it weren't for the end result, would never bear repeating.

Chapter
29

"IL EST PARFAIT," **SAID THE** midwife, as soon as it was all over.

"What do you mean, '*He's* perfect'? She's a girl, *non?*" I asked, aghast.

"Not from this angle," she confirmed, placing the tiny, foreign creature on my chest. "It's definitely a boy. Congratulations! You did a great job."

I looked at Clotilde, wide-eyed, as if pleading with her to confirm that I hadn't mistranslated the sex of my own baby. *What the hell was going on?*

"Ella, it's a baby boy," she said.

"But the ultrasound . . .," I tried to explain.

"There must have been a mistake."

I should have known better than to trust old Doctor Gerard, I thought.

I looked down at my little baby boy, all pink and squishy, grasping, and gasping as he tried to make sense of the sudden change of scenery, and I did the same.

"Clotilde, can you call Serge for me?" I asked.

"Of course," she said, only then letting go of my hand to get her phone. She'd been the most wonderful, if not slightly unexpected, birthing partner, massaging my back through the labor and scooping my shoulders up to assist with the pushing. Despite being squeamish, she didn't react when I'd vomited on her mid-contraction, or when the midwife had suggested that we reach down and feel the baby's head. She had maintained her usual, glamorous sense of composure until the end.

"A quick selfie of 'team baby' before I do," she said, snapping a photo of the three of us, both baby and me looking like we'd just been through labor, and Clotilde looking like she'd just walked off a set somewhere glamorous.

"Serge!" I said when he finally picked up.

"I've just pulled over. Is everything OK?" he asked desperately.

"You're a *papa*," I said.

"I missed it? Is our girl OK? Is my girl OK?"

"*He's* perfect, and I'm fine," I said, and then waited for the reveal to sink in.

"I've been so worried. I'm just outside of Paris. I'll be there in half an hour."

"I can't wait for you to meet *him*," I said.

"Me neither. I will be there soon. I will hang up now so I can keep driving. Congratulations, Bella. I am sure you were perfect."

I looked at Clotilde. "He didn't get it," I said, disheartened.

"Well, he won't be able to miss it when he sees him," Clotilde reassured me.

Shortly after, her phone started buzzing.

"It's a boy?" Serge yelled down the line. "Are you joking with me?"

I laughed. "Nope, Doctor Gerard got it wrong. Or perhaps he was just making sure to keep us on our toes."

"A boy?" It was as though Serge didn't believe me. "And you are certain? They did not switch the babies?"

"It's been confirmed by multiple people," I said.

"This is wonderful news!" Serge said, his voice bursting with pride.

⁓

I got wheeled down to my hospital room, where Clotilde made quick work of ordering some food. I was starving, Clotilde was starving, and I couldn't imagine Serge would have stopped for food.

"What do you feel like?" she asked, scrolling the Food To Go Go app on her phone.

"Sushi. Raw beef. Soft-boiled eggs. CHEESE!" I rattled off everything that I'd missed eating since finding out I was pregnant.

"Right," she said. "And if you were to choose one dish?"

"Let's get some sushi," I said. "Or a burger. God, I'm so hungry!"

The tiny baby in the crib next to us cried out and reminded us of what an adventure we'd been on. I picked him up, and he immediately fell back asleep. It was surreal. Here I was with a baby, *my baby*, Serge's baby. I'd never believed that newborns could smell so perfect, but my little boy did. I felt euphoric with exhaustion, with relief, and with love. Everything Serge and I had been fighting about felt insignificant now. I was desperate to have him by my side.

Moments later, he walked in and threw a bag onto the ground with a loud thud. He kissed my forehead and then sat beside me on the bed, looking tentatively at the little bundle in my arms.

"He looks like you," he said to me.

"Really?" I asked, disbelievingly.

"No, but that is what people say, correct?"

I laughed.

"Here," I said, handing him over to Serge, who apprehensively cradled him.

I felt an overwhelming rush of love, and I burst into tears. Clotilde made some excuse about going to find the delivery guy, and Serge asked me what was wrong.

"Nothing," I said. "I'm just so sorry you missed the birth. It was so stupid coming to Paris like this on a whim. I should have stayed to work things out with you. I didn't even mean half the things I said. I think I was just nervous about having this little guy."

He looked at me gently, his eyes letting me know he didn't blame me for anything. *Maybe holding a baby solves all problems and cures all disagreements?* I thought.

"We should wait until we're out of the hospital to discuss everything properly," he said as a nurse bustled in to check my blood pressure. I began to worry again.

"What's left to talk about?" I asked, as the nurse hooked me up to the machine.

"Nothing that can't wait," he said. "We'll work it all out."

The nurse asked a few questions, gave me some more painkillers, and hurried out. I was about to press Serge further on what was left to discuss, but he interrupted me.

"For now, we need to think of a name," he said, and then, looking down at the tiny boy in his arms: "What would you like to be called?"

"I was thinking Noah," I suggested tentatively. "After my grandfather."

"And we'll go marching two by two?" Serge said, making me laugh. I hadn't considered the biblical reference. "And it is raining," he said, looking out the window.

"You like it?"

"I do. Noah Serge Marais," he said. "It has a nice ring to it."

"It's perfect," I said.

We put aside whatever problems remained to be solved for the time being and we kissed. We hugged our little Noah and just generally marveled at what we had created. It was such a natural thing, but for some reason it felt so epic. Now that he was here, I got the feeling that everything would work out just fine.

Clotilde came back in carrying trays of sushi. We sat around eating and laughing while Noah slept peacefully in the corner. As the sun rose, the nurse came in and, after we admitted that Clotilde wasn't actually my partner, kicked her out. I hugged my dear friend and thanked her for everything.

Over the next three nights in the hospital, which I'd quickly learned was the standard-length stay after giving birth in France, Serge and I tried to sleep, we learned how to look after a baby, and we made good use of the Food To Go Go app.

It felt weird to be in Paris rather than Chinon, but it worked out well, because it meant that visitors kept rolling in. Chris brought coffee every morning and snuck a cuddle with Noah. He told me he was secretly rather enamored with babies, and I assured him that I was happy to trade flat whites for baby hugs whenever he needed. *Clotilde's friend Julie better watch out*, I thought, watching him doting on Noah.

Tim from Food To Go Go messaged to "reassure" me that things would get harder before they got easier. But he wasn't all doom and gloom. He offered some food delivery discount codes to keep us going until we went back to the farm.

Clotilde, too, came by every day to talk with the medical staff and make sure I was recovering properly. She'd transformed into a wonderful proxy-nurse. On the second day, she brought Papa Jean, who came armed with a bottle of chilled Champagne.

"You're my hero," I told him, eying the condensation on the bottle. He poured me a little glass and as soon as the crisp bubbles hit my tongue I sighed. If ever a drink were well deserved, it was this one.

"And this was Clotilde's idea," he said, handing over a large package.

Similar to the experience when I'd first arrived in France, the smell hit me before I could see what was behind it. It was cheese. Gooey, unpasteurized, soft, and stinky cheese.

A nurse walked in and, upon seeing our little hospital room party, said, "I'll pretend I didn't see this," and then backed out of the room, adding, "I'll be back in thirty minutes."

We opened the window and laid out the cheese on my hospital bed. Papa Jean proudly held Noah as we indulged, and I rediscovered everything I loved about Brie, Roquefort, and Sainte-Maure de Touraine. I was still in pain, but it didn't matter. Everything felt perfect. Cheese was the ideal medication.

Mum and Ray arrived the next day, straight off the plane from Australia and horrified that they'd missed time with their grandchild. When I'd told Mum his name over the phone a few days earlier, she'd burst into tears. She told me that Grandpa would have been so proud of me living this adventure in France. I then burst into tears. Clearly emotions were running high.

After Serge and I had introduced Mum and Ray to Noah, Ray offered to take Serge to wet the baby's head.

"We will not," Serge said, aghast.

"Might need to explain the expression, Ray," I suggested.

"Ah, righto. It's simple really. We go for a drink and cheers to the new bub."

Serge nodded and looked relieved. "This I can do."

After the men left, I had Mum to myself.

With all the visitors I'd had over the past few days, it was a relief to have her by my side.

"Now, with everyone else gone, tell me how you really feel," she said.

I looked at her, relieved. She understood me so well. I didn't need to pretend around her. "It all hurts so much," I said.

"You've been through a lot. It'll get better in the coming days."

"And I'm terrified that something will go wrong," I said.

"That's normal, too. All mothers go through a period of sleeping with one eye open."

"And the emotions. Is that all hormonal?" I asked.

She looked at me with a knowing smile and rubbed my arm. "Everything will settle down soon. Now, are you going to tell me why you had the baby in Paris and not Chinon? Were you at risk?" Pragmatic Mum was back.

"Not exactly," I said. "Serge and I had had a disagreement, so I came to Paris to spend a couple days with Clotilde. I really didn't think there was any chance I would go into labor early."

"Well, that was naïve," she said.

"But it's worked out well," I said, ignoring her disapproval.

"And with Serge? Is everything OK?" she asked.

I wanted to say yes and tell Mum that everything was great, but the truth came spilling out. "And I have no idea where we stand. He told me that we could talk properly when we got back to the farm," I concluded.

"Oh," Mum said.

"And what's that meant to mean?"

"Well, it's just that now there's a baby involved . . ." She looked down lovingly at Noah. "You need to fix things quickly. Babies pick up on a lot."

Mum was right. I did need to fix things with Serge. We'd been held together in this magical hospital bubble for the past few days, but soon we'd be heading back to the farm and back to our problems.

Perhaps Noah would be the bridge we needed to help ease the transition. What had felt important to me before was slipping into insignificance as I cared for him. He was, after all, the catalyst for our move to the country, and I felt like Serge and I had both forgotten that to some degree. All things considered, there was a lot riding on his tiny, adorable shoulders.

Chapter

30

DRIVING BACK TO THE LOIRE with Serge and baby Noah, life was looking quite different than it had when we'd moved here last year. Despite Mum and Ray having driven the Citroën back to Chinon so we could hire a sturdier car for baby's first road trip, the drive was still a little uncomfortable, atmosphere-wise anyway.

Both of us were quiet. I hesitated to start the discussion about what had happened before Noah's arrival out of fear of the impending disagreement. It was the first time Serge and I had been alone together without the possibility of interruption from the passing parade of nurses or visitors, and all I wanted to do was sink into his arms and fall asleep.

I looked back at Noah, so tiny in his car seat, and thought about what Mum had told me about making things right. I launched in.

"Serge, we should talk properly about what happened before Paris," I said. As the words escaped my mouth, I breathed a sigh of relief. Whatever was about to unfurl, at least I'd get it over with. Since moving to France, I'd considered myself a girl of action, and often of mis-action, but still, it was better to keep moving forward.

"Ella, I was furious," he said.

I didn't even know Serge could *be* furious, let alone that he could be furious with me. This wasn't the conversation opening I was hoping for. But at least he'd said that he "*was* furious." There was some hope that he'd gotten over it now.

"Then why did you tell Clotilde to show me a good time in Paris?" I asked.

"I asked her to look after you because I was worried. You've never wanted to listen to me when I tried to tell you this, but you cannot expect life to be the same when you are pregnant. There are things you need to be wary of. It is *our* baby. What if something had happened to you?" he said.

I felt like I'd let him down.

"But think of it from my perspective, Serge. It's *our* baby, yes, but I'm the one who did all the heavy lifting, literally. Imagine having to be careful of what you eat, and what you drink—or don't drink—and everything you do. I needed a break from the pressure of that and of being in the country. I guess it was just bad timing."

"Ella, I don't want you to make these decisions without me. We are a duo. We go two by two, remember."

Of course, Serge wants to make decisions together, I thought. *Wouldn't I if our roles were reversed?* I could acknowledge that I'd been self-ish by running off to Paris, but our initial fight wasn't just about us making decisions together; it was also about me spending time with Chuck, and him rushing to help his ex-wife whenever she called. I couldn't just gloss over what had initially set us off.

"And I'm totally on board with us making our decisions together," I said. "Serge, I adore you."

He squeezed my hand.

I hesitated. We could have easily wound up our discussion here and ended on this sweet moment. *Don't quit now, Ella*, I told myself. "But, I need you to be honest with me about Françoise. Is there anything I need to worry about?" I asked.

"Absolutely nothing, *ma belle*," he said quickly.

"Are you sure?" I asked.

"Of course."

"I don't mind if she needs your help every now and again. I just want to make sure that she knows where you stand," I said tentatively. "Serge, you're a nice guy. I don't want her taking advantage of that."

"She's already gone back south," he said, and I couldn't help letting out another little sigh of relief.

We were quiet for a moment, the forthcoming discussion about Chuck still hanging over us.

I, once again, jumped in. "And, going forward, I really hope that I can spend time with Chuck without you rolling your eyes or getting frustrated with me."

"I was only frustrated because you seemed to prefer spending time with him," he said.

"It's not that I prefer spending time with him; it's just sometimes it's easier to speak with someone without any language barrier," I said, although as the words came out, I acknowledged that they sounded weak.

We were both quiet then, and I got lost in thought, realizing that perhaps my friendship with Chuck hadn't just been about bridging a communication gap. I'd gotten caught up in the excitement of spending time with somebody new. And I was flattered that he wanted to get to know me, despite the pregnancy. He complimented me and showed an interest in my plans. With Chuck, I'd felt like a more exciting version of myself. It was easier to imagine living in a country château and zipping between London and France than to imagine being permanently stuck in a run-down French farmhouse. But while I might have envied Chuck's lifestyle, I'd never actually wanted the man behind it.

"And I'm sorry about accepting a loan from him without telling you. That was wrong," I admitted.

"I'm sorry I wasn't able to give you what you wanted," he said, which made me feel even worse.

"So, you understand that Chuck is just a friend. He's my Clotilde out here. My sounding board."

"Ella, I know all this. And I do want you to have friends out here. Maybe I was worried that outside of Paris, you would realize that I was just a simple goat farmer. You ran away from your life in Australia once before, and I was worried you would run away from me."

"I ran away from an idiot ex-boyfriend, not Australia. And besides, I can't exactly up and leave now, Serge. I've built my life out here in the country with you. I chose you, and I still choose you. I can't imagine life without my boys now."

A smile appeared on his face.

"*Je t'aime*, Ella. Forever," he said.

"I love you, too," I said, tears welling in my eyes.

I wondered how I could have ever doubted my relationship with Serge. There would be more fights, I was sure of that, but for now, I knew we'd be OK.

We spoke openly for the remainder of the car ride, except for the little half-hour when I nodded off, and for the other half-hour when we needed to stop to feed and cuddle Noah. We listed things we'd been fretting about separately—the cheese room, sales, renovations—and we worked through them together.

Heading home to the farm as a family felt strangely normal. At no point during our discussion was the idea of leaving even brought up. We were both fully committed to making things work.

Mum and Ray were at the farmhouse to welcome us home. They'd arrived a few hours before to tidy up and cook some food. The warming smell of a beef stew had spread around the house, and Mum had taken down the "Welcome, Baby Girl" wall print that she'd insisted on buying. When I saw the empty frame in the nursery, I laughed. In many ways it had been an even greater surprise assuming I was having a girl and finding out it was a boy only after the delivery.

I settled onto the couch with a cup of tea and shut my eyes, feeling exhausted from the drive. Mum pulled a rug over my knees and took Noah.

"You don't mind?" I asked.

She looked at me like I was crazy. "You rest, darling. He'll let me know if he needs you."

It was a relief to just sit, to know that Serge and I were OK. To know that Mum was here and I could let *her* know if I needed her. I nodded off peacefully.

VICTORIA BROWNLEE

Chapter 31

FOUR WEEKS LATER, AND OUT of that initial baby bubble, things were still manic. The time since we'd been in the hospital had passed in a blur; but, among the never-ending juggle of feeding, changing, and sleeping, what I remember most is my feeling of love toward Serge. And little Noah, of course.

Doctor Gerard had chuckled when we'd arrived with our little boy.

"*Oh là là,*" he'd said with a sheepish look on his face.

I wanted to be angry with him for wrongly guessing the sex of our baby, but I was so loved up on hormones that, when he said that baby Noah had to be the most handsome baby boy he'd ever seen, I forgave him for his previous misstep.

Since the birth, Mum and Ray had been so helpful and had somehow managed to always be around when we needed them, but also to move properly into their new holiday house. Their energy kept Serge and me going as we bumbled through learning how to parent. They, of course, were in their element. Ray in particular, who had never had his own children, took to being a grandfather like Comté took to being aged. He softened every time he held Noah, and I could tell they'd teach each other a lot in life. Mum, too, was smitten. I occasionally had to order her to go to her house just so I could get the baby to myself.

Billie had arrived in France, as planned, a few days before Noah's original due date. She'd wanted to make it over in time for the birth, but baby had foiled her plans. And it seemed as though there weren't enough video chat apps in the world to satisfy her. She was desperate for a newborn snuggle.

"Where is he?" she'd said when she arrived, looking around frantically, after giving me the briefest hug. Mum had picked her up at the train station and dropped her off at our house, along with a box of groceries and some soup she'd whipped up in her spare time.

"Sleeping. You'll have to settle for me until he wakes up," I told her, pulling her in for a proper hug.

I instructed Serge to bring Noah to the cheese room when he woke up, and I took Billie down for a flat white.

We sat on the couches overlooking Ray's increasingly beautiful hedge. It was a sunny day, and it felt nice to get out of the house.

Marie had turned out to be quite the expert café manager, so much so that she made me wonder if I should even come back to work. With her watchful eye and ever-competent hand, she brought a very homely feel to the cheese room and had started moving a good amount of cheese thanks to her local connections.

She also managed to get the French locals drinking lattes, and word of her sweet tarts—and her goat-cheese cheesecake—had spread. She got the café's vision, and added her French flair. Serge was thrilled, I was thrilled, and, finally, the cheese room was evolving as I'd hoped.

As we sipped our Melbourne-quality coffees, I relayed Noah's birth story to Billie. Then I told her about Serge's and my fight, and its resolution, and how things had been since we'd returned home.

"So, life's pretty good in country France, then?" she asked.

"Actually, it is," I said. "I was bored when we first got here, but now I couldn't be less so. There's so much to do, and so much I still want to do. I really think we can build up the cheese room to become a serious destination. And Serge's goat cheese is actually really good now."

"It wasn't good before?" Billie asked, sounding as confused as I had when I'd heard that Serge had made average cheese.

"I don't know what happened to the first few batches," I said. "I guess Serge had trouble finding his feet."

We were interrupted by the man himself, bringing in Noah.

Billie gooed and gaahed, as promised, and fell in love with him, as it seemed that everyone I loved did.

Marie joined us briefly to let me know that she was finishing up for the day. She handed me the keys and after a quick hug with Noah, who was being passed around like a hot potato, headed off.

Serge, Billie, and I fell into a baby stupor, only to be interrupted by Chuck. I hadn't seen him since the train ride to Paris. I looked immediately to Serge to see how he'd react to his appearance here. Everybody remained still as seconds seemed to pass in slow motion. Chuck, perhaps sensing the weird vibes, hung by the door as though waiting to be invited in.

Serge stood up and went over to greet him. The men spoke quietly, seemed to do some kind of mutual nod, and then shook hands. They both walked over to the couches where we were sitting, and Serge slapped Chuck on the back. "I'll leave you to catch up," he said, heading into the kitchen to pretend to be busy. I smiled at Serge. This interaction was a step in the right direction.

"Bravo, Ella," Chuck said, leaning over to look at Noah. "He's charming."

We sat transfixed, gazing at the baby, until Billie nudged me in the ribs.

"Oh, sorry, Chuck, this is Billie, my best friend from Australia."

Chuck finally took his eyes off the baby and extended his hand to Billie. And then something odd happened. Chuck did a double take. If I hadn't known it was spontaneous, I would have thought it had been staged.

"What a pleasure to meet such a good friend of Ella's," he said, smiling. It was the first time I'd ever seen him look at another woman with what could only be described as desire in his eyes.

"The feeling's mutual," Billie replied.

We sat and chatted until Serge came over and said he needed me in the kitchen. I left Noah sleeping in Billie's arms and went to join him.

"And what's going on there?" Serge asked quickly.

"There's definitely some tension in the air, isn't there? I'm glad I wasn't imagining it," I replied.

"He hasn't taken his eyes off her," Serge agreed.

"Have you been spying?" I asked him. He looked at me like he was worried we were about to start another fight, so I gave him a cheeky grin and said, "I haven't been able to take my eyes off them either. Do you think it could be love at first sight?"

"Maybe," he said. "As long as he's not looking at you like that I don't mind whom he falls in love with. Do you think Billie can handle him?"

"Do you think *he* can handle Billie?" I retorted.

I grabbed Noah, and we left Chuck and Billie on the couch in the café getting to know each other. As we walked back to the house, I thought about how lives often ended up entwined when you least expected it. Perhaps now Chuck would reconsider his plan to avoid falling in love while he waited for Natalia. I wondered if I had, in some small way, helped him get over the idea of her.

———

"Well, I'm smitten," Billie said when she eventually made it back to the house. She'd only been in the French countryside for a few hours and had already found a love interest.

"I thought you might be," I said, laughing.

"Well, you didn't tell me he was so handsome," Billie replied.

"I don't think he's *that* handsome," I said in return. "Especially not compared to Serge."

"Different strokes, I guess," she said with a giggle.

"Are you OK? Need a cold shower, perhaps?" I suggested. It was rare to see Billie get like this over a guy. Normally she was so matter-of-fact.

"Don't be dramatic, Ella. It's just that he's so different from the men I've been dating back in Australia. So interesting."

"Well, don't go messing with my friendship. Although I should probably say thank you for helping to finally get Serge off my back about Chuck's intentions."

"I'm here to help," she said with a twinkle in her eyes. "Now tell me more about his château."

I tried to encourage her not to go getting any grandiose ideas when it came to Chuck's castle, but she'd stopped listening, seemingly already lost in imagining her fairy-tale life in the French countryside. I pictured her moving to France but quickly pushed the image from my head before I, too, got carried away. *Best not to get ahead of yourself, Ella*, I told myself. Regardless of my own sage advice, the prospect was thrilling.

"Would you consider living in France?" I asked her.

"You know what? Until now, I've always thought I'd need to be in Melbourne for my work, but perhaps I could do more of it living elsewhere. I've got a good network set up and could easily keep things running from here," she said, and then rushed to add, "If I ever needed to."

"So, you *have* already considered it."

She looked at me sheepishly. "Maybe. But only briefly while chatting to Chuck. But back to you—have we lost you forever to France?" she asked.

"I have no idea. I didn't think I would be here forever, but earlier in the year when I was talking to Serge, he said he had no intention of leaving France."

"And you're OK with that?" she asked.

"I don't know. I guess we'll have to wait and see how things go. There are a surprising number of elements in my life that could go horribly wrong."

"But can you imagine living here forever?"

I'd thought about this a lot since Noah had arrived, trying to figure out what his life would look like if we stayed in France.

Would he go to school here? Would French or English be his native language? Would he grow up scared of spiders and snakes?

"Perhaps not forever," I said.

After a moment's reflection, she said, "Well, France or Australia, you're only a couple of flights away."

"You mean twenty-four hours of flying with a baby in tow?"

"That's another way of phrasing it, yes."

"I don't think I'll be going back for a while," I admitted. "Maybe in a year or two. But with Mum and Ray here for six months, and you potentially moving in with Chuck," I said with a wink, "I might not need to ever go back."

"You don't miss the Australian way of life?" she asked.

"I'm getting my head around the French way of doing things," I said. "And now I'm finally allowed to eat cheese and drink wine again, I need to make up for some lost time."

"Understood. So tonight. Cheese dinner?" Billie suggested.

"Ooh, yes," I said, my mouth immediately starting to water in anticipation. "I'll let Serge and Mum know."

Later that evening, Serge and I were in the kitchen, throwing together a cheese dinner for Mum, Ray, and Billie.

"So, you want to stay on the farm?" he asked me casually, as I was slicing some figs to accompany his goat cheese.

This took me by surprise, because I felt like we'd both, unofficially, already decided to stay; we hadn't even spoken about leaving since Christmas. I wondered what had prompted his question and I considered my response. *Do I really want to stay here?* My gut was saying "Of course!" but I couldn't seem to voice it aloud.

Despite the multitude of hurdles we'd jumped to get the farm up and running, things were starting to get easier; and if we left now, we wouldn't get to benefit from all our hard work. Besides, where would we even go? I couldn't see us taking Noah back to Paris, and Serge would obviously still need some convincing before considering moving to Australia.

I opened my mouth to say as much but, still, nothing came out. I attempted that famous French shrug I'd come to love/hate and rushed out to join the others, figuring Serge and I could finish this discussion later.

We sat down to the cheeseboard and Mum and Billie complained about how they couldn't continue eating like this while they were in France. I called them novices, and Serge and I gave each other knowing looks.

The secret to eating a lot of cheese was not eating too much of any one variety, and not overloading on bread. There was a delicate art to mass cheese consumption. Serge was a pro at it. I only sometimes managed to achieve the perfect balance, but at least I had learned from my mistakes and was improving.

That night, though, I overindulged. There was plenty to love about our life in the country, and it finally felt like it was time to celebrate.

"Of course, we're staying," I whispered to Serge and he gave me a huge grin.

"To life in the country!" I said, raising my glass.

"To the country," Serge echoed in French.

I grabbed his hand and squeezed it, wondering if he ever asked himself how he'd ended up running a goat farm surrounded by a bunch of Australians in the Loire Valley. Thankfully he didn't seem to mind the madness we all brought to his life.

I looked at the cheeseboard and at my family and friends, thinking that every day might not look like this one but, for now, I was happy.

When Serge had first sprung the country move on me, it had felt like a prison sentence, but it had ended up being one of the best things we could ever have done. We'd created a viable business, we'd finally begun our house renovations (although I could already see they'd take years to complete), I'd taken a fun career detour, and we'd become parents. We'd even managed to keep our Paris apartment, although I think I was nearly ready to suggest to Serge that we sell it.

We'd navigated some serious life challenges and had come out the other side. We were still in love, and given what we'd been up against, that was almost miraculous.

Once again, my gaze fell on a slice of Comté. It may have been the cheese that had led me to Serge, but Noah had led us to country France, and for that we would be forever indebted.

Epilogue

"MAMAN, HURRY UP! PAPA'S ALREADY got the car running."

I hobbled out from the bedroom, my shoes pinching my inflamed feet. For some reason, this pregnancy had felt so much harder than the last two. Perhaps my aging body was working against me.

"I'm coming, Noah. Just run ahead and tell Papa to wait a few more minutes."

I grabbed Inès, who was somehow still napping soundly, and wrapped her in a blanket. It was the end of autumn but it could have been winter.

I looked at her sweet little face and marveled at her ability to sleep through anything. I guess growing up on a farm and in a café and with Noah for a big brother, she coped the best she could.

"Shall we go?" I asked, once we were all in the car. We were only driving the hundred or so meters down to the cheese room, but with our current load, it seemed necessary.

"You look like a picture," Serge said.

"What? A picture of an elephant?" I joked. "I feel like I've been pregnant for years."

Serge leaned over and kissed me. He was well used to pregnant Ella by now, and he knew that a little kiss was the best response to these sorts of comments.

"Sorry. I'm nervous," I admitted.

"What? About talking?" he asked.

"No," I said, aghast. "I'm worried about my waters breaking while I'm on stage."

Serge just laughed and told me if they did, it would make for the perfect story. But I wasn't sure Chuck would see the humor in me overshadowing his book launch. He'd worked for such a long time to arrive at this point, and I certainly didn't want to do anything to jeopardize his big evening.

It'd been more than five years since Serge and I had confirmed we'd stay in the French countryside and nearly as long since we'd sold Serge's *fromagerie* to Fanny. Back then, I didn't think life could have gotten any harder than it had been when we were juggling a newborn and a farm. *Oh, how naïve I was!* Now, in comparison, every day felt like I was the protagonist in a French movie—the hilariously ridiculous kind where everything that can go wrong does go wrong, but where love always triumphs. Joining Serge for wine or cheese at the end of most days helped make it all worthwhile.

But tonight wasn't about us, despite Noah's belief that, because I was introducing Chuck, it was. It was about Chuck's book. His epic family saga that spanned multiple lifetimes, and seemed to have taken as long to write. I was so proud of him for finally finishing the draft and finding a publisher. He'd told me that not long after meeting Billie, he'd had a plot breakthrough. I quietly decided that he'd been stuck on something because of Natalia and, by letting her go, he was free to finish writing.

"So, I will take the kids outside while you do your speech if they're looking like they might act up," Serge said.

"But I'll be good. And you will be, too, hey, Inès," said Noah from the backseat while prodding his sister and trying to wake her up. I raised my eyebrows at Serge, who let out a little chuckle.

"And we'll meet back up after Chuck's reading," I said. "And Noah, don't mention anything about what you overheard Grandma saying on the phone. You promise?" I turned to look at him, sitting big and proud. I wondered where the years had gone.

"I promise I won't mention that we are thinking of moving to Australia when the new baby arrives," he said.

"How is it that you can be so eloquent now, but when I ask you to help clean the house you simply grunt and ignore me?" I said hopelessly. I absolutely hadn't wanted to tell Noah about the possible move until it was confirmed, but he had his way of running our house and our lives. In truth, I admired his tenacity.

"Anyway, nothing is certain yet, so best not to tell Aunty Billie and Chuck," I said firmly.

We got out of the car and went inside. Billie greeted us at the entrance with a glass of wine for Serge and water for me. By now, I was used to having her in my French life, but her happy smile would never get old.

"Delicious," I said, sipping my water. "Thank you."

"Not long now, El," she said.

Since Billie and Chuck had met, their attraction had grown into a very stable relationship—more stable than I'd imagined either was capable of, but perhaps Serge and I had set a good example. Or maybe Mum and Ray had, with their ability to effortlessly live in two countries without ever seeming to fight. They'd been in Australia for a few months now, and both Serge and I missed having the extra sets of hands around. Thankfully, they were due back to France before baby number three was set to make his or her arrival. Since the gender reveal and subsequent slipup with Noah, we were still attempting to keep the baby's sex a surprise. Convincing Doctor Gerard not to tell us was a constant battle.

After Noah had arrived, we'd decided to wait a few years before getting pregnant with baby number two. We'd wanted to get everything running smoothly before adding any more variables into our lives. And with experience, we knew what we'd be giving up; at least I did, with the French cheese and wine.

But then when Inès arrived, she turned out to be an angel. She was sleepy and relaxed, and fitted into our lives snugly like a slice of Comté into a baguette. Serge was smitten with her from birth. And with Mum and Ray in town for her arrival, it had felt remarkably easy. So easy, in fact, that we became a little lax on contraception and, whoops, I somehow found myself four months postpartum and pregnant again. Although the timing wasn't perfect—when was it ever, really?—we decided that we could always squeeze one more little *bébé* into our lives. Now we just needed to decide whether that life would be in France or Australia.

"Ella, thank God you're here. I'm as nervous as a salmon swimming upstream during bear season," Chuck said to me after making his way through the people milling around the bar area. He was wearing a shirt and tie and a woolen vest. He looked very authorly.

"Chuck, you'll be great. Have you had a drink? If not, have a quick one for both of us."

"Thanks again, Ella, for doing the introduction. And for hosting the launch. Where would we be without this place?" he asked, motioning to the cheese room.

I hadn't told Chuck or Billie about the opportunity that had come up in Australia. I thought it best not to mention it until we'd made a decision either way. And Serge and I still needed to discuss the idea properly. It would be a huge undertaking, moving ourselves and our brood of soon-to-be three to the other side of the world. My heart rate sped up at the mere thought of the flight home with three children. But then again, it wasn't every day that one of Australia's leading dairy producers asked your boyfriend to move there to manage the production of their new line of goat cheese.

Serge had been flattered by the offer, but had been too nervous initially to even mention it to me; I was busy working in the café and looking after two kids, all the while pregnant with a third. I'd ended up finding out about the offer from Mum, who had eavesdropped on a discussion Ray had had with a dairy farmer. It appeared that Ray might have helped orchestrate the offer by putting in a good word about Serge's cheese-making prowess, although I was sure he wouldn't admit it.

"Shall we just go live in Australia, then?" I'd asked Serge a few days earlier. "Worry about the logistics after you've accepted the job?"

"Sure. I guess it's now or never," Serge had said, somewhat jokingly.

"Do you really want to go? What about the farm?" I'd countered.

"We'd work something out. Get Jacques and Marie to manage things. They've done it before when we've been on holidays," he'd said.

"But would they be happy to do it full-time? Potentially for a couple of years?"

"We can only ask. We could also sell," Serge had suggested.

"That doesn't feel right," I'd said. "Not after everything we've done for this place. Besides, we need a backup option in France in case Australia doesn't work."

"Are you certain that *you* actually want to go?" Serge had asked.

"I don't know," I'd replied. "Let me think about it some more."

So, there we were, at our dear friend's book launch, still trying to decide if we could possibly leave the life we'd created for ourselves here in the French countryside.

I got up onto the makeshift stage to welcome everybody to the café and introduce Chuck. I gave Clotilde a little wave after seeing her slip in through the kitchen. She was wearing a black cap and a baggy black dress, and I wasn't surprised to see that her effort to look clandestine just resulted in her looking gorgeous. Thankfully, her modeling success still hadn't gone to her head, and she continued to make time for her old country friends.

I launched into my speech nervously. "It's not every day an Englishman asks a heavily pregnant Australian woman to introduce his new novel in a country town in France, but then, since I arrived in Chinon, life has never been run-of-the-mill." I looked over at Serge, who was quietly warning Noah to sit still while gently rocking Inès's car seat to keep her asleep.

I continued, describing Chuck's work, and was relieved when I looked over at him to see he'd turned a wonderful shade of red. But he deserved the plaudits. He'd done us all proud.

I invited him on stage for the reading.

I took a seat and drifted into my thoughts, trying to figure out if I was ready to give all of this up. And was I ready to leave France? What had started off as a wild, off-the-cuff adventure to rediscover who I was outside of my relationship with Paul had turned into a very busy, very full life. I had children, I had Serge, and I had a farm and a cheese room. Would I even fit into life in Australia anymore?

"It is this love that brings us together, just as it is love that will help us survive when we part," I heard Chuck conclude.

His reading was met with warm applause, and the buzz in the cheese room as he signed books afterward was intoxicating. *If only I could get tipsy off atmosphere*, I thought as I went to find Serge and the kids.

"How was it?" he asked. "I missed the end."

"It went well. And Chuck was perfect," I said.

"And you?" he asked.

"Still pregnant, thank God," I said.

"I can see," he said, prodding me dangerously.

"Have you thought any more about you-know-what?" I asked Serge, just out of Noah's earshot.

"Maybe we should wait until number three arrives," he said. "Reassess after a few months."

"I think we should go," I told him. "It really is now or never. And as Chuck just read: 'It is love that will help us survive when we part.'"

"You're not planning on leaving me with them, are you?" Serge said, motioning to the kids.

"I wouldn't do that!" I said, and he chuckled.

"Let's just try living there for a year. We'll mark a date on the calendar, see how things go," I said.

Serge kissed me and handed over Inès.

"Sounds like a plan," he said and grabbed our son by the hand. "Come on, Noah, we better eat all the French cheese that we can while we're still on home soil. And I'm going to need a glass of wine."

"What sounds like a plan?" Clotilde asked, having snuck up behind Serge and me and caught the tail end of our conversation.

"Fancy a trip to Australia?" I asked.

"No!" she said.

"Yes!"

Clotilde had somehow understood what this meant without further explanation.

"I'll see if I can sort something out with my agent," she said, just as somebody recognized her and asked her for a photo. It appeared her disguise wasn't as effective as she might have hoped.

I went to find Billie to tell her the news.

"It was actually Chuck who convinced me to go," I told her.

"I'll kill him," she said with a laugh.

"He made me realize that whether we're here or there, it doesn't matter. Love is all that matters."

"Don't get all melodramatic on me, El," she said, rolling her eyes. "And don't go blaming those hormones," she added as I pointed to my huge belly and went to open my mouth.

"You'll be just fine here without us," I said. "Anyway, we'll be back to visit."

"Maybe I can convince Chuck to set his next novel in Australia," Billie said.

"As long as you're willing to spend the next decade or so there," I told her seriously.

"Oh, dear, I need another drink," she said, dragging me over to the bar.

I looked at the cheese room filled with familiar faces, some French, some English, some friends, and some family, and felt a mix of pride and joy at what we'd established. I knew that Marie would keep things running beautifully, but I would miss it.

I wondered what Australia would have in store for us. It was hard to imagine arriving there, setting up a new life, and I had no idea whether we'd be able to enjoy it as much as France. But I felt ready for a change.

It'd been a monumental adventure arriving here, and now I could honestly say I was excited about embarking on the journey home.

Acknowledgments

ONCE AGAIN, IT'S HARD TO start my acknowledgments without a quick doff of my hat to France. Thank you for being inspiring, for being full of plot twists, and for providing me with a cheese for every occasion.

And then there are my people, without whom I'd be lost at sea. Thank you:

To my agent, Greg Messina for his tenacity and tireless promotion of my work.

To my UK editor, Emily Yau for her thoughtful editing and good humor when dealing with my last-minute changes. And to the Quercus crew for their dedication and hard work in promoting this book.

To my US editor, Cherrita Lee and the teams at Amberjack and Chicago Review Press for their ongoing support and for making beautiful books.

To my foreign language publishers and translators for bringing Ella's adventures to new readers: to Goldmann Verlag in Germany, Garzanti in Italy, Metafora in the Czech Republic, and to Lars Rambe and the teams at Hoi Förlag in Sweden and Denmark.

To my friends and family for their love and encouragement. Thanks in particular to Mum and Jules, for their perpetual willingness to chat about plotlines, fictional goat farms, and country-house renovations.

Finally, to my husband, Jamie, for nearly always being willing to read, edit, or talk about this manuscript; *je t'aime*. And to my darling Clementine for providing plenty of inspiration for this book and for being so damn cute.

About the Author

VICTORIA BROWNLEE is an Australian-born food writer. She's spent the best part of the last decade eating her way around the world, including a two-year stint in China where she was the Food & Drink Editor at *Time Out* Shanghai. In 2016, she traded dumplings for cheese and is now settled in France with her husband and daughter. Her debut novel, *Fromage à Trois* was published in 2018 and has since been translated into five languages.